Praise for Francis Cottam

SLAPTON SANDS

'Cottam's crisp prose carries a good story
Newcastle Journal

HAMER'S WAR

'*Hamer's War* skips backwards and forwards in time, obliging the reader to fit together the story of Hamer's life like the pieces of a puzzle . . . very effective in building the suspense in this unusual and unpredictable love story' *Irish Independent*

'A compelling and well-written narrative with excellently drawn, three-dimensional characters' *Big Issue*

An exciting and significant read' *Sunday Herald*

'Sensational' *Good Book Guide*

THE FIRE FIGHTER

'A cleverly crafted, unusual tale that combines romance, intrigue and acute historical atmosphere' *The Times*

Francis Cottam was born in Lancashire in 1957. A full-time journalist, he has lived and worked in London for the last twenty years. He is the author of two previous novels, *The Fire Fighter*, shortlisted for the W H Smith Literature Award, and *Hamer's War*.

SLAPTON SANDS

Francis Cottam

POCKET
BOOKS

LONDON • SYDNEY • NEW YORK • TORONTO

First published in Great Britain by Simon & Schuster UK Ltd, 2004
First published by Pocket Books, 2005
An imprint of Simon & Schuster UK Ltd
A Viacom company

1 3 5 7 9 10 8 6 4 2

Simon & Schuster UK Ltd
Africa House
64–78 Kingsway
London WC2B 6AH

www.simonsays.co.uk

Simon & Schuster Australia
Sydney

A CIP catalogue record for this book is available from
the British Library

ISBN 0 7434 6152 5

Typeset by SX Composing DTP, Rayleigh, Essex
Printed and bound in Great Britain by
Bookmarque Ltd, Croydon, Surrey

For Lisa. Always for Lisa.

ONE

Canterbury, June 1976

The ground sloped gently from where they were gathered on the high slope of the hill. In the distance she could see the cathedral. It lay beyond a long descent of yellow grass and scorched hedgerows. The stumble of buildings at the margin of the city was indistinct from here. But even through the haze of summer heat, she could see the cathedral, a mile and a half away, impossible and real.

Heat plucked at flesh under calico and cheesecloth. The wine was white and sweet and warm. Someone had put a portable stereo system on a tabletop and had shifted plates of cheese and pineapple pieces on cocktail sticks and trays of glasses filled with Liebfraumilch to accommodate its shiny metal case. The speakers looked feeble, but their sound carried with a bright clarity. Joni Mitchell was playing on the little stereo. The song was a familiar one to the ears of Alice Bourne. She owned the album. It was an album everyone seemed to own or share and play that summer. It had been released the previous autumn, when the critics had coldly received its charged lyrics and jazz inflection.

1

Since then it had insinuated its way on to the playlist of every party that liked to think itself smart and discerning. Alice liked the album, and she didn't. She liked the song, and she didn't. Joni Mitchell sang it like a reproach.

She was glad at least that they were playing something recent. Old stuff, familiar stuff, was an ordeal to listen to. It was an Englishman who had made that famous remark about the potency of music. Cheap music, he'd insisted. Cheap or otherwise, it was true. Stuff from home was sometimes bruising to hear. Homesickness was bad enough without melodic encouragement. She stood on the slope of the hill and wondered if she would listen in the future to music first heard in England and miss the place with the same melancholy longing. She'd heard John Martyn for the first time here; she'd heard Traffic and Roy Harper. The guests at the tutorial party clinked and chattered in hermetic little English groups on the dead grass, young women and young men, self-conscious in hats and silver jewellery, louche in wispy beards and linen. The music now was harsh with treble in the bright heat. No, was the answer to the question. No. She didn't think she would.

She looked down towards the pale shape of the cathedral. It rippled, too stubbornly solid for a mirage, too far distant for detail in the shimmering heat of the day. In her mind she sheltered for a moment in the shade of its cold stone. She explored with her memory its arches, its carved grotesques. It was the oldest structure made by men she had ever encountered. As a child she had travelled with her family to

Monument Valley and Yosemite, to the Grand Canyon. The structural achievements of nature were awesome enough, but they were random. They were no more really than spectacular accidents. But the cathedral had been built almost a thousand years ago, with skilled deliberation, by men. Those men would never be dead to Alice Bourne. They lived on in their accomplishment. They had constructed history. And history, as Professor Champion insisted, was Alice Bourne's abiding substitute for faith.

The heat of the day stirred smells: tepid wine, cigarette smoke, cheese softening on sharp little stakes. She'd thought the pervasive scent of the English would be something, well, *English*. She hadn't thought the entire nation would smell of wet tweed and horses, any more than she'd thought they'd smell of coal soot and carbolic soap. But the collegiate passion for Alliage perfume and Tabac aftershave had dismayed her nevertheless. She could smell them now, on ripening skin. Alliage and Tabac. It hadn't occurred back in the unknowing anticipation of home that the British would wish it upon themselves to smell so Continental. Champion detached himself from his circle of pretty people just then and came over to where Alice stood.

'Splendid isolation,' he said. 'Or just fortress America?'

He was a good-looking man, apart from the moustache. Straight men of Champion's age never wore facial hair like his at home. The moustache still looked to Alice like a melodramatic attempt at disguise.

'I'm sorry. I'm just not great at mixing,' she said.

3

He glanced the way she was still looking, out over the scorched ground towards the city and the cathedral. 'They say it's the hottest summer for five hundred years,' he said. 'Forest fires combusting spontaneously. Rumours of water rationing. But you look pale, untouched by it all. Are you quite well?'

Joni Mitchell sang, the song sinuous and sardonic. Alice thought she had preferred the singer in her folky, confessional phase.

It was true that she was pale. She was sleeping badly. She had persisted in dreaming what she thought of as the cormorant dream. She always awoke from its jarring strangeness and always found it difficult to get back to sleep again. Perhaps the heat was part of that. Champion was right: the weather was unrelenting. She'd seen smoke herself, in distant columns rising from English fields. She'd seen flames billow at dusk from a burning barn. She'd seen fire consuming a field of corn stubble. She'd dreamed the dream again last night.

'Maybe you'll be forced to reconsider,' Champion said, smiling behind the concealment of his moustache. 'If the South-West of England starts to ignite, you might find your destination unreachable.'

'Forest fires won't stop me,' Alice said. 'I grew up with them. And the place I want to go to is on the coast. If they close the roads I'll hire a boat and sail there if I have to.'

'You're that determined.'

'I am.'

He turned to faced her. 'You should, you know. Reconsider.'

She didn't answer him. In the cormorant dream, it occurred to her that she could smell as well as see. The cormorant itself smelled harsh with salt and tar. There were fish blood and the iridescent scales of fish smeared on the bone of its beak.

'It's too recent,' Champion said. 'The subject lacks the concealment of time. It's transparent, isn't it?'

Alice was silent.

'There's nothing to discover.'

She didn't want to antagonize him. He would be marking her graduate thesis. Others would read it, but his was the assessment on which the merit of her work would finally be judged. Her chosen subject was an event that had taken place on the Devon coast thirty-two years earlier. How did you define recent? She was of the belief that there was nothing much to be gained yet by poking through the still-spilling entrails of the Watergate affair. But it was already on the history curriculum here. The overthrow and death of the Marxist President Allende, whatever hand the CIA had or had not had in the coup, was also considered a fit subject for seminars. Yet the ink was barely dry on the Chilean leader's obituaries. The history department were happy to study events far more recent than the one she wished to explore. It was a question more, she thought, of emphasis than chronology; of the sway of academic fashion. On the literature curriculum, they examined Allen

Ginsberg's poetry and analysed the protest songs of Bob Dylan; studied whole litanies of domestic American disenchantment. There prevailed an end-of-empire mood in the history department. The United States was an empire in terminal decline and Vietnam had been the proof. Now was not an expedient time to say good things about Americans.

Joni Mitchell was proving the point. The record was playing for the third or perhaps the fourth time. Champion fixed Alice with his eyes and appeared to read the direction of her thoughts. It was a disconcerting talent, if he did possess it. 'Strikes me this whole album's about the vacuity at the heart of affluent America,' he said. 'Yet it's quintessentially a West Coast sound. I didn't know you people harboured anything like this artistic capacity for self-criticism.'

'I don't know that we do,' Alice said, looking towards the bright silver box spinning the record under the sun. Quintessentially, the singer-songwriter who'd recorded it was a Canadian.

'Have you been having bad dreams again?'

'It's the weather, I suppose.'

'You should get out of Whitstable. The place would give anyone nightmares,' Champion said. 'Come and live in the town. Much more accommodating.'

'Maybe,' she said, not meaning it. She'd thought Whitstable was a town. Canterbury was a city; the cathedral made it so. 'Maybe I will at that, professor. When I get back from my trip to Devon.'

His mouth twisted under the moustache, and he kicked dead grass with the toe of his shoe. 'You're set on it, then?'

'I am,' Alice said.

'Military history,' he said. 'With your mind. Three thousand-odd miles, to come and beat a bloody drum.'

Champion receded from her, and she shivered in the heat.

The cormorant dream was always the same. The pitch and toss of the waves and the tear of the wind would bring her to. She'd be hauled, wrenched out of sleep, swallowing back bile, queasy aboard some kind of boat. The boat had a shallow draught but was high-sided, and even standing, which she was forced to do in its comfortless hull, she could see only sky except when the craft rolled to starboard and the land formed a quick, ragged curve above the gunwale. Water sloshed around her knees at the bottom of the boat, and its plywood fabric groaned when the weight of the water it carried shifted through each barrelling roll. Its hull was flimsy and shuddered with the heavy slap of waves. Then, with bewildering suddenness, all land was gone, the pitch to starboard showing only a swell, green and glistening under early light. And then, with an eclipsing spread of black wings, the cormorant landed on the gunwale just above her and she flinched from it as it settled, its eyes empty above the beak and dense slick of feathers. She'd be filled with revulsion at the presence of the bird, recoiling from its stink and strange proximity.

★

Champion was talking to two of his undergraduates. There were two kinds of undergraduate guest at his party. There were his star students and there were those whom he couldn't escape, allocated as their personal tutor. These two looked to Alice like the latter, in that neither appeared remotely bookish or ingratiating. One was dressed in denim and the other in a summer suit showing signs of dishevelment. The denim boy was on the university boxing team, she'd seen him through the window of the gym, skipping, on her way to the tennis courts. He had a head of Pre-Raphaelite curls that sat helmet-like above heavy features. His friend was trying for a more stereotypically bohemian look. He seemed, at the least of it, successfully drunk. The thirty-two-year-old catastrophe on to which she hoped to shed light had claimed the lives of boys no older than the two she now watched sharing wine and conversation with their tutor on a June afternoon. Could those boys possibly have been as callow as these two? She doubted it. She'd seen the boxer studying his mirror image as skipping rope, fast, in the heat of the gym, flayed sweat from his sculpted body. Narcissism was no great quality in a fighting man, but at least, unlike his wobbling friend, he'd have passed his army physical.

At last, someone had changed the music. They'd put on Silk Degrees. Unless there was some seismic late shift in location or taste, this would for ever for Alice Bourne be in memory the summer of Boz Scaggs and Little Feat and Joni

Mitchell. The Pre-Raphaelite boy had put the new record on. Now he came over to her. Dark curls descended to his shoulders, and there was a stud in one of his ears. He smiled at her. She looked at him and waited for him to say something. This ability to smile at strangers was a social skill she didn't remotely share.

'I saw you skipping in the gym,' she said.

'I know. I watched you walk by.'

'You looked like you had eyes only for yourself.'

His smile widened. 'The mirror is more an aid to technique than a tool of vanity. I know how it looks. But it works.'

'Are you a good boxer?'

'Not bad. Are you any good at tennis?'

'Not bad. We could hit, if you'd like.'

She hadn't meant to say this. She surprised herself.

'I'd need some practice first,' he said. 'When an American says they're not bad, they're usually pretty good.'

'Oh? And when a British person says it?'

He pulled a face. 'It means they're not terrible. But usually they are.'

He said 'thee' for 'they'. The vowels in his speech were flat and short. It was an accent she had not heard before, she thought from the north.

'I'm Alice Bourne,' she said.

'I know. Professor Champion told me. David Lucas.'

He extended his hand, which surprised her, because shaking hands was something almost nobody she had met

9

in England seemed to do. It was endearing, in a way that the stud in the ear and the curls were not. She didn't believe him about the mirror.

'What did Champion say about me?'

'That it would be hard to make you smile. He was right.'

'Anything else?'

'That you want to waste time and considerable intellect lavishing an entire thesis on some obscure wartime accident out of nothing more than misplaced patriotism. I'm paraphrasing.'

She nodded and considered. 'You seem quite bright.'

'Thank you.'

'For a boxer.'

His dishevelled friend came over then. David introduced him as his flatmate and coursemate, Oliver Deane. Oliver wore a white shirt she reckoned had sat in the machine, neglected perhaps for days, following its most recent wash. Fatally wrinkled, it had then been ironed into a latticework of tiny creases. Oliver, drunk, did not shake hands with Alice Bourne. Instead he dipped his head slightly as was the fashion, like a reluctant horse testing bit and bridle, Alice thought. He began to speak, his voice slurry and public schooled, but Alice didn't really listen to what it was Oliver said. Her eyes were on Champion, flirting in the middle distance with a pretty girl in a pretty dress with a tightly ruched bodice. It was hard to concentrate in the heat. In the cormorant dream, her clothes were stiff and constricting and weighed heavily on her, she remembered then. And her mouth tasted tarry and sweet. It was odd, this ability to taste and smell in a dream.

'Are you OK?' It was David Lucas. 'You look pale.'

'I'm fine. Really, I'm fine.' 'Hotel California' was playing on the portable record player. She wondered if Champion would go home with the girl in the pretty dress. She thought about the weary walk up the lane to the bus stop and the toiling bus ride back to her digs in Whitstable and endured a sudden and intense stab of homesickness then.

'I'm going to go,' she said to David, offering Oliver, his drunken friend, an obligatory nod, turning to fetch her bag from where she'd left it in a pocket of shade under a tree on the slope. She'd taken the time and trouble to come to the party on the grass outside the college less to meet people than to try to win Champion over.

But Champion had other things on his mind. And her professor didn't honestly seem the winning-over sort. That discovery was the small accomplishment she would take away with her.

She thought about the northern boy with the curls on the bus ride back. He'd said he wasn't a bad boxer. According to his own reasoning, that should mean he was terrible. She didn't think he would be, though. She thought it an odd pastime for someone with any claim to intelligence. But boxing hadn't yet inflicted any damage to his face.

Jocks and nerds were separate species in American collegiate life. But the dichotomy she was so familiar with from home didn't seem anything like so clear cut or prevalent in England. She'd encountered really stupid sportsmen here, of course, brawny and privileged, doing courses with titles like land economy and agrarian science. She'd come across the rugby crowd, half-naked and bellowing lewd songs as they thumped out their drinking games in college bars. But almost everyone at Kent seemed to participate in some sort of sport. They played scratch soccer matches on the yellow grass of the campus. They flew kites. They played tag. They threw frisbies. There were incomprehensible games of cricket. Racing bikes were ridden along the undulating roads. A number of people drove to Broadstairs or Pegwell Bay to swim. Alice wondered why it was she found all this so strange. She swam most days herself off Whitstable beach, despite being pretty sure that amid the queasy panic of the cormorant dream she was quite unable to swim. It was strange because she'd thought the English sedate, stifled by a sort of class- and history-driven decorum. But the English played all the time. They frolicked under the sun.

Alice Bourne occupied a room in a large house at the Seasalter end of the shoreline. She lived on the ground floor. She could always hear the water breaking in waves on the steep slope of shingle beyond the sea wall outside her window. The house had wooden floors, and sometimes she could hear the scrape of a crutch from above. The physics postgrad living up there had broken a leg in a motorbike crash, and the rubber ferrules on the tips of his crutches squeaked on the floorboards with his agitated movement. The crash had been a bad one, the break severe. He couldn't get down the stairs very easily and was almost always up there, pissed off, fidgety. She could usually hear King Crimson or Genesis playing loudly on his reel-to-reel. Long John Silver's crutch music.

But Alice liked Whitstable. She liked the ice-cream parlour in Tankerton with its knickerbocker glory glasses and chipped marbling on old tabletops. She liked the taut slap in the wind of rope against the mast that held the harbour flag. Rigging thrummed in the harbour, beating a homely tattoo. She liked the painted-wood Victorian houses on Wavecrest. The reclusive actor Peter Cushing was rumoured to live in one of them, when he wasn't elsewhere making horror films. There was a market near the railway station where the cheese was always processed and they sold confectionery that had a suspicion of fire damage about it. But the market was friendly, and the local fruit was good and cheap. Once she'd got used to their frankly weird opening and closing rituals, she'd come to feel comfortable in the Whitstable pubs. She'd eat half a pint of prawns in the Pearson's Arms or sit on the breakwater outside the Neptune and watch the water, oily at sunset, stretching towards Sheppey as the sun descended, seeing out the day, sipping a glass of tepid Kentish beer.

She did this now, noticing milky jellyfish on the placid surface of the sea, hundreds of them, brought here, she supposed, by the unfamiliar heat, the slow, relentless raising of the water's temperature through this unprecedented summer to something almost tropical. The sea was new to her, an elemental novelty still, as it must have been to many of the men whose fate thirty-odd years ago she intended to explore despite the reluctance of her professor fully to sanction the project. Patriotic drum-banging. Mere military history. Jesus! She hadn't come over three thousand miles to explore blind alleys.

The lights were coming on now on the Isle of Sheppey. There were lights strung along a late fishing boat, and the flat shape of a dredger was outlined in electric lamps on the horizon as darkness deepened the sky. The sea at south Devon would not be like Whitstable, she knew, with its shingle and groynes and snug little harbour. The sea where she was going was capricious and exposing, its swell powered in tumbling waves along a vast wilderness of shore.

She sat on the breakwater outside the Neptune and wondered if anything ever washed up on Slapton Sands. Were badge caps and buttons and rifle bolts lightened by rust and corrosion on the sea bottom ever cast back on to the land? Was there a beachcomber living in the bay nursing a careful hoard of clues about the catastrophe? Alice Bourne was a historian, not a marine archaeologist. But when she arrived, knowing nothing after the struggle just to go, it would be interesting to see some tangible relic of the men who were rumoured to have perished there.

She'd sat in Champion's campus office and waited to plead

her case while he'd taken an important telephone call that interrupted their meeting almost at its outset. The blind over the single window was drawn against heat and glare. A spindly electric fan failed to create much of a breeze, noisily, on his desk. A collection of precise brass rubbings hung on one wall, long medieval faces in thin, gold leaf frames. It was hard for Alice to imagine such features ever having belonged to the living. Titles Champion had authored were given pride of place in his bookcase. They consumed almost a full shelf. He sat leafing through her proposal as he spoke into the phone, a habit she hated, regarded as dismissive, cavalier. She noticed that his moustache was stained with nicotine at its centre. He finished his call and lit a cigarette from the flame of a heavy desk lighter shaped out of onyx.

'Why have I never heard about this event?'

'Because it was covered up?'

Champion smoked and considered. He held the cigarette between the fingers of his right hand so that when he spoke and gesticulated smoke rose in a ragged column in blinkered sunlight through the blinds. 'So how did you hear about it?'

She'd been on a collegiate skiing trip to Colorado. It was January and shudderingly cold. She'd walked towards the close of the day with her friends into a bar that was really nothing more than a shack, freezing, tugging gloves from clumsy fingers and stamping snow in melting clumps from their boots, inhaling woodsmoke, feeling the radiant creep of heat from an iron stove. At the back of the bar she'd seen a photograph of a man who looked like the bar owner's son, in uniform, outside a whitewashed house at the wheel of a Jeep. Only it wasn't his son. It was the bar owner in another life. Beside the Jeep, blinking into the sunlight, were two women in britches carrying hoes. She'd asked about the photograph.

'Where was that taken?'

He still wore his hair in the crew cut he'd probably worn under his field cap then. It was grey and soft, like ermine, now. It would have bristled, salt and pepper, then. 'You tell me,' he said.

Alice Bourne considered the picture. 'The architecture looks like rural Ireland. But they're land girls, aren't they, in the photograph with you? So it must be England.'

'Very good. It's England all right. It's Devon. And it was taken in 1944.'

The bar proprietor had talked about his war service overseas. He'd talked cautiously at first, with some self-consciousness. But he'd recollected more easily when he realized how well informed his listener was about the period in which he'd most intensely lived his life. And as her friends sipped buttered rum and nibbled at potato chips, thawing out, this veteran had mentioned Slapton Sands to her. And she'd absorbed from him, in his words, the whole incomplete, horrifying mystery.

'It's an anecdote,' Champion said now. 'In context, I mean. It was a training accident. Logistically, I suppose they were unavoidable. Their scale reflected the scale of the enterprise. You want a cover-up, you should look at Watergate. That's a cover-up. And that, my dear, is real history.'

A sergeant called Delroy Boone had taken the photograph in the bar. Boone had been killed in Normandy, cut to pieces by machine-gun fire like hundreds of his comrades on Omaha Beach. The fact could be used to illustrate Champion's point. To illustrate but not to prove it, Alice Bourne thought.

'And the old boy in the bar was probably exaggerating,' Champion said. 'I'd embroider a tale in front of an audience as comely as you undoubtedly looked, snugly wrapped in ski clothes. It's only human nature. Probably his way of flirting.' He ground out his cigarette. After a short silence between the two of them, he took another from the packet on his desk and lit it. There was more silence. It wasn't really silence, with the odd call or cry of laughter carrying from the student world outside, behind the shuttered blind over the one window, but it seemed like silence to Alice in the smoky seclusion in which they sat. When Champion spoke again, he spoke softly. 'We're talking here about your doctoral thesis. You've an original mind. I won't stop you writing about whatever did or did not happen at Slapton Sands. But I would sincerely recommend you look for a subject more suited to your undoubted gifts.'

She said nothing. She looked at her linked fingers in her lap, waiting the moment out.

'Military history,' he said. 'It's like writing up a game of dominoes.'

'The military say it didn't happen.'

'Watergate happened.'

'Watergate is still happening,' Alice said. 'I'm an historian, not a journalist.'

'That's that, then,' Champion said, dismissing her.

He'd been ushering her out of the door when he mentioned the tutorial party taking place the following week. An opportunity for her to meet people, he said. Can't live your life in a scholarly vacuum of reading and research. She briefly pictured jugs of Pimm's and cricket sweaters. Dappled, sunny aphorisms. Leather and oiled willow. But her departing smile was forced.

Water lapped against the breakwater outside the Neptune, everything dappled and flushed in the water's reflection under the descending sun. Alice lifted her glass and sipped beer. It tasted warm and hoppy. The sky was empty, apart from a few torn threads of vapour trail, remote, almost at that reach where the sky became space. She thought a boat slipping out of the harbour must have caused the brief agitation of the water. Otherwise the stillness was complete. She felt remote from everything, without purpose and more isolated than she could ever remember having felt. In a few days she would travel to Slapton Sands, brave a journey west across the smouldering country to discover what she could about what had really happened there over a few days in April in 1944.

The known facts were straightforward enough. The American army had needed to rehearse for the invasion of France. They chose this particular section of the Devon coast for their practices because it so resembled the coast of Normandy. Slapton Sands looked strikingly, eerily similar to Utah Beach. Slapton Leys, the shallow, gravel-bedded lagoon beyond the beach, was as close in conditions and topography as they could approximate to the flooded hinterland of the Cotentin. Action was sanctioned in the autumn of 1943. The whole of an area known as the South Hams would be evacuated: seventeen thousand acres of farmland, two thousand, seven hundred and fifty people, six miles of coastline, the villages of Blackawton, Strete, Torcassow, Stokenham, Chillington, East Allington and Slapton itself. The people were told they had to leave in meetings held at their village halls on the evenings of 12 and 13 November. They were given a deadline for departure of 20 December. The decision was taken in private, never even discussed by the full War Cabinet of the British government. The American ambassador to Britain lobbied and Winston Churchill agreed. So it was that families who had lived in south Devon since the compiling of the Domesday Book were given six weeks to leave with no offer of compensation or assurance about when they would be able to return. There were protests, which were futile. There were suicides. But the deadline was met. And when the soldiers of the United States army's 4th Infantry

Division arrived in their twenty-six-square-mile Devon domain, they marched along empty roads, through fields glutted with forgotten crops, past schools and shops, post offices, pubs, churches and cottages which lay silent, empty and abandoned.

Summer darkness had almost come. Light through the window of the pub pitted and scarred the old stone of the breakwater. Jellyfish glowed pale and thick as spawn now on the water. She'd take a train to Totnes and then a taxi to the guesthouse she'd located in Strete. She didn't have a car. She didn't have a telephone or a television either, come to that. These absences seemed unremarkable in England.

There was a TV room in each of the colleges, but it was a long way to go to watch television and anyway a kind of censorship was imposed, an insidious insistence on what it was and wasn't ideologically proper to view. That dim friend of David Lucas, Oliver Deane, had grumbled about it at the party earlier in the day. David had wanted to watch a televised world title fight involving some Panamanian champion called Duran. But boxing was ritualised brutality, considered too thuggish for the student union rep in charge of the TV watching in Elliot, the college among the four colleges at Kent of which Lucas was a member.

'David called her an Apache,' Oliver said admiringly. 'Told her she was an Apache.' He sipped wine. 'To her face.'

Some of the students on the campus brandished copies of *Bury My Heart at Wounded Knee* with the same totemic pride with which copies of *Zen and the Art of Motorcycle Maintenance* were just then being routinely flourished. In the year of the bicentennial, treatment of its native tribes was one more stick with which to beat America. But Apache was not, had not for a long time, been a term of disparagement. Quite the opposite, in fact.

'You're sure he didn't call her something similar-sounding to Apache? Apparatchik, maybe?'

'Absolutely not,' Oliver said. 'Well. Maybe.'

He looked keen to change the subject. He produced a matchbox from a pocket and began to fumble with it. Alice watched, for want of anything else to occupy her attention. When he managed to open the matchbox, it was full of small, circular pills.

'Blues,' Oliver said to Alice. 'Billy.'

'Billy?'

'Whiz. Speed.'

'Amphetamine isn't very good for you.'

'I know. I've got a death wish.'

'It rots brain cells.' Though to be honest, the damage looked to be done.

'Would you like one?'

'Thanks. I'll pass.'

'Come again?'

'She's wisely declining,' David Lucas said, returning from a visit to what they all called the loo. 'What have you two been talking about?'

'Sitting Bull,' Alice said. 'Little Big Horn.'

They both looked at her, the one appraising, the other clueless. David Lucas was very good-looking, she decided. It was only a shame about the embellishments.

Alice decided to have another drink before leaving the pub. It was fully dark now. The black bulk of the oyster sheds formed a solid rectangle of darkness concealing the harbour from where she stood, but the lights of Sheppey twinkled prettily enough across the sea. She'd been born and raised in the middle of her home state of Pennsylvania and never tired now of the novelty of the coast. So she lingered over the night view for a moment before going into the saloon bar to order another glass of bitter and listen to whatever was playing on the Neptune's old jukebox. She didn't know enough about the English to establish whether it was someone's ironic joke, but a high proportion of the records on the jukebox had a nautical flavour about them. You couldn't escape Chicago's terrible dirge, 'If You Leave Me Now', that summer. And Elton John and Kiki Dee were for ever warbling their duet. But when she walked through the door of the pub, the regulars were playing their games of darts and bar billiards to the Fleetwood Mac instrumental, 'Albatross'.

Alice was served by the landlord. He was a brusque man with little time for students. But he'd been a pilot sergeant in the war and seemed to appreciate how knowledgeable she was about events then. She was a good listener and had opened him up to an extent that she thought had surprised and perhaps even embarrassed him. He was naturally reticent, as so many men were recalling their part in the conflict. She persisted, though, because she thought oral history was important, and she knew that it was finite. He told her once about the briefings they were given prior to duelling with German fighter-bombers in what later became known as the Battle of Britain. Principally, these talks concerned the importance of fuel economy, he told her. They listened to pep talks on how to save petrol as they washed down Benzedrine with mugs of weak tea. Historians like Champion were efficient with statistics and dates, but they had no real experience of the world. Men like the Neptune landlord did. Alice owed this insight to her father, whose own life and death had taught her an indelible lesson.

She would not ask the landlord about the war tonight, though. She was tired, and he had an intolerant look that tightened his smile of welcome to something near a grimace. She'd had enough of conversation for one day at the party on the yellow grass. She would have loved a proper talk, full of the ease and intimacy of home; but it wasn't to be. The only way she could reach home was through shovelling coins into the telephone box outside the Salvation Army citadel on the high street, with its broken panes of glass and a receiver that smelled faintly of old saliva and cigarettes. There was no intimacy there; only unwarranted expense and the dislocating awkwardness of satellite delay forcing pauses that prevented conversation.

Besides, who was there at home for her to swap intimacies with?

Looking at the wisps of vapour trailing the sky earlier, she'd thought of home. She'd read somewhere that some English flight tycoon was selling transatlantic returns for a hundred pounds. But she hadn't really envied the passengers in the jets that left those soft streaks of white earlier daubed on the sky. And it wasn't homesickness that kept her now in the light and comfort of the pub. As she found a vacant table and sat down with her fresh drink to the sound of Procul Harem and 'A Salty Dog' (surely it had to be a joke, didn't it?), she was honest enough with herself to admit the fact. She was there not because she craved company or fresh stories about sorties over the Kent Weald from the horse's mouth, or even the beer, hoppy and pale and still challenging her stubborn will to acquire an acquired taste for it in its glass on the tabletop. She was there because she didn't want to go home and slip into sleep over a book and dream the cormorant dream again.

Alice thought of herself as comparatively tough, fairly resourceful, independent by circumstance, if not by nature. But each time she dreamed the dream it found some fresh detail to insinuate forboding into her. She'd awaken chilly with dread in the close heat of this strange English summer. And sleep would prove elusive after that.

She studied the other people in the pub. Nobody there smelled of Alliage or Tabac. Those were scents more potently grouped on the campus, in the college bars. Here there were mostly students in denim, much of it embroidered, the girls in smock tops and clogs and the boys shod in clogs or cowboy boots. Alice thought most English university student fashion arcane, rural even. Location didn't seem to have too much bearing on this. The same arcadian dress code applied equally in the pubs in Camden Town she'd visited on her one real weekend in London since her arrival in England. You'd see the odd dyed David Bowie wedge cut on students from the school of art in Canterbury. But most pub males dressed in the biker-farmer hybrid style pioneered, if that was the right word, by the ramshackle bands they listened to. There was a lot of unkempt hair, a lot of rolling your own, a surprising and possibly even dismaying amount of corduroy. She'd saved hard doing two vacation jobs for her own wardrobe and had had to tone it right down here to avoid looking hopelessly out of place. She didn't really understand this deliberate dressing down among the men. Even if you were really, really into Jethro Tull, you surely wouldn't want to be reminded of Ian Anderson when you studied your reflection. Would you? And the dressing down among the women was even more baffling.

Alice Bourne had been brought up poor. She hadn't been dirt poor, but she'd learned an appreciation of the good things in the most emphatic way possible. She hadn't had any of them. Every material possession in her life, like every intellectual accomplishment, had needed to be earned. She had never resented the fact. You played the hand life dealt

25

you. But the modest circumstances of her upbringing had taught her to like good clothes and good shoes. English folk wisdom insisted that a person never missed what they had never had. Alice considered this to be total horseshit. But her suits and her skirts languished with her leather briefcase in the wardrobe of a Whitstable room while she strove for the drab conformity of the general student body.

She'd worn her good clothes in England only twice. The first occasion was her formal interview with her supervising tutor, Professor Champion. She'd considered it a necessary formality, a demonstration of respect. He'd seemed loftily indifferent to how she looked. It hadn't been a mistake, at any rate, because the interview had gone well. He'd thought it necessary to reminisce about the carpet bombing of Cambodia, deride the peanut farmer striving for the White House, name-check Gore Vidal and Ruben Hurricane Carter and Gil-Scott Heron. But it was the bicentennial year and he was a liberal historian and, anyway, she was getting used to it.

It was the second time she wore her good clothes that got her upset. She wore her Bill Blass suit from Bloomingdales to the cathedral. And a woman with cropped hair in a boiler suit and work boots had sneered in the transept and offered Alice the unwelcome information that she looked like a hooker on the make.

She had not personally sanctioned the carpet bombing of Cambodia. She didn't mention this fact to Professor Champion. She didn't mention either that her older brother, Bobby, had been a casualty of the seventy-seven-day battle of Khe Sanh, dead at twenty, killed by septicaemia thirty-six hours after he was hit in the chest and legs by grenade fragments as his platoon tried and failed to hold a desperate position from being overrun. And she didn't say anything in reply to the hooker remark. What was the point? The feminist agenda here seemed unalloyed, unmitigated, unremarkable in its predictably fixed hostilities and hard-core resentments.

She was angry, though, about Bobby. She was angry whenever English students and campus academics aired the theory about the draft conspiracies that tried to solve America's social problems by sending its ghetto dwellers in disproportionate numbers to fight in Vietnam. She'd seen no evidence of this as an adolescent in Pennsylvania, where the draft had seemed pretty indiscriminate and she'd not been aware of a single case of a boy trying to avoid it.

She'd been reminded about Bobby at the tutorial party earlier that day when David, the cute English under-graduate, had commented on what a tragedy it was that Muhammad Ali, in what would have been his best years in the ring, had been prevented from boxing for refusing the draft. What kind of a tragedy was that, she had wondered. A sporting tragedy? An aesthetic tragedy? She'd enjoyed Ali's courage and grace in the ring herself on television. Who hadn't? But tragedy for Alice Bourne was her drafted brother dying in the bewilderment of delirium on a foreign battlefield. She burped surreptitiously and sipped hoppy

27

beer. Smelling patchouli oil and hand-rolled Old Holborn, she reminisced, for a few seconds of indulgent weakness, about jukeboxes devoid of foghorns and barnacles, about cold draft in chilled jugs and pizza and voluble, civilized, Ivy League sanity.

Champion had suggested that she study a subject with what he insisted was greater substance. He suggested the Marshall Plan and its catastrophic effect on Britain's post-war economy. Or what about the segregated black GIs in Britain in the 1940s, he said, and the appalling racism they endured from their own army? She could investigate whether the crime wave enabled by the London Blitz was anything other than folk myth.

'It's your best interests I'm thinking about,' he'd said. 'I've a mind to publication. What you suggest sounds more appropriate for one of those popular paperbacks which discuss Krakatoa and the Kraken and alien abduction and the Bermuda Triangle.'

She'd said nothing.

'Don't you want to be published?'

'Eventually. Of course, eventually. It's not my principal motivation, though, for this.'

In Colorado, in the fug of stove heat and the late light of a short winter day, she'd listened to the old infantryman tell his story, incomplete and staccato, like all true war stories were, he insisted, except for those concerning the generals, who were the only people privileged to see the picture in its entirety. To other ranks it was not quite chaos, because they had discipline and training and the comfort of routine. But it was sometimes close to chaos because they were men confined together, in huge numbers, in an alien place, operating in conditions of absolute secrecy, some of the men very raw. And in the sea they were confronting an element most of them had seen for the first time only when they embarked for Europe in convoy from New York aboard passenger liners hastily turned into troopships for the task.

'I say it wasn't quite chaos,' he told her. 'But it was chaos all right that April, when I came back from London.'

He'd gone to London because that was what they did after weeks of drills and punishing night endurance marches and small arms practice and confinement with other men in a Nissen hut. They did it even though it meant a long bicycle ride to Totnes Station and a cramped ride aboard a train in blackout conditions to Paddington. At least on the way back they'd be too hungover to care about the length of the ride or the suffocatingly small compartments or abiding absence of refreshment of any sort. They went to London because the alternative was the Red Cross Club or a Totnes pub serving weak cider drunk among farm hands until they were forced to leave at half-past ten when the place was obliged to close. They went for sex and hard liquor and bustle and anonymity; for the chance to sing and brawl and misbehave and do it all in the relative safety of a metropolis under an imposed and absolute darkness.

'Most of us thought we were going to die,' the Colorado veteran told Alice Bourne, rolling a cigarette, deliberately, between steady fingers. 'The Germans had been in France a long time. They were a battle-hardened army of occupation. We didn't know where we'd be landing, but we assumed the coast of France. The beaches had been mined. Tank traps had been constructed, pillboxes built, all the machine-gun emplacements would have unimpeded fields of fire. Field Marshal Rommel had masterminded those coastal defences. They would be thorough, formidable. We thought we were going to die, all right. Most of us.' Years of mountain sun and tobacco had seamed his face. His features had not altered since the taking of the picture at the wheel of a Jeep on the wall. But time and the habit had drained all the youth out of him and lined him in those places in his face where youth had once been deposited. He looked like he had been mined for his youth. 'Course,' he said, 'we assumed we were going to die fighting.' He smiled. 'All of us assumed we'd be dying at least in battle, for a cause.'

So making the most of life in the face of death he'd gone to London and painted the town on a two-day pass and returned late in the evening to a changed atmosphere of silence and empty billets and armed sentries strung along the shore as though they were expecting to repulse invasion rather than practising carrying out an invasion of their own. A field hospital had been hauled together out of canvas and

SLAPTON SANDS

wood behind Slapton Leys. He'd heard the stifled cries of casualties under sedation and seen the yellow lights they used in makeshift operating theatres creeping like glow-worms along seams of canvas through the blackout.

'I couldn't get any information,' he told Alice Bourne. 'I didn't see many guys I recognized, which was curious, but those I did recognize weren't talking. Then a captain told me to shut up and sit tight or I'd be doing plenty of talking of my own to our MPs. I must have looked pretty upset. I didn't know it then, but I'd lost a lot of friends. Anyway, this captain, he relented a little bit. Sit tight until morning, soldier, he said. Things'll be a lot clearer tomorrow than they are tonight.'

Alice nodded. Behind her, she could hear her skiing friends becoming louder in their laughter and talk with warmth and alcohol.

'He was lying. I don't know, maybe he was just trying to be sympathetic. Either way, he wasn't telling the truth.'

At first light, the Colorado infantryman had gone down to the shore. A thin, persistent rain was dimpling the sand and the still water, and the grey horizon rested no greater distance than what seemed a pebble's throw away. The sentries were still there, strung along the shore, slick in watery light in their green rain capes. But the gulls had gone, which was unusual. And the shallow sky was grey and seemed absorbed with a roof-like silence. Start Bay extended to either side of where he stood, a shallow curve stretching as far as it was possible to see in the wet,

31

diminished light. Water in salt droplets gathered and dripped from the brim of his field cap. The bay, the featureless sea and dimpled sand, looked like a place harbouring secrets.

'But the sea gives up its secrets,' he told Alice Bourne, thirty-odd years later in the warmth and comfort of his little bar. 'An infantryman in full kit will sink, weighed down by his boots and his ammunition. But corpses bloat on the bottom. Belts, clothing – they're shrugged away by the currents under there. The bottom of the sea is a restless place. Pretty soon, bodies started washing up. And they didn't just restrict themselves to the six miles of beach we'd seconded. No. Those boys washed up all along the south Devon coast and beyond.'

'What killed them?'

He'd looked at her for a long time. He took a drink of the whisky he'd poured himself. 'I don't know. I do know that far too few of them found the burial proper to them.'

'How many of them were there?'

'I'd be guessing,' he said.

'An educated guess.'

'Don't patronize me, miss,' he said.

'I'm sorry.'

'It's all right.' He shifted in his seat and drank. 'I'm used to it. It comes with age. But my guess is educated. I'd say over a thousand men. I'd say we lost close to fifteen hundred.'

'Jesus.'

He'd smiled when she said that. 'I don't think Jesus was at

Slapton Sands, miss. Not ever, I don't think. But certainly not on that day He wasn't.'

Maybe that's my true historical gift, Alice thought now. Finding out from bar-owning war vets about the conflict as seen through beer-soaked, ageing minds. As she left the Neptune for home, Whitstable fully dark now, she looked out over the sea wall and was surprised to see that the jellyfish had gone. Where they had loomed and coalesced in white clouds under the water was only a smooth blackness reflecting the sky in starts and winks of jittering, silver light. Some jolly acoustic ditty followed her out of the closing door of the pub, something by Steeleye Span or Fairport Convention about a day trip to Brighton that had become a hit after being used on a television commercial for butter, or for bread. She'd heard Long John Silver playing it in the room above hers and thought it a departure from his usual aural diet of austere progressive rock. Then she'd heard the squeal of his crutch tips and remembered he had a telly as he dragged himself across the floor to turn it off, she supposed, in disgust.

The song was folky, nostalgic. They employed nostalgia often to sell things here. It was a weird thing about the English, she thought, their reluctance to divorce past and present. They seemed infinitely more beguiled by the past than people were at home. Even in Camden Town they wore collarless shirts and corduroy, and wood and leather clogs or nailed boots, such as a rural labourer might have had no choice but to wear a century ago. You'd see a character straight out of Thomas Hardy at the wheel of a Volkswagen Beetle stuck in a London traffic jam. Yet nobody seemed to think it incongruous. The green man leered out at you from the labels of beer bottles. There were harvest festivals and morris dancers and none of the shops opened on a Sunday. You couldn't see a movie on a Sunday either. They were extremely reluctant about refrigeration, even in this record-breaking heat. They viewed ice cubes as an exotic and impractical affectation and seemed to consider food a necessary evil, something to be endured only because one had to endure it in order to avoid weakness and eventual death. They stuck stubbornly to traditional recipes, few of the listed ingredients actually qualifying as food. Tripe. Black pudding. White pudding. Suet pudding. Steak and kidney pudding. That stuff they called spotted dick. Did any other country seriously consider a whelk edible? Then there were their austere, ration-book beverages. Marmite. Horlicks. Ovaltine. Could anybody convincingly explain Ovaltine?

It was morris men that baffled her most. Alice believed, intellectually, in assimilating other cultures. But she'd happily risk accusations of closed-minded bigotry to exclude morris men from this general principle. Then there was John Barleycorn. What place did John fucking Barleycorn realistically occupy in the late twentieth century? The key, clearly, was to get yourself on to the capricious and bizarre agenda propagated by the morris men. Alice paused, extended her right hand, felt the rough granite of the sea wall against her fingertips, warm despite the night, the stone, to her touch. She was drunk. Tiredness and sun had conspired to make her drunk on a few glasses of pale Kentish beer. She took a couple of deliberate breaths, tasting stored heat in old stone and salt from the supine Whitstable sea. And she thought of the Apache and his friend, Sir Lancelot, drunk, at the party that afternoon. It seemed a long time ago now. He'd been cute, was cute; but both of them had stressed to her the gulf in maturity that stretched all but unbridgeable between the undergraduate and postgraduate student. Their study was a diversion still, while hers was a cause. Then she hiccuped and laughed at herself, at her own drunken pomposity. We're not supposed to do that, she thought, hiccuping again. We're not supposed to be able to laugh at ourselves, we Americans. We don't possess that sly, ironic English gift.

She was almost home. She'd never felt further from home. She fumbled in her bag for her key. She looked up, and the night stars winked back at her conspiratorially. Had Peter Cushing capered past her then in Hammer Horror resplendence, she wouldn't have turned a hair. But she opened her door begging herself not to dream the cormorant dream that night.

'I'll fix myself a Horlicks,' she mumbled, feeling her familiar way around the confines of her room. 'Or an Ovaltine. Maybe a Bovril.' She hiccuped again. 'A Bovril. Beef extract. Jesus. Bound to do the trick.'

She switched on her desk lamp. She sat on the bed and took off her shoes. The giddiness ebbed out of her. It was here, after all, that she dreamed.

By student standards her room was uncluttered. She didn't have candles, scented or otherwise, despite the fashion for them. And she didn't like the big paper globes popular as lampshades for overhead bulbs. Alice thought them a dreary fire hazard so ubiquitous it was a wonder students weren't nightly incinerated. Her room was illuminated by an Anglepoise and a bedside lamp from Habitat in Canterbury. When she had moved in, there had been posters on the walls. The dead girl in the lily pond and the blown-up movie still of Butch and Sundance about to meet their maker she had rolled and secured with elastic bands and stored beneath the bed. The painting of Gandalf she'd ripped up and put in the bin. An area at the bottom left of the poster had been carefully torn off, probably, she thought, to be used as roaches. The paper was laminated and the subsequent joints would have tasted disgusting. But she was glad of the justification for throwing the image away. At the age when these things are decided, Alice had opted for Narnia over Middle Earth. She'd been eight. Aslan was cool, the White Witch cooler. The Hobbit, by contrast, was a jerk.

Her walls were decorated now with historical photographs. She had the famous Frank Capra taken at Normandy. She had a Lee Miller shot of Ernest Hemingway having dinner with Marlene Dietrich at Jack Dempsey's restaurant in New York. There was a very primitive photograph of Abraham Lincoln atop his makeshift platform delivering the Gettysburg Address to a blurred multitude. The raising of the flag at Iwo Jima. A strutting Theodore Roosevelt. Kennedy reading the Robert Frost poem on the bitterly cold morning of his inauguration. Christ, she thought for the thousandth time, what heartbreaking promise had resided in that frozen moment of time. There was a picture of a wounded Panzergrenadier officer lying on a cot in a field hospital with an SS Gruppenführer standing solicitously over him. Winter plumed the senior officer's breath as he patted the wounded man's shoulder with one gloved hand. The final shot showed an English firefighter, unshaven face gaunt with soot, sitting, spent, on coping stones at the edge of a ragged pyramid of smouldering rubble. One of the tin helmets made mandatory in the London Blitz lay upturned like a melancholy relic between his boots.

People studied history for all sorts of different reasons. Alice Bourne thought that she was being educated in a time and in a place when the principal function of the study of the past was justification for the political ideologies of the present. That wasn't her motivation, though. She thought it was probably that of her professor, and explained Champion's glee in using the bicentennial anniversary to turn his gift for analysis to America's historical short-comings. They were doing that at home, too, of course. And recent events in American history made it an agonizing process.

But it wasn't why Alice studied history. If she had an axe to grind, she was honestly unaware of it. She was fascinated by the past and by its secrets, that was all. And she preferred the study of the recent past because it seemed sometimes so tantalizingly close, as if almost within touching distance.

You could study medieval history, but it was so speculative a subject as to be almost abstract, she felt. Whatever awe and admiration she felt for the men who had built Canterbury's cathedral was felt a substantial remove away for what she felt about the people in the pictures that decorated her walls. They were real, they were corporeal. You could source documentary evidence to discover exactly how successful Abe Lincoln's career in law had been before politics claimed him. Champion's brass rubbings, by contrast, thin faces in their parsimonious frames, portrayed people so remote from the secular world that Alice felt inadequate to get inside the meat and mystery of their lives. Perhaps this was because she was American and came from a youthful country.

It wasn't that she lacked imagination. She would never know who the young German tank killer was in her picture on the wall. But she knew that abiding strength lay beneath the trauma and blood loss that had drained his face of vigour. She wondered if he had lived to regret the appalling purpose to which his strength was being put. But she was in no doubt that he had lived, had survived this wound, this particular episode in his life.

The English firefighter sitting uselessly beside his pyre of

Blitz desolation had eyes that reminded her of those she'd seen staring from the faces of grunts pictured after combat missions in Vietnam. Desolate; they were desolate eyes. It was a look not just beyond consolation but beyond reproach. His eyes signalled that he had put his mind somewhere distant from all encroachment. His uniform displayed a rank beyond his years, and that was a puzzle to her she knew she would never solve. But after studying his face, she'd have bet money that this was a man who had seen things so awful that if he dreamed at all it was all his survival allowed him to do, to dream in monochrome.

Champion insisted on thinking that she wanted to investigate the tragedy at Slapton Sands simply to commemorate the deaths of brave American boys happy to leave their homeland to fight the abstract concept of fascism. Her motivation was patriotism, pure and simple, he'd decided. She wanted to gain her doctorate by celebrating the courage and idealism of young American men who had paid the ultimate price for freedom. He had this phrase, did Champion, in her tense dialogues with him over whether Slapton Sands was or was not a fit subject for her thesis.

'Let's look at the salient facts,' he would say. But there weren't any, not really, which was really her point.

Whatever had gone wrong in Devon had occurred in conditions of utmost secrecy, and the American military establishment seemed determined to keep it that way. She had tried and failed to get any kind of official response to queries about casualties incurred during training. So far as the US army was concerned, all casualties were casualties of war. The US navy said the same. She'd found some reference to Slapton and the Arlington Military Cemetery in a Senate sub-committee report after trawling for days through microfiche, but whatever had been discussed had been subjected to censorship then or since, which made the transcript meaningless.

'This is not an article for *Stars and Stripes*,' she'd said to Champion.

'It's a footnote,' he'd said, reiterated. 'It's an anecdote. It's a waste of a keen and resourceful mind.'

And maybe it was, and maybe the professor with the moustache that made him look a bit like Joseph Conrad was right. But the thing was, she wanted to know. And she felt that this was something knowable. She had nothing of what her cop father would have termed 'stuff we can take to the bank'. She had only the oral account of a soldier who'd missed the event getting drunk and laid in London's Piccadilly and the discrepancies she'd discovered in casualty figures when the units involved had got to Normandy. But her instinct insisted there was something significant there. She felt that finding out the facts, solving the mystery, was important. And it wasn't detective work to Alice Bourne. And it wasn't an anecdote. To her, it was history. And its authentication, its telling as irrefutable truth, would provide her justification. It would also perhaps provide a fitting epitaph for the uncommemorated dead.

History for Alice Bourne centred on values largely

immune to cynicism and trends. History for her was about proof, fact: justification in truth.

She was shuddered into consciousness, shivering, bewildered. Smoke lingered strong and acrid in the dream's bitter aftermath. But she could not remember the dream. Its images had emptied from her mind. She gathered her duvet about her head and closed her eyes. But the smoke was real. Smoke hung, hazy, in the early light of her room.

Alice lifted back her duvet and swung her legs out of the bed, smelling the unfamiliar smell about where she slept. Alone, she slept naked. She opened a drawer in her bureau and took out a clean T-shirt and a pair of knickers and put them on. She opened her curtains. It was only just getting light, the day breaking raw and insubstantial over the sea through the window. The T-shirt she had pulled on smelled strongly of cigarette smoke. Fear brushed her skin, and she felt a kind of claustrophobic panic she thought it necessary to fight. Then she saw the ashtray on her desk. It had been placed next to her typewriter, just to the right of the little Olivetti portable which had been her father's gift on her last birthday before his death. The ashtray seemed a familiar object, circular and made of white, opaque glass, crenellated like the walls of a castle to accommodate the width of cigarettes rested between puffs. Didn't they have these in the Neptune? Was it a souvenir from the pub? She hadn't been that drunk, didn't possess that jackdaw, student compunction for random theft.

Anyway, the ashtray wasn't empty. It contained a single

cigarette stub. The stub was white, unfiltered, fouled heavily at its end with nicotine. And it wasn't hers. Alice Bourne had never smoked a cigarette in her life.

She felt cold. She fancied she could hear the snap and thrum of rigging on the harbour masts in wind grown terse, urgent. Water gathered and roared and hissed into shingle in her ears. Rubber insinuated squeaky crowded noises on the floorboards above her head. But none of this was real. The wristwatch on her bedside table told her it was five-thirty in the morning. There was no surf on the beach. The harbour was half a mile away. Long John Silver was sound asleep. The wind caterwauled only in her head. But smoke hung sour in the room, and the ashtray sat on her desk as its obdurate proof. Alice Bourne dressed quickly and fled. She escaped despite the fact that it was too early on a Sunday morning for there to be anywhere in Whitstable to go. She gained the beach and walked the tide line, trying to lose herself in its litter of rope braids and bleached plastic fragments and bits of waterlogged wood. She walked, hoping the breeze would tear the tobacco smell from out of her clothes. But the wind was somnolent and the day heavy already with its promise of burdening heat. No matter. She would walk for as long as it took.

Alice was familiar with incidents of shock and trauma from the stories her state trooper father had brought home and regaled her and her brother with over family dinners. They'd lived fifty miles north of the tough industrial Pennsylvania heartland of Easton and Allentown. Her father's district had been a sometimes bleak and difficult place to police, made mean by land recession and the shocking decline of Pennsylvania's staple industry, which had been steel. Some of his tales were lurid, disquieting in their randomness and detail. Crime is a question of approach, he'd always insisted; of preparation. Cops expect bad things to happen. No one else does, not really; not all the time, not the way cops do.

She'd been well enough schooled by her dad to know that it was shock now that prevented her from being able to consider properly the extent and implications of the weird violation she'd been subjected to. Perspective might come later but was impossible now. Beyond the fright and indignation, what she did have was the detail. And she needed to focus her mind with clarity on that. Her door had not been forced. Nobody had climbed through her window. The physical evidence of trespass comprised the cigarette and the ashtray in which it had been extinguished. The ashtray was ageless, characterless, generic. The cigarette, though, was not.

The English all seemed to smoke. Which wasn't to discriminate against the Scots and the Irish, who seemed to Alice Bourne to smoke even more than the English did. They smoked brands here called Benson & Hedges and Rothmans and Peter Stuyvesant. Many of them smoked Marlboro, bought in stiff cardboard packs. But walking the tide line, Alice knew that the cigarette stubbed out in her room was none of these. She knew because her dad and his

43

state trooper buddies had played cards once a week, the card school rotating around a route comprising each member's home. So once every six weeks, four or five of her dad's colleagues would descend on their dining room and fill it with poker hands and cop vernacular and beer drunk from the neck of the bottle and smoke. In the morning she would help her brother clear the room up after them. She'd seen enough to know that the discarded butt in her room in Whitstable belonged to a Lucky Strike.

Professor Champion smoked Gitanes. She didn't know why that fact came to her then, but it was a fact, and it did. A Lucky. The cigarette butt ground out in the ashtray in her room was American. As she stared out over the sea towards Sheppey, it seemed an incongruous detail. But it was nothing like so troubling as having had the man who'd smoked it in her room uninvited while she slept. And it had been a man, she was certain of that detail, too. He'd left his own smell, oily and masculine under the sour odour of smoke.

Now, she took a deep breath and turned her eyes back towards the sleeping town. She couldn't go home. She couldn't, just now, entertain the idea. She'd had the presence of mind to bring her bag out with her. It contained her travelcard and her cash and her pass for the campus library. She'd go up there, wait for the library to open, sit at one of the blond wood carrels and work. Maybe if she was lucky she could scrounge a cup of morning coffee from one of the college kitchen staff. They brewed Kenco coffee in Kenco coffee machines. They brewed it with British indifference. It wasn't great. But it wasn't at all bad either, and it was a hell of a lot better than nothing.

The Apache said: 'You don't think Peter Cushing could in some way be involved?'

'I highly doubt it,' Alice said. Without enthusiasm, she sipped beer.

'Exotic smokes,' Oliver said, persisted. 'They had to come from somewhere other than Whitstable. And nobody else living there is a film star.'

'The Hammer Horrors are made at Borehamwood,' David Lucas said. 'Nothing exotic about Borehamwood.'

'But he's not at Borehamwood, is he?' Oliver said. 'Has somebody coughed?'

'Nobody's coughed,' David said. 'Where is he, then? If he isn't at Borehamwood?'

'My brother drinks with a lighting rigger who happens to be working on his new movie. It's science fiction, this one. Nothing to do with vampires and werewolves. Cushing plays a top-ranking baddie, apparently, on this orbiting arsenal called the Death Star.'

'And they sell ciggies on the Death Star, do they?' David said.

'Someone's definitely coughed,' Oliver said.

'You're double-bluffing, Ollie,' David said. 'On the coughing front.'

Alice wasn't following this any more. She looked at the

Apache. 'How would Peter Cushing get Lucky Strikes on the Death Star?'

'The Death Star is an entire planet,' Oliver said. 'As such, it's bound to have toilets, cafeterias and so on. Toilets and cafeterias generally have cigarette machines.'

'Where is this Death Star?' David asked.

'Deep space,' Oliver said.

'OK. Where's your brother's drinking pal rigging his lights?'

'Elstree,' the Apache said. He looked deflated. 'Embassy Number One territory, Elstree, I suppose.'

'Even aboard the Death Star,' David said.

'I'm sure someone's coughed,' the Apache said. 'I'm going to the loo. Sorry.'

'What's this coughing thing?' Alice said to David when he'd gone. 'Does he think there's a tuberculosis epidemic or something?'

'It's a euphemism for farting,' David said.

'Oh.'

'You know. Like letting one go. Squeezing one off. Pooping. Trumping.'

'I get the general idea,' she said. 'Trumping?'

'You don't have trumping in America?'

'Not to my knowledge. We don't find flatulence as endlessly funny as the British seem to.'

David looked at her across their table. 'Then you're missing out.' Alice smiled. The Apache returned and sat back down.

What had happened didn't seem remotely so bad, sitting here discussing it with these two. It didn't somehow seem particularly odd.

She'd spent the day at the library, sourcing every detail she could about the area of Devon she intended to visit. She had immersed herself so deeply in study that the day had passed without much thought of what she had awoken to that morning. Then, at about five, the information had started to run out and hunger had anyway broken her concentration. She'd got a drink of tepid water from the water fountain in the library basement and a gluey Mars bar from one of the vending machines there. She had punched and bound the photocopies she had made and notes she had written in the file she was compiling. Then she'd gone into the TV room in Elliot College just to be amid the safe anonymity of other people. In the darkness, a small sea of pale, earnest faces reflected *Songs of Praise*. Try as she might, she didn't really get the appeal of its presenter, some fat guy called Harry Secombe. It was disconcerting, the way Harry Secombe kept bursting into religious song on clifftops. Then there'd been a documentary about Polar Bears that had been quite good, splicing modern natural history footage with blurry black and white film taken on one of Amundsen's polar expeditions. The great explorer himself had shuffled in and out of shot on snow shoes, elusive as a ghost in grey fur and goggles against the grey landscape.

★

The pubs opened in Canterbury at seven on a Sunday evening, and she'd been thinking of walking down to the City Arms for a drink, when her two new friends from Champion's summer party had wandered in. Well, not wandered, exactly. They'd walked into the television room with a real sense of purpose. Oliver had even looked at his wristwatch as they found chairs and sat.

'*Poldark*,' David Lucas said in the City Arms later, when she asked what had brought them up to the campus.

She took this in. 'The eighteenth-century guy with the bad skin and the ponytail, right?'

'Thought you were a historian,' Oliver said. 'His skin isn't too badly pockmarked. Not for the period. They didn't have vaccinations in those days, you know.'

She looked at them both. Neither of them was smiling. '*Poldark*,' she said. 'Is this, like, a homoerotic thing?'

'Look,' Oliver said. 'It's Sunday night, right? They used to have *All Creatures Great and Small* on. Then that finished. Now they have *Poldark*. It's pretty gripping, actually.'

She looked at David, who shrugged. 'Don't knock Ross Poldark,' he said. 'Not from a position of ignorance.'

She decided to let it go. She was grateful for the company. And she filled the ensuing silence by telling them about the circumstances in which she had awoken that morning.

'Fucking odd, if you ask me,' Oliver said. Which she thought about the most redundant sentence she had ever listened to. Then he brightened up. 'You hadn't taken any drugs, had you?' Then he aired his Peter Cushing theory.

'You can rule Cushing out completely,' David said, after Ollie returned from the loo. 'I read a magazine article about him once. He's been a recluse since the death of his wife. He's a recluse and a non-smoker. He speaks to his wife on the other side. And he goes for long walks on the beach. He isn't even very cosmopolitan. And, as you've confirmed, he's filming in Elstree.'

Oliver was staring at his friend. 'What kind of magazines do you read?'

David looked uncomfortable. 'It was at the dentist,' he said. 'There was a limited choice.'

'Do you two think this is funny?'

'I think you were followed from the pub,' David said. 'If we rule out the bloke upstairs with the broken leg, it's pretty obvious what happened. An attractive woman, drinking alone, possibly a bit the worse for wear . . .' He shrugged. 'Maybe you need to change your locks. Maybe you need to talk to the police.'

'I thought England was safe.'

'Yeah,' Oliver said. 'Safe from the Black Panther. Safe from the Cambridge Rapist.' Alice and David looked at him. 'Safe as houses,' he said. 'Sorry.' He got up abruptly to go to the loo again.

'What did your friend just apologize for? Did he fart again?'

'I don't think so. It's a reflex. It's a public school thing.'

David sat opposite her making circles in spilled beer on the wooden tabletop. The City Arms was one of those pubs where they didn't bother to put beer mats out. He'd look much better, she thought, with shorter hair.

'Do you like those bodice rippers with James Mason and Margaret Lockwood?'

He lifted his eyes. 'Just *Poldark*. You don't want to read too much into it.'

She nodded and tried not to smile.

He sighed. 'I like listening to Taj Mahal and Mahalia Jackson. I've just finished reading *Zen and the Art of Motorcycle Maintenance*. What a page-turner. Unputdownable. Ingmar Bergman is my favourite film director. I've probably seen *The Seventh Seal* more often than my gran's seen *The Sound of Music*.'

Alice sipped her beer. English beer was still an effortful ritual for her. 'Is any of that true?'

'I'd stand a better chance of sleeping with you if it was. Better than none, anyway. But the truth is I like listening to the Faces.'

'And watching *Poldark*. And Roberto Duran.'

'How do you know about Duran?'

'I read the papers,' Alice said. 'He's a world champion.'

David nodded. 'There's more to you than meets the eye. Even more, I should say.'

'Why do you box?'

'My father and grandfather boxed. I've been doing it

since I was eight years old. It's college that's the novelty, not the boxing.'

She took another, willed sip of her beer. The City Arms was a Whitbread pub. She was drinking a draught beer called Trophy A. It was what they insisted was an acquired taste. She thought Trophy C-minus would have been a better name for the brew. 'So what is your favourite film? *The Woman in White*? *The Scarlet Pimpernel*?'

He smiled at that. But he said: 'You really ought to go to the police. And you should stay well clear of that flat until you do.'

'My dad was a cop,' she said. 'I'm not innocent about crime.'

Even to her own ears the claim sounded stupid.

'So,' she said. 'I take it your favourite movie is not *The Seventh Seal*?'

'I don't go in for lists. If I did, *The Godfather* and *The French Connection* would be pretty near the top.'

'No foreign movies?'

'They're both foreign movies. This is England.'

'And Lucky Strike are foreign cigarettes.'

'Chain-smoked by jumpy GIs flushing out Japs with flame-throwers on Iwo Jima,' David said. 'Proffered to blondes in cocktail bars by private eyes in trench coats and trilbies.'

Smoked by state troopers, she thought, risking a week's pay over a single hand of cards in her father's den. But not commonly found in Whitstable.

51

The Apache returned then from what Alice could only imagine had been a festival of farting in the gents. The guy was turning out to be a clear and present danger anywhere near a naked flame.

'You know what I mean,' she said to David Lucas. 'You know what I mean by foreign movies.'

'He likes *Enter the Dragon*,' the Apache said, catching on to their subject with surprising speed, for him. 'And that was filmed entirely in Hong Kong.'

Alice Bourne didn't go home that night. She stayed at the house, on a road to the rear of the campus, shared by David and Oliver and three of their undergraduate friends. One of the sharers was on a geography field trip and she slept on his bed, in a sleeping bag borrowed from David, after fish and chips eaten from the paper it came wrapped in at closing time in Canterbury, grossed out by Oliver's saveloy and the pickled egg he swallowed whole in an evident bid to turn flatulence from an affliction into a quest. She slept under the *Easy Rider* poster Blu-Tacked above the bed head in the field tripper's room, alert to the smell of dope that permeated the bedclothes and the carpet and an easy chair spilling its grey and foamy innards.

Maybe it was the room. Maybe it was the gloomy nihilism of Lou Reed's Berlin, Oliver's choice of late-night listening before they all turned in – or, in his inevitable terminology, crashed out. But she awoke sweating at a quarter past six in David's sleeping bag having dreamed the cormorant dream. And this time the lurching craft had been full of the hack and stink of Luckies, harshly smoked.

In the morning, she used their bathroom gingerly. English hygiene, she'd discovered, was a haphazard pursuit lacking commitment or persistence. Soap softened into green Communion hosts in shallow pools on the sink beside either tap. Neither sliver produced suds. The water was cold. Not truly cold, of course. Water would need to be drawn from some deep artesian source to emerge truly cold in the sweltering, ambient heat of that summer. But it wasn't hot enough to encourage suds. Someone had at least put out a cleanish towel for her, though. She didn't remember it having been there from brushing her teeth with David's borrowed toothbrush the previous night. Strange, she thought, scrubbing her teeth again, the purposeful mood a Monday had compared with the limbo of an English Sunday. She already felt focused, energized. She didn't feel as shaken as she had in the past by the cormorant dream. Perhaps she was getting used to it. And yesterday she had awoken to a worse shock than nightmares provided. She felt angry at herself, though, for not having gone to the police. Yesterday the intrusion into her flat had felt bruising and inexplicable. Today it felt like an opportunity spurned, a crime scene gone cold because of her own panic and hesitancy. She was outraged by the trespass, deeply angered by the fact of the violation now that the panic had dissipated. She wanted the offender caught and punished. Except that objectively there had not been much of a crime committed. Everything of it was in what might have happened and what might happen still. Alice felt under threat but knew that the best chance of dealing with that threat had gone. The police would not take seriously a complaint made more than twenty-four hours after the alleged committing of an offence.

She rinsed David's toothbrush and put it back in the toothbrush mug in the bathroom cabinet. The cabinet had a mirrored door into which he no doubt looked at his reflection every morning. Except that most of the mercury had peeled with time and damp off the back of the mirror so that any reflection was incomplete, streaked with absence. He probably thought that his long hair made him look like one of the Faces. Or perhaps he planned to pull it back into a ponytail like the one so fetchingly worn by Ross Poldark. Poldark's hair was bushy but straight. The Faces had straight hair, too, teased into those urchin cockatoos they all wore. The trouble was that David's hair was curly, and worn in the style he had it made him look like something out of a Burne-Jones painting. It put his appearance comically at odds with his nature, she felt, with that blunt accent and surly sense of obligation. He really wasn't Sir Lancelot. No more than his friend was an Apache. Oliver also wore his hair long. And he could have passed for a band member, his youthful face having that corrupt quality that drugs use sometimes inflicted. Inflicted or endowed, depending on your point of view. If Oliver was aiming for the debauched choirboy look of a Brian Jones or a Jim Morrison, he was succeeding. She couldn't imagine him trying for anything less clichéd. He was the sort of young man who wanted to remind you of someone dead. That's what he had meant when he'd claimed to have a death wish. What he really wanted was the safe kudos of resembling closely someone drugs had killed. He was probably very popular with the girls. She imagined they both were. Unless there really was some homoerotic quality to their Sunday-evening television viewing. That *Poldark* business was, frankly, a bit worrying.

She'd rinsed out her underwear the previous night and strung it across a hedge in their back garden to dry. It wasn't as if there was any risk of rain. It seemed this summer like it would never rain again. Rain seemed impossible, more of a folk myth than the persistent feature of the English summer weather she had read about before her arrival. She couldn't remember having seen a substantial cloud. Now, wrapped in her towel, she retrieved her bits of laundry. Doing so reminded her that she would at some point have to go back to the flat in Whitstable. Her things were there. It was her home. She would have to do it today. But even if she accomplished her return in the daylight, night would come and she would have to stay there. In one way, though, going back was going to be a relief, she thought. She had begun to doubt the fact of the intrusion. When she went back she would see the physical evidence. She'd have the fact of it affirmed before she aired the room and discarded the cigarette butt and threw the ashtray away.

And she would have a witness. David Lucas had offered to come back with her and help her put a deadbolt on her door and window.

'Is this a ploy, David? Like brandishing a copy of *Zen and the Art of Motorcycle Maintenance*?'

'Whether it's a ploy or it isn't,' he said, 'it has more practical value than those strategies would. From your point of view.'

'That's true.'

'It isn't, by the way. It isn't a ploy.'

'Good,' she said. 'I wouldn't want to think you were wasting your time. I'm very grateful, though.'

He smiled. The smile was inward, for him rather than her.

'What?'

'You're pretty tough, aren't you?' he said.

'Maybe American women are different.'

'I've met American women before,' he said.

'I'm not that tough, David,' she said. 'I'm not so tough as I think I'm going to need to be.'

Her therapeutic Sunday in the library had yielded few salient facts about Slapton Sands. On the Monday she did better. She sourced a Church commission report concerning claims of looting and vandalism levelled against departed American troops once the native population had been allowed back into their villages in the late summer and autumn of 1944. Pictures, plate, gold Communion goblets, even christening fonts, had disappeared from churches that had afterwards been smashed into ruins, their stained glass shattered, their roofs torn and holed. Subsequent papers, including the answer to a parliamentary question, showed that the contents of the churches had in fact been removed, faithfully inventoried and painstakingly stored. The damage to the fabric of the churches turned out not to be the work of bored and drunken GIs made vindictive by a bout of homesickness. The churches had been damaged by shellfire. The American military had used live ammunition in its practice assaults on the Start Bay beach heads. Some of the shells had gone astray. Tacitly, it was assumed that some of the churches and other blasted buildings had been used for target practice. It was hard to hit a target precisely with a gun mounted on a moving platform. And a moving platform was exactly what a battleship comprised in a ten-foot swell.

She'd found aerial photographs of Slapton Sands taken for the purpose of updating Ordnance Survey maps in the summer of 1948. There had still been rationing in Britain then, she recalled, examining the black and white prints on an epidiascope, adjusting the focus, searching for detail, for clues. There had still been hundreds, perhaps thousands, of unexploded bombs in Britain's Blitz-damaged cities. Much of London still lay ruined. Regeneration was a decade away, the bravely symbolic Festival of Britain on London's South Bank still three years hence. Britain then had been insular, monochromatic, engaged in the grim economic hardship of victory.

The aerial pictures were of very good quality. They had needed to be, taken as they were for the purpose of precise geographic reference and plotting. They began to get grainy only when magnified to a point where the features they showed became so large they were abstract anyway, unreadable out of the context of landscape. They showed a beach and hinterland heavily cratered with shells. Even three winters after the end of the war, one of those winters very harsh, the violence done to the shore and the gravel lagoon beyond it was shockingly obvious. If men had been there when the shells responsible for this damage had exploded, she didn't see how they could have survived the barrage. Is that what had happened? Had an American cruiser bombarded American infantry on the beach during a live-fire exercise? Had the dead infantry been blown to pieces by their own fire power unleashed by their own navy? The pictures she was looking at meant that Alice Bourne could not dismiss this as a possible explanation of the casualties. But the Colorado veteran had made no mention of the carnage she was projecting from the epidiascope on to the wall. He'd mentioned sentries, strung out along the shore after the catastrophe, and he'd talked about the rain and how subdued the sea had been on that hungover April day. But he'd said nothing about the beach having been shelled. Before coming to England, she'd travelled back to his bar with her notebook and interviewed him at length. She would have to read the notes again, but recalling them now she was sure he had said nothing to her about the shelling of Slapton Sands.

It seemed impossible. If more than a thousand men had been blown to pieces there, he'd have seen body parts on the sand. He'd have seen dropped packs and water bottles and discarded rifles. There'd have been shattered landing craft at the edge of the sea and more listing, sinking in the water. But he'd seen, or mentioned, none of these things.

One of the Ordnance Survey pictures showed the hull of a Higgins boat hauled up on to the sand. Rust ran down to the sea from its corroded metal fittings in a trough behind the craft. It was submitting with ferocious speed to corruption, its hastily bolted-together panels crumbling and dissolving under the assault of wind and salt. Alice felt deflated looking at the wreck, felt for the first time that Champion might be right and that her trip to Slapton was nothing more than conceit and folly. What could she hope to find? What secrets could an English beach hope to surrender after thirty-two years of ravaging weather?

It was hot in the library, hotter over the epidiascope, with its little electric motor and its electric lamp and the faint smell of burn that always arose from machines that have been left to grow dusty, when someone switched them on and they started to hum and get hot. She got up out of her chair and went over to one of the large windows set in the south façade of the building, overlooking Canterbury. She was on the library's fourth floor, and from the campus hill the view over the city and the Kent countryside was panoramic, the projection of an epic film. But nothing much was happening on the screen. In the centre distance,

59

the cathedral rippled, spires and fancies lost to dissipating heat. Trees heavy with defeated leaves endured the sun. The Stour twinkled in a narrow strand whenever banks and bridges allowed a sight of the diminishing river. It was not hard to imagine Spitfires cartwheeling through the sky, barrage balloons strewn across it, smudges of smoke from wing-mounted cannon oily against the blue vastness.

She'd read that three million American servicemen had been based in England at various times between January of 1942 and December of 1945. American airmen had flown missions over Germany from US bases in East Anglia. An army of invasion had been trained in secret for the assault on Berlin through France. They'd come here from Maryland and Nebraska, from the Bowery and the Bronx and the patrician districts of old Boston and the race-hating, rancorous stew of the old South. The 29th Infantry Division had been in the South-West of England for more than a year and a half before finally leaving its shores for Omaha Beach.

She could do what Professor Champion wished and add her ten cents' worth to the dead debate about the causes of the Peterloo Massacre or the reason why President Nixon had escaped impeachment. Or she could travel to Devon to try to discover how more than a thousand American men brave enough to come halfway across the world to fight for freedom had died instead on one calamitous day on a stretch of the English coast.

'Their story deserves to be told,' she said to herself, with her head on the thick glass of the window through which she looked. 'If nothing else, they deserve its telling.'

She turned away from the view. Across by a bank of carrels, two English girls were looking at her curiously. Probably think I'm bitching to myself about the lack of air-conditioning, she thought. Which in a building less than ten years old I'd have a perfect right to do. She went over and switched off the epidiascope and went to put the survey photographs carefully back in the map drawers where she had located them.

She had arranged to meet David Lucas after his early evening training session at the university gym. The session took place between five-thirty and seven o'clock. Alice was reaching the point at which any more of Champion's salient facts would come only with her imminent trip to Slapton. By six-fifteen she'd done as much as she honestly could in the library.

A walkway ran across the top of the gym building's interior. It was intended as a short cut to reach the upper floors of adjacent buildings. But it made an ideal viewing gallery, particularly if you didn't wish to be observed doing your viewing. She had arranged to meet David at seven-fifteen, after he'd had time to shower and change. Instead she drank a cup of coffee from a machine and got to the gym walkway fifteen minutes prior to the time when the boxing training was scheduled to finish. He was in the practice ring, sparring with a West Indian boy with dreadlocks like those worn by Bob Marley and Peter Tosh.

He had on a sparring helmet. The sparring looked pretty lively to her unschooled eyes. The two boxers were trading punches under the vigilant supervision of a well-built, grey-haired man in a tracksuit who had one hand gripping a stopwatch and the other clenched in a fist around the top rope of the ring. Both boys were glossy with sweat, and David Lucas had red weals on his paler skin where he had been caught by the laces on his opponent's gloves when they closed and clinched before the man with the stop-watch shouted 'Break!'

She watched three rounds of sparring before their coach finally ended the session. Then the boxers touched gloves and patted each other on the head. The dreadlocked boy spat his gumshield into the palm of a glove and said something that made David Lucas laugh and take out his own mouth guard and reply. They walked in these little anti-clockwise circles in opposing corners of the ring, cooling down, she supposed, all the time talking. Alice thought they seemed pretty friendly, considering what they'd just been doing to one another. Then David pulled off a glove and unbuckled his helmet. He peeled the thing off and handed it to the coach and looked up, blinking into the roof lights, at the gantry. His eyebrows and cheekbones and the bridge of his nose were streaked with Vaseline. The grease blurred his features in the flat glare of electric light. One nostril showed a thin trickle of blood. And his hair had been cut, cut off, sheared to within an inch or so of his skull. She recoiled slightly in surprise, and he grinned at her.

Once he had showered, they went back to Elliot College. He had bought a deadbolt for her door and window locks to fit at the flat in Whitstable. He'd borrowed tools for the job sourced by the college porters' office. He picked the stuff up from his locker, and she checked her pigeonhole for fresh correspondence. There was a bill for books from Foyles in London, where she had opened an account. There was a note from Professor Champion, too. She recognized his handwriting on the buff envelope.

'You don't quite see eye to eye, do you?' David said as they walked the lane to the bus stop on the Whitstable road. He'd seen the handwriting on the envelope before she put it into her bag.

'He has a problem, I think, with Americans.'

David nodded. 'Stems probably from the problem he has with America.'

'Who was the black boy you were boxing with?'

'Cliff. Clifford Lee. Why?'

'He's good.'

'He's bloody good. He'll probably box in the Olympics.'

'Where's he from?'

'St Paul's.'

'Is that like St Kitts, or St Lucia?'

David laughed. 'No. It's in Bristol. Good job you're not doing your doctorate in geography.'

Her bedroom still smelled faintly of smoke. She thought it might be her imagination. But she saw David wrinkle his nose in something more than a show of sympathy. He went over and picked the cigarette end out of the ashtray and held it up to the late light coming through the window. 'No lipstick.'

'It was a man.'

'Yeah, you said.' He put the stub back.

'It's a man's brand.'

'It's weird, is what it is,' David said. 'Really weird.' He put the canvas bag of tools he'd been given on the floor and took out a drill and started to look for a power point for its plug.

'I could do that myself,' Alice said. 'I'm perfectly capable.'

David was screwing a bit into the head of the drill. 'We'll do it together,' he said. 'It'll be quicker. And then, if you'd like, we'll go for a drink, maybe a bite to eat.'

'Fine,' she said. 'So long as it's on me.'

He triggered the drill in his hand and it whined and gave off a hot, oily smell. She picked up the ashtray and its contents and walked past him to the door.

'Where are you going with those?'

'To a bin. Any bin so long as it isn't mine. There's a palladin bin a ways along the sea wall.'

'It's evidence.'

'Of what, exactly? My dad was a cop. I'm getting rid of it.'

They had a drink on the breakwater outside the Neptune. After, they walked along the top of the beach towards Tankerton. It was almost nine o'clock by now and still light. The seafront houses got smaller the further they walked from Wavecrest. They were fishermen's cottages, narrow, roofed in weathered wood, no two the same. The cooling shingle on the beach smelled of heat and tar and salt crystals caught the light of the sun here and there, as though someone had slipped silver coins between clusters of stones. You couldn't help but look at those twinkles of brightness, Alice thought. It was a longing for treasure. It was the avaricious impulse of a child.

'You like the sea, don't you, Alice?'

She breathed it in through her nose and nodded. 'I'm still getting used to the sea. I was brought up a long way inland. It's one of the things that fascinates me about Slapton Sands. Many, probably most, of those soldiers were seeing salt water for the first time when they embarked for Europe. Slapton must have seemed very different to them from what they were used to.'

David didn't say anything for so long that she thought he wasn't going to respond at all. 'They crossed the Atlantic,' he said finally. 'Jesus. In convoys. Chased all the way by U-boats. They'd have docked where? Liverpool?'

Alice nodded. 'Some of them via Ireland.'

David was thoughtful again. 'There's the sea and there's the sea,' he said. 'Slapton Sands will seem very different to you from this.'

They ate dinner in the basement bar of the Pearson's Arms, seated near the fishtank on the wall, with its lurking population of taped lobsters and crabs. Alice watched David Lucas eat, which he did methodically, without comment

65

about the quality of the meal. He had good enough table manners but ate like someone taking on fuel rather than enjoying the experience of food. He was probably very hungry. The skin of his knuckles was still reddened from the blows he'd landed on his sparring partner. He looked once at the fishtank beside them and shuddered. Alice asked him what it was he was thinking and he shook his head. So she persisted with the question.

'Cannibalism,' he said, wiping his mouth with his paper napkin, pushing his plate away. 'If their claws weren't taped, they'd try to eat each other.'

She nodded. 'How are you spending your long vacation, David?'

'Working,' he said, brightening. 'They're renovating one of the old sea forts in the Solent. Do you know about them?'

'Built to repel French invasion.'

'Very good.'

'You surprise me,' she said. 'I'd have thought you'd be travelling.'

He smiled. He looked younger with his hair cut short. 'Subsidized by what?'

What was he? A year younger than she was? Two? 'That's a Rolex on your wrist,' she said. 'I thought Mummy and Daddy might pay.'

He fingered the watch, a big diver's model on a steel bracelet, turning the bezel so that it clicked with the calibrations. 'This is my dad's. He's a diver. He works for a

French company prospecting for oil in the North Sea, and they supply them all with these. He's separated from Mum. She asked him for a contribution towards my college costs, and this turned up in the post with a note saying I could swap it for three hundred quid or the equivalent in any city in the civilized world.'

'You don't see him?'

'Not since I was fifteen.'

'That's tough.'

He didn't say anything. His eyes were focused on a triangle of buttered brown bread on a side plate amid the debris of the food on their table.

'None of my business,' she said.

'No.'

'Do you dive?'

'Not since he left. I didn't enjoy it. Too claustrophobic.'

'Boxing. Diving. Your dad sounds like something out of Hemingway.'

'Except that my dad never wrote a book. I don't think he's even read one, to be honest. Unless you count those little Commando comics.'

Alice Bourne didn't say anything. She didn't know what a Commando comic was

'I suppose he must have read diving manuals,' David said. 'Credit where credit's due.'

'Will your summer job involve diving?'

'It's all diving,' he said. 'But it's paid work. It's not groping through kelp and plankton on the sixty-year-old wreck of a scuttled German warship in a freezing current at Scapa Flow.'

'You've done that?'

He smiled. 'I'll get us another drink.'

'I'll get them,' she said. She stood but, gathering her not-quite-empty glass, looked crestfallen.

'You should try Pils,' David said.

'What? And end up like your friend the Apache?'

'Holsten Pils. It's a new beer that comes in bottles. They might have some on the cold shelf. It isn't American, which is greatly to its advantage. But it might be closer to what you remember from home.'

They talked and drank until the pub closed. Then they walked back along the sea wall to her flat. Alice took David's arm and with her free hand played with the key to her new lock, turning it over and over in her fingers until it grew slippery with the sweat that heat and tension had slicked across the pads of her fingers and palm. The Pils had made her mouth dry without it providing the Dutch courage she had hoped for. The sea and the town were quiet. The tide was out. A few lights burned on Sheppey, and a beacon warned of sandbanks, from a buoy flashing in the channel. But the buoy did not bob, and the beacon was static on still water. To their left the small houses were dark. You could see down into their back yards from the sea wall, and some of the houses had small boats leaned prow upwards on their rear walls and nets set out to dry on hooks and over fences. There were blocks and tackles in these yards, bits of rigging, oars and rolled sails and pots for catching lobster and crayfish and crab. There was the mingled smell of tar and creosote, cooling in the night after the burning day.

When first she'd arrived here, there had seemed a bogus, theme-park quality to Whitstable. Excepting the small and shabby co-op supermarket branch, every store on its narrow high street was a business independent of a chain. There were scrolled proprietorial names on scrupulous antique frontages. There were hand-painted pub signs batted back and forth by the wind in their proud gibbets. It had all seemed too self-consciously picturesque, too Dickensian, the way Dickens might be done by Disneyland. Then someone had told her that Dickens had lived in Chatham and known intimately this part of the Kent coast as a child. And over weeks she had seen the shabbiness under what had appeared to her indiscriminate tourist's eye merely to be picturesque. And she had realized that Whitstable had endured rather than been re-created. The town had depended on the oyster trade and was actually dying. Established by the Romans, it had dwindled through centuries until the Victorian appetite for oysters had funded its final, short-lived pomp. But culinary fashions had changed, and it was a town dying now, subsidizing its demise by student rents and odd foreign visitors on the way to somewhere else.

When Alice had arrived, they'd been showing *The Towering Inferno* at the Oxford, Whitstable's decrepit cinema. A month later, by the time *One Flew over the Cuckoo's Nest* opened at the Oxford, she'd grown to love the town.

That had been until the intrusion at her flat. Now she didn't think Whitstable charming at all, but sinister. It was astonishing the difference in a person's emotions that forty-eight hours could bring about. Now she couldn't wait to escape the still, picturesque days and night stillness of Whitstable. If David Lucas made the pass at her she assumed he inevitably would, she'd send him away with as much tact as she could summon. But she knew the night to come would be an ordeal after his departure.

'What are you thinking about?'

'About English girls. About how promiscuous they are.'

He appeared to take this in. He nodded, as she pretended not to be looking at him.

'Bit of a generalization.'

He didn't sound so drunk as she felt. He was capable of a polysyllabic word, pronounced without slurring. They were on the sea wall, seated, feet dangling seawards. It was late. She didn't want to go back to the flat.

'What happened to the Apache, after Champion's lawn party?'

'Went home to bed, eventually. Managed to undress himself. There was a minor drama concerning one of his Doc Martens, which he couldn't remove. After his frenzied struggle with the laces, which functioned as a sort of tourniquet, I managed to get it off him.'

'He was carrying enough amphetamine to kill a horse.'

'Lost it. He has a way of losing his drugs. It must be a survival mechanism.'

'You saved his life.'

David didn't react to this claim.

'His foot, leastways. You saved his foot.'

'Do you give everyone a nickname?'

'Survival mechanism,' she said. Sir Lancelot. It didn't suit him, not with the shorn hair. It never had. 'They don't last, the nicknames. Not if I get to know the people involved. I make snap judgements about people that always turn out to be wrong.'

'It's the pill, Alice. It's the times in which we live. The pill and penicillin and feminism and the ratio of females to males at the college. To some extent it's environmental. Isn't it the same in America?'

It took her a second to realize the talk had got back to sex. 'Not really.'

'With role models like Janis Joplin and Joni Mitchell?'

'Joni Mitchell is a Canadian, which I'm frankly sick of telling people. And it's only really like that on the West Coast. I don't think America is as permissive as Europe is. Not sexually. Bertolucci wouldn't have made a film called *Last Tango in Washington*.'

'Woody Allen might,' David said.

'Nope,' Alice said. 'Woody Allen's strictly New York.'

'Anyway, you're right,' David said. 'If you weren't American, I'd have been reasonably optimistic about tonight.'

'You're quite conceited, aren't you?'

'Not particularly. I'm optimistic. Most people are at our

age, you know.' He got to his feet. 'You can relax. I won't try and grope you or anything. I'll see you home, walk back to the phone box outside the Sally Army and ring for a minicab.'

Alice stood and brushed sand from her skirt. She smiled. 'I wouldn't have wanted to come between you and Oliver anyway.'

'He'd have been all right,' David said. 'He's always got Ross Poldark.'

The new key felt stiff in the new lock. But there appeared nothing different about the room from what they had left behind, hours earlier, when it was still light. There was a faint smell of raw wood from the door, from the drilling and chiselling done by David in fitting the new lock, from the waste-paper bin into which he'd dropped sawdust from the work, swept up with a dustpan and brush. And it was colder, more accurately cooler, than it had been then. But her duvet lay tautly stretched over the bed, and the sheet of typing paper rolled into her Olivetti portable still sat pristine and blank.

Alice had evolved a theory concerning the visit to her room. She had come to believe that it had taken place prior to her return from the Neptune. Drowsy and preoccupied, she had not noticed the cigarette smoke or the Lucky Strike stub or the ashtray on her desk. She'd come back from a smoky pub, after all. Her landlord had a key and for some reason had visited, or had someone visit the property on his behalf. She didn't have a telephone. He may have alerted her to the need for the visit by post, but mail deposited in college pigeonholes could easily go astray. He lived in Ashford, her landlord. She had met him only once. He was middle-aged, shy and obliging. Until she managed to catch him in, and she'd telephoned him twice now without success, she couldn't confirm her theory. But it seemed to her more plausible than any other. It had occurred to her only today. Her dad, who had been a very good cop, would have been appalled at how long it had taken her to reach the obvious conclusion. In mitigation, she thought, she did have rather a lot on her mind at the moment.

David Lucas was looking at the pictures Blu-Tacked to her walls. He seemed fascinated by the picture of the wounded Panzergrenadier. Then he studied the picture of the firefighter. He turned to Alice, who was standing with her backside resting on the edge of her desk and her arms folded under her breasts. 'Do you think it's cold in here?'

'Colder than it is outside, obviously.'

He frowned. 'It feels damp to me. And it smells of the sea.'

Alice laughed. 'It's next to the sea. Is damp so unusual – ' she nodded at the window ' – so close to all that water?'

'It smells foggy,' David said. He was frowning. 'What do I know?'

She couldn't sleep after his departure. She wished he hadn't said what he'd said about the cold and the damp. It was merely the power of suggestion, she knew, but it did feel chilly, and there was an odour in the room – that corrupt smell a tide leaves when it recedes across an area of soft sand or marshland. She'd smelled it further up the coast, on a walk at Swalecliffe. She'd walked without thought, lulled by the featureless nature of the flats, until the ground betrayed her feet and she was sucked into stinking mire up to her shins.

Alice lay without sleep and thought about her father. To reminisce in this way was something she didn't allow herself to do very often. She found such great comfort in the warm memory of him that afterwards his absence from her adult life seemed all the crueller and more bewildering. She'd lost her mother to cancer at the age of two. Her father had reared her. He'd done a great job, in her opinion, which was the only opinion on the matter she thought anyone had a right to.

Being the daughter of a cop had got harder as she had gotten older. When she was very young, she had only the social stuff to contend with. But because she was a bright child, as she got older she tended to share her classrooms with children from far more moneyed backgrounds. Their fathers were publishers, bankers, high-flying members of the legal establishment, physicians, dentists; professional people, they were fond of pointing out to her. To her classmates, cops were corner automatons who smoothed the winter traffic flow in rain slickers and white gloves. Cops were little more than street furniture in the ongoing, epic unfolding of their own lives.

When she came into contact with campus radicalism,

cops represented something far worse. State policemen like her dad were tarred by the same dirty establishment brush as the trigger-happy National Guards at Kent State, or the municipal cops who'd attacked delegates with batons and teargas at the Democratic primaries in Chicago in 1968 at the bidding of city boss Mayor Daley. The uniform, the badge, the vehicle and the gun; all symbolized something the vast majority of her college contemporaries found ideologically unacceptable. To them, she believed, her dad was probably no better than the sinister prison guard in the reflective shades who'd shot Paul Newman's Cool Hand Luke just because Luke had refused to call him 'boss'. No better and fundamentally no different. But she never lied about what her dad did for a living. She never hid him. She'd never have begun to apologize for him. Her con-temporaries, in the full flush of their bright and unfeeling radicalism, might have smirked behind their hands at his Sears & Roebuck suit and heavily polished Floresheim shoes and brutally brush-cut hair when he attended her graduation ceremony. But she was as proud of her father as he was of his daughter. They hadn't held his hand like she had at his side when they lowered her brother into the earth draped under the flag at Arlington. They hadn't felt the grief and strength alternate in currents of competing force through her father's shuddering grip.

Lying in bed, she remembered the first time someone in England had asked her about her family. The question had been posed by a girl whose own father was a veterinary surgeon. For some inexplicable reason, being a veterinarian seemed a particularly prestigious job just then in England. When the question was asked, Alice was still suffering the culture shock of her first exposure, the previous night, to the full awfulness of British television, with its three miserable, choice-free channels.

'Did your father carry a gun?' the girl had asked, her mouth twitching with horror. 'Did he shoot it at people?'

'Nah,' Alice had replied. 'My dad was more like those two cops on TV in *The Sweeney*. When the bad guys pulled their weapons, my old man just took them to a bar and drank them to death.'

The veterinarian's daughter hadn't really seemed to get the joke.

In truth, Sergeant Patrick Bourne had been well enough armed. There'd been a heavy-calibre revolver strapped to his hip. There'd been a pump-action twelve-gauge clipped under the dashboard of his car. Neither weapon had saved him on the night he was shot to death, forced to kneel on corn stubble, executed outside a derelict barn on the outskirts of Emmaus.

Her collision with the vet's daughter had been the first of the many culture clashes Alice had experienced in the relatively short time she'd been in England. Whether she had endured or provoked them was a matter for debate. She didn't think of herself as being particularly confrontational. But a kind of low-level anti-Americanism seemed to pervade all aspects of English life. It felt after a while like one of those flu bugs they had here. It made you feel lousy without debilitating you to the point where you needed to consult a doctor and have antibiotics prescribed.

In her first week, Professor Champion had invited her to sit in on a seminar. He ran a course of his own devising called the American Century. It was a very popular course. His American Century seminars were held one afternoon a week. Entering the room a couple of minutes late, Alice was almost felled by the heady, combined assault of Alliage and Tabac. Champion was chain-smoking, but doing so next to a window. Looking at the eight or so faces around the table, it was tempting to think that the professor cast his students for their looks more than for their brains. The subsequent discussion did nothing in her mind to challenge this view.

They were talking about American films. The best French and German films apparently addressed Issues. The most influential American film of recent times starred a vindictive rubber fish and had emptied beaches. This was not considered by the group to be a pertinent achievement. That's why mainstream Hollywood studios made *The Candidate* and *The Parallax View* and *Three Days of the Condor*, Alice thought. That's why they were all solid box-office hits. But she didn't say anything, because she'd been invited to observe. We don't address issues. That's why Pakula was right then having to shoot *All the President's Men* on a shoestring, forced to resort as his leads to those two underground actors, Redford and Dustin Hoffman.

The group moved on to cultural imperialism. Coca-Cola seemed to be the principal culprit in this particular area of discussion.

She cracked when they began to talk about Norman Mailer and Allen Ginsberg and Bob Dylan as representatives of America's counter-culture.

'I don't think you can be part of the counter-culture if your work forms window displays in Barnes and Noble,' she said. The words weren't out of her mouth before she remembered that Professor Champion had written a paper on the lyrics of Dylan in the context of something called the American Dissident Tradition.

'You don't think Dylan has anything authentic to say about what is wrong with his country?' Despite the heat and cloying odours in the room, the professor's tone was arctic.

'I think he was always a middle-class, urban boy performing in borrowed clothes. I think Woody Guthrie was a phoney, too. All that riding freight was just romantic posturing. They're troubadours, not itinerant labour. They are to popular music what Jack London was to literature. There's a new blue-collar hero on the scene. A fellow called Springsteen. His credentials are equally bogus, and I'm sure he'll be just as successful. Probably even more so.'

They were all staring at her.

'Oops,' Alice said.

She kept quiet after that. But it was a long two hours before she could escape the room and what she thought of as the smug and lazy preconceptions of its collective occupants.

She lay in bed and remembered the debacle of her single American Century seminar and still she couldn't sleep. She wished David Lucas had not said what he had about the temperature of the room. It did feel cold. It felt cold and clammy on her face and forearms, the bits of her above her duvet, and there was that faint, insistent, saline insinuation of rottenness. It could have been coming from the shore, must have been coming from there, but there was no wind to bring it, because the night was still. Whitstable was still. The town was sleeping, except for her. And it slumbered silently.

She thought about David Lucas. He was strong and very good-looking and quite intelligent, and she felt sorry for him in her heart. She could see him as a child on the pillion seat of his father's motorcycle, with a pair of boxing gloves knotted around his neck, on his way to be dropped at night outside some church hall in a Liverpool suburb to be educated in the bleak pragmatism of the noble art by bigger boys only too eager to inflict the lesson. She could see him in an oversized wetsuit, struggling under the weight of an air tank, his face lost inside a face mask belonging to his father, its rubber straps stretched and bunched in buckled knots at the back of his head. He'd been frightened of the big creatures that lurked under water in his child's imagination, and his father's solution had been to take him

79

for a weekend in Scotland and put a lead belt around him and bully him into dives down into the peaty blackness of Loch Ness. She'd had to tease this stuff out of him over dinner. He didn't offer information, he surrendered it.

She thought again about her own dad, in his Floresheim shoes, with his brush-cut hair and the kind look on his pained, honest, Pennsylvania cop's face.

David Lucas had called Alice Bourne's face beautiful. And she had known he'd been telling her the truth. Her looks were to her as some alchemic miracle. Her dad had not been a remarkable-looking man. If she looked at the family album now, with sincere objectivity, she saw her dad's expression as stolid-featured and redolent of the fortitude he'd certainly required in life. Her mother was elusive in the camera's eye, never more than a suggestion, a filled-out shadow of how she must have looked. Her mother's pictures suggested a wistful impermanence they'd been sadly accurate to portray. But these two people had produced a daughter, somehow, who was beautiful. It had been often and dispassionately remarked on. It was a truth. You play the hand you're dealt. You do.

Someone had said that at forty everyone has the face they deserve. Was it Orwell who'd said it? Auden? It had been an Englishman, she was sure. Well, she had seventeen years to play with before she earned that questionable fate.

She was lying on her back. She coiled her body to the right, succumbing to the instinctive shelter of the foetal position. You play the hand you're dealt, was Alice Bourne's last thought before sleep claimed her.

Once again the dream left that thick taste of caramel sweetness in her mouth on waking. She flung off the duvet and tiptoed naked to the lavatory. She lifted the lavatory seat and spat. She remembered then how the bottom of the boat had been swimming in sea water and vomit in the dream and she almost retched over the lavatory bowl. She could feel goose bumps, bumpy as Braille, when to warm them she ran her fingers up and down the flesh of her bare arms. She was shivering. She flushed the toilet and fetched her dressing gown from its hook on the back of her bedroom door.

She would make herself a cup of coffee. There was a small refrigerator in the kitchenette off her room and an electric coil on an enamel platform with a plug for heating pans. She'd located no proper coffee in Whitstable. Her method was to heap two spoons of decent instant into a cup and pour near-boiling milk over the grains. It wasn't coffee. But it wasn't a bad improvised beverage in the sense that it provided something hot to hold and sip between linked fingers. It was a focus separate from her fear. She'd put sugar in it. She'd read that sugar was a good antidote to shock. She'd bought sugar in theoretical consideration of the guests she'd never entertained at the tea parties she'd anticipated, looked forward to, but never hosted in her time in England. She had milk for her coffee, reasonably fresh, in a bottle in the fridge.

It was five-thirty in the morning. It was ridiculous. But sipping her makeshift brew, barefoot on the tacky linoleum of the kitchenette, Alice did not want to return to her own bedroom. Was it the dream? She'd dreamed the dream before. She'd endured its wrenching dislocation and bewilderment, the sick churning of the sea and the vertiginous feeling dreamers always suffer in nightmares of witnessing their own fate fleeing their control. She'd been dismayed at the gargoyle grip of the cormorant's talons on the hull of the boat over many nights. It was prehistoric, this bird, its scaly malevolence its own dream within a dream. She'd lurched and slapped on the sea, toyed with. What was new? Nothing, she decided, steeling herself, rubbing the rash of goose bumps on her arms like energetic friction would make the Braille go away. It didn't. Heat from the electric plate did not radiate either in the kitchenette. It was the smell that was different. The smell of her coffee substitute could not dispel that rancorous, rotten odour. Where was that smell coming from? She shivered. Damn David Lucas and his sensitivity to temperature. She wished he was still here. But he wasn't here. She strode in her bathrobe back into her bedroom. And she saw it immediately and wondered how she could have missed the thing on awakening.

The Olivetti portable on her desk looked diminished, naked. This was because the single sheet of white A4 Alice habitually wound into its roller had been removed. She looked for it first balled up, the consequence of some sleepwalking episode, in her waste-paper bin. But she did this with a sinking heart, as someone might performing a pointless duty. For Christ's sake. She'd never sleepwalked. When she looked properly around the room, she saw the shift in its arrangement almost immediately. A single sheet of white paper had been newly affixed to the wall. It had been stuck up above her bed head, diagonally opposite her cluster of historical photographs. Words were printed at the centre of this otherwise blank sheet. It tried to crawl in on itself up the wall from its time in the roller. The words had been printed in the upper-case font familiar from her typewriter. It was a good machine, but the letters were slightly misaligned, as though the legend had been hammered out by someone inexperienced at typing, either in haste, or perhaps anger. The words, the message, were, however, clear.

'GO HOME,' it said.

So he'd been back.

The note had been glued above her bed head with something other than student Blu-Tack. A stain at the top centre the size of an English ten pence piece was sweating through the paper. Blu-Tack didn't sweat. She carefully peeled off the sheet. A disc of pink gum adhered to the wall. In the dim light and saline stink of the room, it resembled, for a moment, a bullet wound. Alice looked at the gum. Its edges were whitening, drying palely. It was moist and sticky still at its centre. She lifted her arm and watched her fingers prise the wad away from the wall. It wasn't warm, thank

God. Thank God at least for that. She held it close to her nose and smelled it. The smell was cloying, American, almost nostalgic.

Thinking of her dad, Alice tore the piece of gum in half and sniffed it slowly again. Gum and tobacco tar. She spat. Bubble gum and Luckies. The taste would be familiar to her. A woman who had never smoked, she'd spat that taste out of her mouth each morning, she now knew, after the cormorant dream. She took another look around the room. The books she'd bought from Foyles and borrowed from the university library occupied a narrow, two-shelf bookcase. On its top sat the anchoring weight of shells and stones she'd brought back from walks on Whitstable beach. On her bedside table was a framed family photograph taken just before Bobby's first tour of duty in South-East Asia. Alice had been fifteen when it was taken. Bobby had never posed for another family portrait.

'I'm not leaving, you fucker,' she said aloud. 'I'm staying until I'm done. And I'll fucking nail you, I swear to God.'

She felt better after saying this, but still scared. Her father, she knew, would have insisted she check the new deadbolts on the door and window. But Alice Bourne did not now think there was any point.

There was only a duty sergeant present at the police station. He listened to what Alice said to him warily, making no notes with the pen poised over the incident log in front of him. The log rested on a mounted width of ancient timber, scarred and pitted with carved graffiti, which formed a division in the room behind which the policeman stood. He could have sat; there was a stool for him back there. But he stood, leaning over what Alice assumed was his incident book, and explained that as the sole officer on duty he couldn't leave the station and would have to telephone for an officer to come from Canterbury.

'Will an officer come?'

'Oh yes, miss,' he said. 'An officer will come all right.'

She sat on the wooden bench in the station vestibule and waited. The floor was tiled and the plaster walls painted to a head-high border in a shade of institutional green and then in ivory beyond that. There was no traffic sound from the high street outside. The space was lit by a single bulb, screwed to the high ceiling under wire mesh. There were cobwebs in the corners and a smell of hops and vomit stirred under disinfectant. It was a dispiriting place, deliberately so, Alice thought, wishing she had brought something to read as the smells gathered strength in the heat of the morning. Occasionally the desk sergeant looked up at her from his pantomime of logging Whitstable's crime epidemic in the large book in front of him. He tried not to let her see him doing this. Her story was a curious one. Unless he was just taking in the view. There was that possibility. She thought he'd probably be outside, sneaking a smoke, at least from time to time, if she hadn't been there.

For something to do, she rummaged through her bag. She opened and read the note Champion had left in her pigeonhole the previous day. She'd forgotten about the note altogether, and only remembered it seeing the hand-addressed buff envelope. Three cordial lines enquired about her general wellbeing and invited her to supper that evening. She didn't know what supper was. She'd heard of the Last Supper, but didn't think Champion was planning an event on a similar scale. This one took place at his flat near the Cathedral Gate at seven-fifteen.

It was still quiet enough an hour later for her to hear the small engine of the police car pull up outside. She couldn't believe how puny were the cars driven by the English police. Stumpy and underpowered in their blue and white livery, they made her father's state cruiser look as sedate and powerful as a battleship.

One of the two police officers who entered the station was a woman. Alice was surprised to note that she was obviously in charge. Alice stood.

'Detective Sergeant Sally Emerson,' the policewoman said. 'I take it you're Miss Bourne?'

'Alice Bourne.'

DS Emerson nodded. 'This is Constable Rennie.' She looked to be aged in her late twenties and was slim in a pinstripe trouser suit. Her eyes were a startling green and her hair, cut short, was strawberry blonde and trying to form ringlets even at the length she wore it. Alice could imagine the dull, dyke, canteen jokes. She was flattered they'd sent a detective. She nodded an acknowledgement at the constable.

Emerson said: 'We'll visit the crime scene first, if that's tolerable to you?' If there was sarcasm there, it was sarcasm too subtle for Alice to detect.

They insisted on putting her in the back of their Ford Escort and driving her the five hundred yards or so to where the alleged offence had been committed. Rennie drove, which could have been chauvinism but was probably protocol, Alice thought. She had a sick feeling of impending dread thumping at the wall of her stomach. It was not to do with the warning gummed above her bed by a stranger as she slept. It was to do with Professor Champion. She had no idea of the protocol at the college when it came to matters involving the university with the police. Was there a college policy? Was there a student policy? When she'd arrived at the campus, an acrimonious and damaging occupation of the senate building had been under way. Files had been destroyed, graffiti painted and items of furniture tossed, alight, from upper-floor windows. But she hadn't seen any police. Perhaps there was an unwritten rule that the college policed itself. Perhaps it was written, but she hadn't been aware of it. Here she was, a stranger from an unpopular country, studying a begrudged subject for motives thought dubious. And now she'd tried to ally herself with an agency people like David's friend Oliver thought of as the Filth. But David himself had chastised her for failing to alert the police after the first intrusion. Instinct told her what she had chosen to do would not sit well with her professor. Instinct told her, too, that she'd done the only thing she could have.

★

The ice-cream parlour in Tankerton was open by the time they arrived. Rennie looked relieved, driving the little police car back to Canterbury and sanity. He'd have a choice tale for his canteen pals, Alice thought. It didn't require any great speculative gift to postulate on unwanted one-night stands, pranks provoked by drinking games and the ingesting of a species of mushroom growing in wild abundance locally that never made it on to toast. Ho fucking ho. And that was just him warming up. That wasn't even pre-menstrual hysteria, or the suggestibility of a neurotic American woman living four doors away from an actor who starred in horror films.

Sally Emerson put two cups of coffee down on the fake marble table between herself and Alice Bourne. She sat and lit a B&H gratefully from a pack of twenty without offering one. She hadn't forgotten. She was sharp and precise. And sexy, Alice thought. She was a woman thriving in a world made of machismo and prejudice.

'You didn't like Constable Rennie?'

'I don't have a problem with men on principle.'

'Maybe you're just a good judge. He won't go further than constable. He's in because his dad was in. His dad was a fascist, too. Nearly shot a war hero in a pub here in 1940, apparently. Thought the war hero was a Fenian.'

'Was he?'

The detective shrugged and smoked. The smoking was furious with nicotine debt. 'Fellow called Finlay.

You never know. Doesn't strike me as a Fenian name.'

'Sounds Scottish,' Alice said.

'I don't think Whitstable was much fun during the war,' Emerson said. 'I'll fill you in on the Finlay incident one day, if you're interested.' She smiled over her coffee cup. 'We should go for a drink some time.'

History, because history was what Alice did. Alice wondered how far someone as good as this would get if she were a man instead of a woman. A long way. A bloody long way, as they liked to say here.

'What will happen to the evidence?'

'The sheet of typing paper and the wad of gum will be dusted for prints and filed as possible prosecution evidence in tamper-proof evidence bags. This will be a pointless exercise, since what evidence there was has been hopelessly contaminated by you.'

Emerson had placed her cigarette packet facing her, hinged by the lid and leaning upwards. She picked her next cigarette, Alice thought, the way a marksman might select his next bullet.

'You don't have many friends here.'

'There's been no time to make them.'

The policewoman smoked and looked at her. 'Nor inclination?'

'Americans are not very popular here just now.'

'We don't have a great deal of contact with the university,' Emerson said. 'Marxist orthodoxy makes America a post-colonial bully. Marxist beliefs are fashionable among students just now. Americans are very popular with the Canterbury Chamber of Commerce. They represent polite behaviour and substantial tourist revenue. But up there on the campus, among the politically active, America mostly means napalm and Agent Orange and the My Lai Massacre.'

Alice didn't say anything. She knew all this.

Emerson said: 'Which begs the question: why did you come?'

'I've already told you. My doctoral thesis concerns an event that took place here in England. Kent University has a strong history department and a number of distinguished specialists in American history. I couldn't have done it three thousand miles away, not thoroughly, the way the subject deserves to be examined.'

'When do you leave for Slapton Sands?'

'In two days' time. What do you think is happening?'

Emerson looked out of the window. It was just after eleven o'clock in the morning. The sky was blue and the light already brilliant, intense. The ice-cream parlour's door was open, and the warm, ozone smell of the sea mingled with the pink sweetness of candyfloss and buttery popcorn oil. A transistor radio sat on the counter between the window and the soft ice-cream machine. Elton John was beseeching Kiki Dee not to go breaking his heart. A piercing treble characterized the sound coming out of the little radio. The table between the two women was fissured in its plastic marbling with countless tiny cracks, mapped by age and grime. Alice could see fine, tiny hairs on the policewoman's chin under a thin coating of foundation. The make-up had been hastily applied and was uneven over her skin. It occurred to her again that this was not a country equipped for the relentless exposure of detail obliged by this summer's unearthly weather. England was a country that suited shadows and flat, diminished light. Exposed like this, it looked shabby and somehow amateurish. It looked fraudulent, not really up to the job of being what it represented to the world. Or to itself.

Emerson had astonishing eyes. In this light, grey and yellow particles of colour flecked the green. Those eyes focused on Alice now, unblinking. 'Student radicalism is usually confrontational,' she said. 'They'd sooner shake a fist or wave a banner in your face and scream slogans at you. Exhibitionism is a strong part of it. Subterfuge for them wouldn't be stealing into your room insinuating subtle messages in the night. It would be setting fire to the contents of your pigeonhole with a cigarette lighter. It would be daubing graffiti on your locker door, dropping a dead mouse in there after forcing the padlock.'

'Charming.'

'We can dismiss Long John Silver, as you call him. He's apolitical. His record collection alone pretty much rules him out as a sex pest. And he has a leg in plaster.'

'Sex pests don't listen to Genesis?'

'No,' Emerson said. She sipped her coffee. 'Not as a rule.'

'What do they listen to?'

Emerson appeared to consider this. 'Hawkwind,' she said.

Alice put her hands on the tabletop and half-rose to leave but sat down again when Emerson said: 'The obvious suspect of course, is David Lucas.'

'Why?'

'Nothing happened until you met him. The first incident occurred only after you had met him and he'd discovered you lived in Whitstable. He fitted the locks that failed to prevent the second intrusion. He finds you desirable, but sexually reticent. Maybe if he makes you feel vulnerable and grateful enough, he can get you into bed that way. You're predisposed to thinking of him as the shining knight. Maybe he's intelligent enough to be aware of that and callous enough to exploit the fact.'

'I don't believe any of that,' Alice said.

'Neither do I,' Emerson said. 'Except perhaps for the last bit.'

'So I'll ask you again,' Alice said. 'What do you think is happening?'

Something softened in the policewoman's posture, or expression, or perhaps in her tone. It was no one thing Alice could have identified, even in the bright shrillness of the ice-cream parlour and fully alert. But it was there, unmistakable, a sympathy when the woman spoke. 'What I think is that you are alienated and homesick. I think there is some deferred grief from the deaths of the two people you loved most. The subject of your thesis is American dead in a foreign war, a theme bound to make you think of your brother. Your father died in violent circumstances, only

92

relatively recently. Subconsciously, I think you are looking for a reason to go home. And you are providing it for yourself. There was no intruder, Alice. Not unless it was someone capable of walking through walls.'

Alice didn't say anything. She looked down at her hands resting on the tabletop. A skin was forming across the surface of the coffee in her cup. They put milk in it without waiting to ask whether you wanted milk in your coffee or not. They did it every damned time.

'You've taken too much on,' she heard the policewoman say.

'Are you going to charge me with wasting police time?'

Emerson laughed. It wasn't unkind laughter. 'I'm going to pay for a minicab and give you a lift up to the university, if that's where you're going.' She closed her cigarette packet and unhooked her bag from the back of her chair and put her cigarettes and lighter away. She put the bag over her shoulder. Alice sat with her head bowed and her eyes fixed on the cracks and fissures of the tabletop.

Emerson reached over and squeezed her hand. 'Go home, love,' she said. 'Go home. The mystery of Slapton Sands will wait a while longer to be solved, you know.'

'The thing is,' Alice said, 'I saw you shiver. A summer morning during what they keep telling us is the hottest summer in England for five hundred years, and I see you shiver in the room where I sleep. And I believe you smelled the smell, too. Dank and dead, like spilled fish guts from something that feeds on the bed of the sea.'

93

★

When she reached the university, Alice tried for as long as her concentration would allow to read about south Devon in the library. The pre-war economy there had depended heavily on agriculture and fishing. Both were little more than subsistence industries. They provided a few large-scale farmers and one or two fleet captains with a decent enough income, but Devon was neither a breadbasket for the British economy nor, obviously, the industrial powerhouse of the nation. Its prettiness was often enough remarked on, but tourist income was a scant, negligible consideration beyond those coastal towns equipped with promenades and piers. The residents of south Devon occupied villages and eked out modest livings. And its population growth had been catastrophically stunted by the casualties sustained among its young male population during the Great War. It had been a place in the early 1940s disproportionately high in its demographic ratio of elderly men, ageing widows and bereft mothers reaching pensionable age. Many of its dwellings had at that time still been without electric light. Indoor lavatories were a scarcity. The roads were ill lit, narrow, poorly maintained and with the signs removed and maps deliberately falsified to confound invading Germans, difficult to navigate. The railways were better. The trains had been primitive in terms of passenger comforts by American standards, but the rail network was comprehensive and left largely intact by enemy bombing raids. The trains ran frequently, if not strictly to timetable and always, at night, in the imposed gloom of blackout conditions.

Entertainment was confined to the church hall and the pub. Religion and drink tended to exist as opposing cultural forces in America, but here they seemed to coexist quite happily. Perhaps this was because they didn't compete. The church espoused the traditional values of community and nuclear family and faith. The pub was strictly a place for men. It represented a threat to family economy if a man spent all his time and wages there, but it wasn't a place to which he strayed in search of adulterous adventure. Not in rural Devon, it wasn't. The pub seemed to function there as a place of warmth and refuge as much as beer; a forum for debate and the exchange of information and opinion. Alice had long held the view that men were much more inclined to gossip than were women. The character of the English pub, its enduring popularity and unchanging nature, supported her in this belief.

Much had remained the same, she thought, about England. But she thought south Devon in the early 1940s would have seemed a terribly alien and isolated place to the young men arriving there in uniform from the States. This would be equally true whether they came from the wheatfields of Idaho or from the tenements of Little Italy. It was a place with a settled and unchanging population, where tradition meant much and any shift in the routine imposed by the cycle of the seasons would be interpreted as an unwelcome threat. The Americans were not there to protect the people of Devon from invasion. To the people of Devon, they were invaders. And this would have been particularly true for those forced at short notice to abandon their homes.

Alice packed up and left her library carrel and bought a sandwich from the Elliot College shop. The sandwich comprised limp lettuce and sweating Cheddar cheese between slabs of white bread that had been dabbed at with margarine. Oh well. She ate it on the slope behind the college under the shade of a tree. It was one-thirty now. At two she had arranged the showing of a film in a small lecture room at the university's Gulbenkian Theatre. One piece of begrudging advice offered by Professor Champion had been to look at the films of Will Hay and George Formby and Old Mother Riley if she really wanted to understand the England of the Slapton Sands era. But these films, though Formby's were occasionally shown on television, were very difficult to view on demand. She had located and borrowed a copy of the Will Hay feature *Oh, Mr Porter!* through the college film society. Godard and Bergman being their usual fare, they'd been pretty sniffy about the request. They did agree to borrow it from an archive when she explained she wasn't watching it in the hope of being entertained. But viewing the film still required a room, projector and technician to change the reels and balance the sound. She had to pay the technician an hourly rate to perform the task, adding some mysterious extra surcharge described to her as 'ancilliaries'.

Oh, Mr Porter! didn't initially appear very promising. It was set in rural Ireland and had been directed by a Frenchman. But Champion said it was a good choice, a film that reflected the values of the 1930s in provincial Britain, poking subversive fun at such shibboleths as the Empire and the police. Not much changed between the 1930s and the 1940s, Champion told Alice. Not in south Devon it didn't, anyway.

Much to the obvious disgust of the technician, she found the film hilarious. She found herself wishing she'd bought popcorn along instead of a notebook. This version of England and its manners was sly and gentle and monochromatic and could have been set a hundred years ago. Men still took watches on chains from waistcoat pockets to tell themselves the time. Leisure clothing did not exist. Ceremony was stood upon by everyone at every possible opportunity. In its comic re-creation of a life its audience needed to recognize to find funny, the film revealed a quaint and primitive place low on clutter and amenities. The telephone was an object of terror and the wireless of wonder to its crafty, workshy inhabitants. Was this England? She left the theatre smiling, thankful to Champion, four pounds fifty lighter to the smirking technician as he let her out and spooled the feature back into its pile of tarnished silver cans.

Will Hay was an old music-hall comedian who had starred in ten successful feature films between 1934 and 1941, each with the same two character actors in principal supporting roles. Hay apparently always played the pompous bungler. Graham Moffatt played the fat, pompous bungler. And Moore Marriott played the bungling, pompous codger. Alice recognized all three. They were not so much stereotypes as faithfully exaggerated portraits taken from English life.

Had Devon been like Will Hay's England? If it had, it must have seemed arcane and basic to its invading army of young Americans with their dollars and lust, their Jeeps and motorcycles, Hershey bars and bubble gum. The principal difference between then and now, she thought, having spent an hour and a half looking at the film, was that this was an England that had liked itself. It was its own idle, self-serving, pompously incompetent universe. It had charm, innocence and unsullied optimism. It filled you with nostalgia for something you had never experienced. Will Hay's England had been comfortable with what it was and therefore inured to any urgency to change. Walking into the vaulting sunshine of the afternoon, momentarily blinded by it, she did not think that was anything like so true of the England to which she had come. She left the projection room very much looking forward to her first George Formby film.

She wanted to see David Lucas. She wanted to see the chief suspect in the crime that the Canterbury detective was sure had been committed only inside her own troubled head. She didn't believe she had done it herself, the grief-stricken somnambulist tapping out upper-case instructions to herself in the dark. Nor did she think David Lucas had anything to do with what she had awoken to find. She just wanted to see him. She didn't even want to tell him about waking to the piece of paper gummed to her wall. She wanted company, that was all. And the company she most wanted, was his.

David wasn't in the gym, but Clifford Lee was there, hammering a malevolent tattoo in the heat on the heavy bag, his head rested on the cylinder of plumped leather as he shaped into a series of punishing hooks. Alice stood on the gantry above and watched him work. His punches spread staccato echoes around the gym. He worked with evident grace and a brutal economy with the delivery of his shots. But the grace was incidental. Anyone watching was watching violence, or at least a demonstration of violent capability. Eventually he stopped and raised his head. Sweat left an intimate smear on the bag where his brow had rested for the body work. He opened his mouth, gulping air, and looked up, grinning through his gumshield. Christ, she thought, he even does his bagwork wearing his gumshield, in this heat. Clifford Lee spat the guard on to the parquet floor and smiled at her.

'Is he any good? Is he as good as you?'

'Nah. He's shit.' Deadpan.

'Really?' She felt crestfallen, childish for feeling so.

She had fetched tea for them from a vending machine in the entrance area of the gym. Clifford Lee was wrapped now in a tracksuit and towels. He was making weight, he'd told her. He blew on his tea as if to cool the brew. But he didn't drink it. He just smelled it in gulps, gathered in the aroma under his nose.

'Boxing's more or less been outlawed now at the universities,' he said. 'There's us. There's Bath. There's Oxbridge and there's the army boys at Sandhurst. There's Edinburgh in Scotland, Trinity over the water. That's it.'

'I don't see your point.'

'To get any competition, we have to go local. We have to go to the clubs in Dover and Folkestone and the like.'

'And?'

'And they take liberties with the college boys. Or they try to. Now, you take a liberty with Davey, and you pay.'

Alice took this in. 'So he is good?'

Clifford Lee smelled his tea again. 'Good isn't quite the word I'd use. Bad is more accurate.'

She nodded, not saying anything.

'Here's the deal,' Clifford Lee said. He inhaled steam off his tea. 'Where will Ollie Deane be in five, ten years?'

'I have no idea,' Alice said. She didn't.

Clifford smiled down at his feet, and his skin tightened over the bones in his face in a vision of premature age. 'He'll be an estate agent. Somewhere like Putney, Hampstead. He'll sell posh properties in that public school drawl. He'll have an occasionally unfaithful wife, attend London–Irish home games and buy his two-point-four kids a pedigree puppy.'

'Breed?'

'How the fuck would I know?' He shrugged. 'Jack Russell. Irish Wolfhound.'

'Kids' names?'

He looked at her.

'Come on, Clifford. You started this.'

'Ben. Josh. Rory.'

'Girls?'

'God help them,' Clifford said. 'Celia. Sophie. Alice.'

She laughed. 'And David?'

'Five years from now? I don't know. A mercenary. A priest.'

They were silent for a while. Alice wondered where Clifford Lee would find himself in five years from now. She supposed pretty much wherever he wanted.

'He says your speciality is the American occupation of Britain during the Second World War.'

'Occupation?'

'Invasion, my grandfather called it. That's what it seemed like in the South-West of England, he said. He was a merchant seaman on the convoys. He said there were a lot of Yanks in Bristol.'

'Are you interested in the war?'

'Not particularly. You know how it is. When people get older, they like to reminisce. Very fit, the Yanks, he told me. Well fed, they were. Strong. He was invited to spar with their boxers sometimes. Fought the odd exhibition bout.'

'I wasn't aware inter-racial boxing was allowed.'

'I don't know that it was,' Clifford Lee said. 'My grandfather is white.'

Universities were funny places, Alice thought. On the way to the gym she'd walked past the campus bookshop, where they did a brisk trade selling Arthur Rackham fairy posters to young adults toiling for competitive grades in pure sciences. From where she sat she could hear the faint chanting of the anti-apartheid protestors outside the campus branch of Barclays Bank. There were always at least three or four students picketing the bank, and since she'd been here she'd never seen a black face among them. When Clifford Lee shifted where he sat, muscles like lazy grapefruit ripened on his upper arms.

'Aren't you going to drink that tea?'

'I'll gain less weight just enjoying the aroma. Aren't you going to ask me where he is?'

She was about to knock on the door when she thought she heard her name spoken from within. Her hand hesitated. The voice had belonged to Oliver. It was Oliver's posh, corrupted drawl.

'And those men's jeans they all wear that make their arses look like crisp bags. And Earth shoes. Make their feet look like they've been put on back to front, Earth shoes do.'

There was a silence. No one from within the room filled it. Then Oliver spoke again.

'Charlie Brown. Eval fucking Kneival. And all that metal

they wear on their teeth. "If You Leave Me Now". Fucking
. . . Neil Diamond.'

'Neil Diamond doesn't sing "If You Leave Me Now".'
David's voice.

'You know what I mean.'

'You know what he means.' A third voice, one she didn't
recognize.

'And she doesn't wear braces on her teeth.'

'Those self-supporting socks that Jimmy Connors
prances about in. Naugahyde furniture. Wonderwoman.'

'You can't knock Wonderwoman.' David's voice again.

'You can't. No one would want to argue the point about
Jimmy Connors and his unnatural socks,' the stranger said.
'But you can't knock Wonderwoman.'

'Those electric shaver adverts with that cretin with the
silver hair.'

'Remington,' the stranger said.

'No,' Oliver said. 'I'm pretty sure he's not called
Remington.'

'Victor Kiam,' David said.

'Him,' Oliver said. 'Fucking Victor Kiam.'

She could smell the thick fug of a joint drifting under the
door. Hall and Oates were playing on a record player she
could picture without having to see. They were playing
Abandoned Luncheonette. There would be Wharfdale speakers
on the tabletop opposite the narrow bed, to either side of a
Garrard turntable. Albums in a flat stack on one of the
speakers. An album on Oliver's lap, littered with Rizla

papers and tobacco fragments and burned-down matches.

'He's a bastard, that Victor Kiam.'

It was tedious and disappointing. She was disappointed with herself for being there. If she possessed more of a gift for friendship, she wouldn't be in this situation. Maybe it was more a question of effort than talent. She didn't put the work into developing friendships. Perhaps she deserved her isolation. But believing that didn't make the isolation any easier to tolerate at times like this. Her hand was still raised to rap her knuckles on the door. She let it drop to her side instead and turned to go. Oh well. In the library and the projection room at least, the day had been a sort of a success. Hall and Oates were singing, 'She's Gone'. They were almost right. She was certainly going. David's voice stopped her.

'You know, smoking that stuff isn't really giving what passes for your minds a fighting chance, boys. Don't get me wrong. Paranoia and prejudice can work as the basis for a belief system. But you still need a mechanism for some independent thought processes.'

A silence followed this remark.

'At least we're not punch-drunk,' Oliver said.

'I'm talking about basic stuff. You know. Perambulation. Respiratory function. Toilet training.'

'Do you find you've started having trouble remembering telephone numbers?' This from the stranger.

There was another silence.

'When you leave home,' Oliver said, 'do you have to have your address with you, written down?'

Alice knocked on the door.

The one she hadn't met was an Eng. Lit. student called Larry. He was on a continuous assessment course, and he'd received his latest assessment that afternoon, sweating the verdict before a three-man panel while she had chuckled over Will Hay's grainy comic antics. It was his room. He considered he'd done well. The dope was partly reward, mostly their prelude to a long evening of boozy, narcotic celebration. They were undergraduates. The sun was shining. They were celebrating the last, shiftless days of their final term before the long vacation. Clifford Lee had given her the college name and room number, but not the name of its occupant.

'Great believer in fate, Clifford,' Larry said, patting a spot on the bed where he sat next to Oliver. Larry looked like he dressed out of one of Canterbury's charity shops. His teeth signalled years of neglect. His watch showed base metal through chipped chrome plating on the case and was fastened to his wrist by a nylon strap striped like a scrap of seaside deck chair. He was probably the heir to an estate somewhere, she thought. But his invitation was an uninviting one. To Alice, the bed looked already over-crowded. The beckoning to sit was best ignored. 'A Thomas Hardy man, our Clifford,' Larry said. 'Believes it will all end in tears.'

'It usually does. For his opponents,' Oliver said.

It was funny how they stuck for the duration with the friends they made in their freshers' weeks. At home, the like-minded were funnelled through societies and sororities and frat houses into homogeneous groups. Seamlessly compatible cliques dominated student life. Here, they stuck stubbornly to the haphazard and unlikely friends they made in ther first chaotic weeks at college, usually while half-drunk. Compatibility had nothing to do with it. It was endearing in a way. It was fiercely loyal. But it was mad.

She sipped some of the Nescafé David had made her. Larry had the Christ image of Che Guevara Blu-Tacked to his wall. It shared space with a poster for a production of *Waiting for Godot* staged at the Abbey Theatre in Dublin. There was a picture of Samuel Beckett, stony-eyed as a bird, in some austere Paris café with rain-daubed glass. Trinity College had been one of the many that had offered her a postgraduate place. She wondered if Ireland laboured under the same relentless summer heat as England did this June. She wondered if the Irish were as irritating and incomprehensible as the English seemed to be.

'He must like you,' Oliver said to her. 'Clifford, I mean. He isn't usually so forthcoming with information.'

'Maybe I'm likeable.'

'No,' Oliver said. 'You're not. You're extremely easy on the eye. But you aren't likeable.'

Nobody in the room contradicted him.

'Sorry,' Oliver said.

Alice turned to David. 'Why is Clifford sweating off weight?'

'He can't get into his jeans,' Oliver said.

'He needs to scale a hundred and seventy-five pounds,' David said. 'He's on the scales tomorrow morning for a match made at that weight.'

Larry said: 'What's that in kilos?'

'I haven't got a clue,' David said.

'Kilos are the future,' Larry said. 'Kilos, litres, kilometres. I reckon he weighs about eighty kilos. Alice?'

'Search me,' Alice said. 'I'm an American.'

'Get away,' Oliver said.

'American,' Larry said. 'So you'd be far more familiar, of course, with the imperial scale of measurement.'

Larry and Oliver were doing that dope thing of not daring to look at one another.

'Where'd you get your clothes, Larry?' she said. 'A landfill site?'

She wanted to get out of the room. She wanted David to come with her. He wasn't indulging in the smoking ritual, but he seemed very settled, very comfortable there. She couldn't really drag him away from his friends without appearing to do exactly that. But she'd had enough of Hall and Oates and the skanky smell and claustrophobia of a dormitory space on a stifling day. She'd had enough already of Apache Oliver and Metric Larry. She wanted to sit under the shade of a tree on the slope behind the college down to the city and tell David about the note on her wall and the Canterbury detective.

Abruptly, David stood. 'Let's get some air,' he said to her.

'Don't mind us,' Oliver said.

They could hear the giggles explode against the door as David closed it behind her and they walked together out along the corridor.

'What's his problem with Naugahyde?' Tan Naugahyde had covered her father's recliner, his comfortable, television-watching chair. The Naugahyde chair had been sold along with the rest of the house contents prior to the selling of the house itself. Alice had been told to go home. The truth was she had no home to go to. She didn't think she would ever live in Pennsylvania again. It would be home in the future only ever in her memory.

'Do you know in America they make the bags for bagpipes out of Naugahyde?'

Alice pretended to consider this. 'That's practically sacrilegious,' she said.

She had no home to go to. She'd had a home from home, but that lay violated now.

David said: 'I don't think Ollie has ever actually been confronted by Naugahyde. Not personally. It's more a point of principle. I think he just feels really sorry for all those innocent naugas, slaughtered for their pelts.'

They walked out of the main entrance of the college and turned left down the concrete steps and left again through parked cars on to the scorched grass of the university grounds and the slope that led gently to the city spread under the sun beneath and beyond them. Students as still as corpses sunbathed in places on the grass on towels beside transistor radios. Alice lifted her hand to shield her eyes from the glare of unrelenting light. Saplings, sycamores mostly, wilted strapped to posts in an infant forest all down the slope. If they survived the summer, they would grow over the years into mature trees that would conceal the cathedral entirely from view.

In a little over two hours she was due to present herself at Professor Champion's supper party. She would be expected to swap precise, research-based anecdotes with Champion's careful pick of nimble-minded fellow guests. A supper party. And Whitstable afterwards, her room there dank, dream-fractured, its privacy breached. She wondered if she wasn't losing her mind. Was madness like this?

She turned to David Lucas. He stood watching her with an expression on his handsome face she couldn't read. 'Are you busy just now?'

'No,' he said.

'I'd like to go back to your house,' she said. 'I'd like to lie beside you in your bed and just talk. Not do anything, just talk. Do you think, David, that you'd be OK with that?'

'Of course,' he said.

'Good.' She smiled at him.

So they went back to his house. And they undressed in the heat and the light and went to bed. And, of course, they did everything.

Alice quite enjoyed the supper party. The three principals from the history department attended, or rather presided, and all three displayed the endearing, almost touching ineptitude of clever, closeted people forced to confront the hazards of social interaction. It reminded Alice a bit of a programme she had watched on British television. In it, volunteers representing their towns were forced to compete at activities requiring levels of strength and coordination a trained athlete would struggle to produce. She couldn't recall the name of the series, something to do with knock-out, but towards the finale it always descended into a gladiatorial slapstick, mostly memorable for the way in which its sadistic compere openly guffawed at the willing inadequacies of the competitors.

Sadism wasn't in Alice Bourne's nature. She had never taken pleasure in others' pain or social ineptitude. She felt relieved rather than happy about how uncomfortable the academic staff appeared at Professor Champion's party. If the stars of the occasion were incapable of small talk, it took attention and pressure, she felt, away from her. She still felt she was under scrutiny and a degree of approbation. She wasn't at the university under sufferance. On the contrary, they'd courted her. But they had courted her credentials, her achievements in her own short but bright-burning academic career. The stubbornly insisted-on subject of her doctoral thesis was an immense, anticlimactic disappoint-ment to the department, she knew. Her professor, she now believed, took it as a personal affront.

'You look different,' Champion said. He had drifted alongside her with a vol-au-vent and a lighted cigarette caged elegantly in the same high-perched hand. In her peripheral vision, the head of American Studies shoulder-charged a doorframe, drunk or incredibly clumsy, in a hooped purple and saffron dress. The female academics there were a kaleidoscope of clashing fabrics and clunky wooden jewellery of the Scandinavian sort. The room smelled of Alliage and Tabac and those thin, ornamental Sobranie Russian cigarettes. Through the window of Champion's sitting room, only a detail of the cathedral was visible. The ancient building was fantastically close to where he lived. His flat flanked the Cathedral Gate. Either the university owned the building he lived in or he was affluent beyond the reach of his salary.

'I don't wish to speak out of turn—'

'Don't, then.'

'But you do look different,' he said.

'I'm sorry,' Alice said. 'I didn't mean to be abrupt.' She sipped more wine. It tasted cold and seductive. She wasn't used to wine. It wasn't the time or the place to tell him of her encounter with the Kent constabulary. But she told him anyway, blurted out an abbreviated version of the morning's strange, remembered events.

'Let's find a quiet spot where we can sit,' he said, guiding her, finding places on tables on the way to dump his baked morsel, his half-smoked cigarette. They were in his bedroom. It was austere, cathedral masonry surreally close through the small, polished panes of a single window sunk into ancient stone.

'Sit down,' Champion said.

A part of Alice Bourne thought, then, that it was always coming to this. But her professor did not have on the seductive face he'd worn at his party on the grass.

'How did you find Sally Emerson?'

'Sympathetic. Incredulous. Both of those, maybe not in that order. I don't know. A bit febrile. Clever?' She hadn't told Champion the detective's first name.

He nodded. 'I taught her. She's clever, all right. Took history as the minor part of her degree. Majored in philosophy, which was a shame. Did a postgrad at the LSE and came there to the attention of the powers that be. In the period you're interested in discovering more about, she'd have been whisked off to Bletchley Park to crack Nazi codes. Or maybe she'd have been SOE material. Our intelligence people seemed to enjoy parachuting people like her into occupied France to get tortured and shot by the Gestapo. Outstanding girl. Local, obviously. Faversham.'

Alice nodded. She could hear party noises, but they were polite and dim. It was cool in Champion's bedroom, despite the ambient heat. They were insulated from the worst of it, she imagined, by the medieval thickness of his walls. She could still smell David Lucas on her skin, in her mouth and her hair. She had washed scrupulously in the tepid bathroom water at his shared house. But the smell was rich still in the heat of her mind and memory. She had lied to the English boy. Did she have a boyfriend? he had asked. No, she had said, shaking her head. It wasn't quite the truth. It hadn't felt at the time like a lie. Are you seeing anyone?

he'd asked. Jesus. They were naked together. They were in bed. Yes, she'd admitted. You, she'd said. And that had felt like the truth. Which it was, kind of.

Now, she cleared her throat. 'You don't mind my having gone to the police?'

Champion coughed laughter. 'Your grammar is wonderful, you know. For an American.'

Alice didn't say anything.

'You summoned them and they came to you, apparently. We don't like the police force arriving uninvited on the campus. There's a libertarian issue. There's a clash of ideologies. There are too many drugs, frankly. It might surprise you to learn this, but the use of illegal substances is not entirely confined to the student body.'

Alice nodded. She wondered whether she was supposed to be impressed by this claim. She wondered if it were the reason why the head of American Studies was out there careening into fixtures and fittings.

'But this was a domestic matter between you and them,' Champion said. 'It won't make a paragraph in the less-than-vigilant pages of the *East Kent Gazette*. Even if it did—'

There was a knock then at the door. And her professor shrugged and gave Alice the sleepy-eyed look he'd worn when talking to the pert girl in the ruched dress at his party in the sunshine on the grass.

'How far will DS Emerson go?'

Champion frowned, distracted. 'With a spurious investigation? Nowhere. Obviously.'

'I meant in her career.'

The knocker knocked again on the bedroom door. Champion shrugged, as though resigned to the interruption, to the distraction of the question. 'The civil service do the wooing. There's all this talk of fast-tracking, as I believe it's called. Loathsome term. Do you know anything about the British police?'

The knocker knocked again.

'Go away!' Champion said.

'Nothing,' Alice said. 'I've seen *The Sweeney* on television.'

'Well,' Champion said. He chuckled. His laughter was full of tobacco. 'She'll earn a call soon enough from London. But she won't exceed her present rank at Scotland Yard. Eventually she'll become bored. She'll meet a good-looking fellow officer and marry and have babies. Or she'll leave the force to teach history at a secondary modern.' He drank his wine. 'And maths. They always make the graduates teach maths.'

'Someone's still outside, waiting,' Alice said. 'I can hear her breathing. I can sense her there.'

Champion nodded. 'What did Sally Emerson conclude?'

'Just what you've surmised. The complaint was spurious.'

'I've changed my mind about Devon, Alice. You need Devon. The fields might be burning all across England. But you need to get there, if you can. You need a couple of weeks of study, in isolation and solitude. You've an intellect, I think, that's always thrived on solitude.'

She said nothing.

'How do you know it's a woman? Outside the door?'

'I don't know. I just do.'

'The same way you knew your Whitstable intruder was a man?'

She shrugged.

'No?' he said.

She nodded. She was aware of the indignant weight of the woman on the other side of the door. She was aware, as they rose to leave the room, of how clever and influential was her professor.

'You might solve the riddle of Slapton Sands,' he said. 'You might very well make something out of all this. I've changed my mind about that, too.' He smiled, showing his teeth under the trimmed bristles of his moustache. 'We've high expectations of you, Alice Bourne.'

She nodded again. High expectations. They made a welcome change from salient facts.

The door opened on the woman in the ruched dress from Champion's summer party. She wore jeans now and a white cotton smock top and an expression on her face of indiscriminate fury. Alice slipped past her and smiled to herself. It didn't matter, apparently, how clever or influential a man was. The temptation to crap on his own porch was sometimes an impulse impossible to resist.

She left her professor's flat at eight o'clock on an evening filled with light. She noticed late tourists in family clusters outside the Cathedral Gate and, in the courtyard, a bigger contingent grouped listening intently to a guide. They looked alien to her, in their seersucker suits and trilbies of woven straw, carrying their Leicas and Nikons around their necks, triggering their little Super-8 home-movie cameras, aiming them like harmless handguns at historical and picturesque targets. These were Sally Emerson's welcome Americans, the free-spending ones who swelled the coffers of the Canterbury Chamber of Commerce. It was funny, she had never really noticed them before, the men in their loud, alien accents and the women in their loud, alien clothes. Opposite the Cathedral Gate, students occupied tables outside the pub there, sipping pints of lager and halves of lager and lime or cider, hand-rolling cigarettes from pouches of Old Holborn and Golden Virginia. She looked from the students to the tourists and back again. They were oblivious to one another, these contrasting tribes, as though existing in parallel worlds.

In their Devon domain, the Americans had come thirty-odd years ago and literally created a world of their own. Theirs had been a more compelling agenda than mere sightseeing. They'd been preparing for a war that would claim many of their lives. Perhaps that justified the ruthlessness with which their secret invasion of a part of rural England was carried out. And their cause had been noble enough. No one was threatening to invade America's West Coast, after all, or threatening its eastern seaboard. The American war in the Pacific had been a war of revenge. But in Europe? The conflict in Europe was an ideological struggle. The Americans dispatched to prepare for warfare in Devon might have been overpaid and oversexed, as the English had it at the time, but they were over here in the first place only because they were committed to a fight for freedom.

Outside the cathedral, the Americans were prosperous and middle-aged, gaudy in Crimplene and Foster Grants, loud with questions for their guide framed in the dialects of Missouri and Nevada and New York State. Probably they reclined at home on furniture covered in Naugahyde, listening to Neil Diamond on their stereos. Alice blinked in the sunshine and smiled at the thought. And she thought of the lean young Americans of three decades ago in their brush cuts and combat fatigues, with their Luckies and their straight-edged razors and their murderous ambition to fight battle-hardened German strike troops in the fields and hedgerows of occupied France.

She had asked her veteran about that. She had asked her Colorado veteran about the apprehension the soldiers must have suffered in the prolonged, uncertain secrecy of waiting for the fight. He'd turned his whisky glass on the bar between finger and thumb and then raised his head and grinned at her. And the grin had been cold enough for her to see his youthful ghost staring along the sights of an assault rifle.

'Wasn't so bad,' he told her. 'We were willing enough. The Nazis were evil bastards, miss, if you'll excuse my language. I thought there was every possibility I'd die. The beaches were mined. They had machine-gun emplacements and tanks and fighter-bombers to strafe our columns with. The more we learned about combat strategy, the greater that likelihood seemed. I thought I'd be killed. But I thought I'd kill a few of them first.' The grin deepened. 'Turned out I was half-right, anyways.'

The declining sun had half-dipped now behind a building, and a shadow extended to cover the area in which Alice stood outside the Cathedral Gate. She shivered, thinking of bodies in rain capes, surfacing on an oily sea, the buoyant stink of decay creeping from creped fingers and corrupted organs as the corpses rose in dead battalions to litter the ocean. Had it happened like that? Had they died aboard their landing craft, killed by friendly fire in some catastrophic night rehearsal? Outside the pub opposite, as shade encroached across tables and chairs, the students were gathering their bits and pieces, their bags and books and paraphernalia, and retreating into the pub itself, into comfort and shelter.

It wasn't truly cold. It wasn't even chilly. And dusk was more than an hour distant. But Alice shivered again, thinking that perhaps the supper party wine had thinned her blood. Had it happened like that? Had they been killed by the guns of their own artillery batteries fired on them from the shore? She didn't know. She aimed to find out.

Outside the cathedral, a man had detached himself from the group listening to the guide. He was a slim, insubstantial figure with grey stubble on gaunt cheeks under an iron-grey crew cut. Half-swallowed in the shadow cast by a cathedral buttress, he stopped moving at the moment Alice noticed him and stood perfectly still, as though listening, alert to something other than the well-practised patter of the group guide. The other tourists fiddled with lenses and wound on rolls of film, a couple of them tinkering with tape recorders hanging from thin leather shoulder straps. One dabbed sweat from his face with a handkerchief. The figure who had claimed her attention did none of this. He just stood, lurked almost, in the cadaverous shadow of stone. And then he slipped behind the buttress completely. Alice felt there was something vaguely troubling about the man. He hadn't looked like a tourist, dressed in a neutral shirt, a pair of drab olive trousers hung on bony hips. There was no camera, no straw trilby on his head, no accompanying wife. But it was the alertness that was odd, that slightly troubled her, that didn't sit quite right and perhaps was the thing that made her shiver again. He'd appeared taut, had the man, like wire. Had he been looking at her, from the shade of the cathedral, a hundred and fifty feet distant? Alice shrugged. He hadn't. Had he? Anyway, he was gone.

From the west, she saw David Lucas walking towards her through the narrow shadows of the street. It was eight-fifteen. He was punctual. But with a thousand dollars' worth of watch on his wrist, he had no real excuse not to be. She watched him walk towards her, able to picture him, now, naked under his clothes. She knew now how his body worked, how fluidly the muscles under his skin functioned

119

when he moved. He probably thought her promiscuous, possessed of the easy promiscuity he'd become used to and taken for granted in his student life. Ordinarily, this was far from the truth about how she was, how she viewed sex and regarded intimacy. She hoped there would be time for him to get to know her properly. And for her to get to know him. They'd certainly made a start. It hadn't been her usual way of going about things. Oh well. It was done. About David Lucas, at least, she now possessed some salient facts.

He had borrowed Oliver's car. It was a minivan the Apache was seldom apparently in any fit condition to drive himself. David had parked it in the car park near the West Gate, and they drove from there to Whitstable and her flat to fetch anything she hadn't taken that morning and needed to take with her to Slapton Sands. The flat felt cold when they got there. It was dusk. Alice switched on the light. Traces of fingerprint powder, fine like chalk, had trickled from the space where the note had been above the bed head to stain her pillow in a yellowy drift. She inhaled. That sluggish smell of the sea, of mud and salt decay, lingered about the place.

'It was a ghost,' Alice said. And David stood from where he had crouched, with his back to her, running a thumb over the titles in her bookcase. 'It was a ghost, David. You can feel the chill and dread of him.'

'You've drunk too much wine.'

'No. I haven't.'

'I could smell it on your breath in the car on the way here.'

'I'm not exactly drunk.'

He looked at her. 'Who would haunt you?'

'I don't know.'

He walked across to her and put his hand out, as if to place a reassuring palm on her shoulder. She took a step away from him, and the backs of her knees hit the edge of the bed. She sat, involuntarily, and then just as abruptly stood again. She brushed the backs of her knees with her hands. She looked up at him. 'What's wrong now?'

'You flinched when I reached out to you.'

'I didn't.'

'You recoiled.'

'Don't be so precious. I fell on my ass.'

But he looked hurt.

'It's this place. It's haunted. Can't you feel it?'

David was silent. Through the ceiling, on Long John Silver's reel-to-reel, someone sang the chorus of a song celebrating the Court of the Crimson King. The song was full of a gloomy foreboding. It was growing dark. Alice wanted to leave. She wondered if they should go to the Neptune, sit listening to a jukebox full of sea shanties. In her mind, the pub seemed an impossibly snug and comforting prospect. The pub was Jack Tar dancing the hornpipe to the music of a wheezy accordion. It was not the Crimson King and the cruel antics of his malevolent court. But the pub was probably a bad idea. David Lucas already thought her drunk. She filled a string bag with books and packed a few items of summer clothing. The Bill Blass suit stayed with her other good pieces, carefully stored on hangers or folded between sheets of tissue on shelves in the wardrobe. It wasn't the weather for Bill Blass. And Slapton Sands was not the place. 'What are you doing?'

David was standing by the wall, running his finger along a seam of wallpaper above the bookcase. 'Looking for signs of damp,' he said. 'There aren't any. It's bloody odd. No damp, no condensation. But you can feel it.'

'Let's go.' It was fully dark outside now. The doomy music thumped against the ceiling from upstairs. Alice thought, imagined, she told herself, that she heard a footfall, soft, on the linoleum of the kitchenette.

'I wonder how a barometer would react in here?'

Alice said nothing. David gestured at the portable Olivetti on the desk. 'Aren't you taking that?'

Fuck it. 'Let's go to the Neptune,' Alice said. 'Like now, David?'

He shrugged. He seemed genuinely reluctant to leave the little typewriter to abandonment and damp. She didn't want it any more. It angered her that the machine had been a present from her dad. She knew with certainty that she would never touch its keys again.

In the pub he told her about his summer job. St Helens Fort had been one of a series of defensive forts built by British Prime Minister Lord Palmerston to protect the South of England from attack by sea and principally to defend the naval base of Portsmouth harbour. The threat of invasion had supposedly come from French Emperor Napoleon the Third. The cost of construction had been astronomical. Work on St Helens had begun in 1867 but had been hampered by subsidence. It wasn't finally completed until 1880. This particular fort defended an area of strategic importance on the Isle of Wight and lay close to Bembridge. It had been used as a platform for anti-aircraft guns in the First and Second World Wars. It had been garrisoned as recently as the early 1960s but now lay decommissioned and derelict, the site of a proposed diving and navigation school, should the exploratory work carried out by David and his underwater colleagues prove its structural fabric to be sound.

'I don't think any of the forts ever fired a shot in anger,' he said. 'They proved pretty useless in the last war, when it came to defending Portsmouth from air attack. The dockyards and city were hard hit during the Blitz. An awful lot of the historic city was destroyed and of course a lot of lives were lost.'

Alice nodded. She was thinking of her good clothes gathering mildew, tendrils of damp, the strengthening insistence of decay. Her typewriter keys would clack with rust under the cold compulsion of unseen fingers in an empty bedroom. She would never go back there.

'It's a violation of a sort, when war is brought to your home country,' David said. 'It's an intimate sort of destruction. Rows of houses and shops and schools don't possess the neutrality of a battlefield.'

'You sound as though you've studied the subject.'

He shook his head. 'My dad was a teenager in Liverpool. Until they evacuated him to Wales. He ran away, lied about his age, joined the merchant navy.'

'At what age?'

'Dunno. Fourteen?'

'He didn't like Wales?'

'Lots of the evacuees were just child labour. He didn't appreciate digging spuds in a field at four in the morning.'

They were silent for a moment.

'You do know what a spud is?'

'Sure,' Alice said. 'Spud. As in Spud Murphy.'

The minivan belonging to the Apache needed a new baffle on its exhaust. Or it needed a new exhaust. This unless someone had bolted a twelve-cylinder engine beneath its modest hood, Alice thought. Even above the noise of the exhaust, she could hear a half-full can of gas sloshing about in the area behind their seats. She stretched around to look back. The steel gas can was holstered in some kind of bracket above a rear-wheel arch. There was a tartan picnic blanket spread across the rear interior. Brown bottles of beer, or maybe cider, rolled and chinked in collision. There were even scatter cushions, tumbling back there when they climbed the hills and the baffle roared like that of a preening dragster on the modest, four-mile ascent to Canterbury.

'Passion wagon,' David explained.

'It's the vehicular equivalent to a slum, David.'

'Say that word again. Say "vehicular" again.'

'So that you can record me? So that you can ridicule me in front of the Naugahyde Apache and his faithful sidekick, Metric Larry?'

'That was very funny, Alice. About the landfill site.'

Despite herself, she rested her head against his shoulder. It had not been the longest day of her life. The two candidates for that distinction had both featured gravesides. But it had been a long day. She was tired. It seemed weeks, not hours, since her interview with the Canterbury detective in the ice-cream parlour in Tankerton.

'Put the radio on.'

David reached forward and depressed a toggle on the dashboard. Elton and Kiki came on about halfway through 'Don't Go Breaking My Heart'. David pulled a face and searched for another station. There was a lot of static, something to do with the weather, apparently. Heat afflicted transmitters, made the stations remote. He got the Steve Miller Band and 'Fly like an Eagle' and Alice leaned into him.

'Do you like American music?'

She felt him shrug slightly. 'Some. Soul, mostly. Marvin Gaye, Curtis Mayfield. Blue Oyster Cult, however, you can keep.'

'Gee, thanks. Neil Diamond?'

David laughed. 'A genius.'

The road ahead of them was dark and narrow in the feeble beams of the Apache's passion wagon. Alice wondered what precise quality it was about this modest pocket of yellow light that told her she was in England. In Pennsylvania, in June, the windscreen would have been smeared with the corpses of flying insects. The road would not have undulated so. There would be a greater sense of space out there; the void, the absence that the bleak plains of North America always suggested to the night driver. England and Wales combined occupied about the same volume of space as the state of Colorado. By American standards it was tiny and densely populated. Did it seem bigger, in the countryside, at night? She thought it did. She thought of this little country as a place that harboured secrets beyond its size.

'Do you know anything about Slapton Sands?'

He lay beside her in bed for a long time before answering. They had not made love again. She wondered again what he had concluded from what they had done in the afternoon. But whatever his thoughts, they evidently didn't include the assumption of ready sexual availability. He was naked. They both were. It seemed a natural enough state between them. She felt relaxed, lying there beside him. Perhaps it was a reaction to shock. Perhaps it was fatigue. And she thought him beautiful to look at, lying next to her, his profile nubbed by starlight in the warm night.

'It's not my period,' he said.

'You think I'm wasting my time.'

'I think only time will tell.'

She remained quiet for a while, aware of her own breathing. She wondered if he was sleeping. She said: 'Do you? Think I'm wasting my time?'

He lifted himself on an elbow and leaned over her. 'You told me you lost your brother at Khe Sanh. He was a soldier killed in a war most Americans don't think was worth fighting. The men who died at Slapton Sands had joined the fight for civilization. There was nothing ambivalent about their cause, or their sacrifice. But I think somehow it's grief for your dead brother that's got you into this.'

'And my ghost?'

'It's your brother haunts you, Alice. I don't think you've buried him yet.'

'Thanks.'

He reached for her hand, which was unresponsive.

'I'm sorry.'

'No. But you're honest.'

TWO

The South Hams, 1943

His grandfather had been a sharecropper. His father had joined the army at fourteen and learned his soldiering in Cuba with Teddy Roosevelt's Roughriders in the Spanish-American War. By the time the Germans sank the *Lusitania*, his father wore three hard-won stripes on his sleeve and was one of very few Americans with combat experience that could in any way be called military. A year after the sinking, Bob Compton found himself a platoon commander on the Western Front. He saw plenty of action, enough anyway to come home with a chest full of medals and a persistent cough caught from a French whore in Amiens. Johnny Compton, his only son to survive past infancy, was reunited with his dad at the age of six, a fortnight after the armistice amid the panic of the flu pandemic in 1918. Bob Compton survived the flu. His wife, Johnny's mother, did not. His French whore finally killed Compton senior in 1927 when he died of tuberculosis in a public ward in a Tennessee hospital. Johnny was fourteen then and determined to follow his illustrious father into the army. He was at his father's bedside when the old man, by that stage of the TB an accurate description rather than any term of filial affection, finally passed away. Just before the last shallow breath left what little remained of his lung tissue, Bob Compton beckoned with a finger for his boy to hear his final words.

'Hiram Maxim was a genius,' he said to his son. And then he winked at Johnny and he died.

When Germany invaded Poland, Johnny Compton was a sergeant among the ranks of an American professional army numbering something under 200,000 men. Most of the infantry were armed with single-cartridge bolt-action Springfield rifles manufactured for the First World War. The cavalry boasted fewer than twenty tanks, and the senior officers were by and large West Pointers allocated field commands on the basis of age rather than any aptitude for strategy. It wasn't their fault. America hadn't fought a war for more than twenty years. The only experience of combat the army had was spates of sporadic strikebreaking prior to the Depression.

By the time Johnny Compton was shipped to England, America had sixteen million men under arms, two-thirds of them conscripted. The army had gone from being a refuge for criminals, chronic alcoholics and the dispossessed to a machine equipped for waging war on the world stage. Army pay had doubled. Overseas bases were provided with recreation officers. Rations were so generous that each man received a pound of meat a day. They were awash with coffee, with fruit and vegetables, with chewing gum and chocolate and cigarettes.

Compton didn't dislike all the new men. Some of the new brass were an improvement. He'd been sent to give the benefit of his technical expertise when George Patton established his vast training camp in the Californian desert in the summer of 1942. There he'd been impressed by Patton's single-minded thoroughness, by the ruthless way in which he schooled the best of the new recruits and discarded those who didn't come up to scratch. War was principally about killing as many of the enemy as you could in the most efficient way possible, and Patton had seemed, to Johnny Compton, to have a good grasp of that. He'd even been invited to dine with the general. There'd been only twenty officers in the tent, and he couldn't afterwards recall having ever heard a speaker funnier or more profane.

It was the draft that bothered Compton. The volunteers were one thing, you could forgive them their inexperience for their commitment to the cause. But the draftees did not deserve to be getting what they were. It wasn't just the pay they drew and the rations they ate. Equipment, weaponry, transportation – everything had improved beyond measure since the outbreak of the war. Compton had been proud to wear the uniform when the pay had been piss poor and the chances of glory non-existent. Now he was forced to attend lectures on how to maintain the morale of men who might grow bored of drills and succumb to homesickness. He found himself marking men out for petty acts of retribution for slights he knew in his injured heart were largely imagined. He harboured a particular grudge against New Yorkers. He didn't object to the Negro soldier. He never had. But New Yorkers, with their wheedling and their wisecracks and their sense of city-boy superiority, he was growing more and more to detest. He'd look at them, seated before him in their half-circle on the sand of an English beach, submitting to the illusion of cross-legged obedience, and he'd see the smirks spread with the speed of an epidemic among them when he opened his mouth and they heard him lecture them on Hiram Maxim's killing machine in an unschooled voice of the South. It was a good enough voice for George Patton's high table, he'd thought more than once. But it fostered a sort of furtive mockery among those dragged overseas to fight for their country from Queens, from Little Italy, with their peacetime professions and their paper qualifications from the public education system. The number men. The citizen soldiers. He sensed their civilian distaste for saluting, fatigues, kitchen patrol and kit inspection. Chickenshit was the term the draftees used for the everyday stuff of army life. 'In the army but not of it' was the phrase frequently used to justify their sneering distaste for men like himself.

England, however, he liked. He'd come over on the *Queen Mary*, embarked from New York after a two-day furlough featuring one hooker, countless beers, a bottle of Wild Turkey bourbon and three fights if he didn't count the fight involving the hooker. He'd won his three fights, so far as he'd been able to recollect. But the third, the one involving a saloon bar bouncer, had been tough. He'd embarked for Europe nursing bruised ribs and a jaw too sore for the doughnuts that were supposed to provide sustenance on the five-day voyage.

It was standing room only on the boat. He'd found himself in possession of greater space when what seemed like the majority of his comrades in arms embraced portholes and lavatory bowls and ship's rails to void their stomachs of doughnuts when the sea turned choppy a few miles out into the Atlantic. Johnny Compton, by contrast, discovered to his surprise that he was a natural sailor. Perhaps he should have joined the navy, he mused. He sipped coffee and dozed on his feet and hoped that what they had said about the ship being too fast for U-boats was true. The voyage gave him the opportunity to sober up. His jaw stopped hurting, and the bruises on his ribs purpled and yellowed in a pattern he admired in the steel mirror reflecting them when he eased off his shirt in the can. A lesser man might have resolved at that moment to avoid future confrontations with the doormen guarding the speakeasies of the Lower East Side. Johnny Compton had never seen himself as a lesser man. He reckoned his accent gave him a split-second edge. Opponents heard it and couldn't help but think of cornball pipes and slow days on hick porches squinting at the sun. Johnny was slow like a mongoose was slow confronting a cobra.

He kept himself to himself on the ship, easy enough

among reluctant sailors too busy fighting nausea to engage in conversation. Then they docked at some port in Ireland but were not allowed off the boat. A day later he climbed up on to the deck and saw the coast of England, the city of Liverpool bleak and smudged above a river dull with silt and shallow enough for the great Blue Riband liner he'd travelled aboard to need six tugs and a pilot boat to nurse it into harbour. England is in black and white, like a newsreel, like a lesser sort of movie, was his first impression. The city was soot-stained, cobbled, bomb-battered, grim.

He stopped in Liverpool only long enough to relish his status as a weapons expert called to the fray individually for what he knew and the value of what he could impart to others. It meant he didn't travel any longer with the herd. War had given him a freedom and a status that were still novelties. In the cocktail bar of the Adelphi Hotel, he admired his reflection, his new uniform, his officer's cap in the mirror behind the bar. He tipped slightly too lavishly and studied the English women. Like buds they were, he thought, with their pale faces and their puckered, painted-over lips. He thought them pale blooms after two or three Tom Collinses, these women, ripe enough for the picking.

He caught a ramshackle train to a big railway junction called Crewe and then a train full of narrow carriages to what a polite ticket inspector confirmed would be his final destination. The seats were cramped and greasy and there were blackout drapes over the windows as the train clanked and he rocked and dozed through a series of fitful little stops.

When Johnny Compton awoke, it was light and he looked out of the window. The land was lush and green. It was another movie. Another country. He found himself sitting opposite two boys. They could have been ten or eleven, he supposed. They wore gas mask cases on canvas straps across pale-blue school blazers edged with a violet trim. The trim looked hand sewn and clumsy. Maybe their mother had done it. The boys offered him lemonade from a bottle stoppered with a plug of paper. Parched, he took a swig. The boys tried to engage him in conversation. Eventually they gave up. People always did, Johnny found, if you gave them enough encouragement.

His destination was the Assault Training Centre set up between the villages of Woolacombe and Appledore on a stretch of coastline in the north of an English county called Devon. Here, he was supposed to school assault troops in the strengths and weaknesses, the capabilities and tactical limitations of the machine gun. He didn't feel the machine gun as a defensive weapon had too many characteristics on the deficit side.

He'd misheard his dying father's parting aphorism. He'd thought the old man had said something like: 'Hire a maxim. Be a genius.' He knew that 'maxim' was a fancy word for a slogan or a motto, and he puzzled over it. But the puzzle remained unsolved. His daddy had been cold the better part of a year when Johnny Compton read on the trivia page of a magazine in a Mississippi barber's chair that Hiram Maxim was the name of the Kike inventor responsible for the machine gun. He whistled, which made his Adam's apple bob under a freshly stropped blade. He wasn't cut. But he'd have taken a nick as the price of the posthumous wisdom his father finally imparted.

The ATC occupied an area of coastal land Compton thought shockingly cramped. He'd known that England was a small country. He'd seen it on a map. But he had done his own tactical training in the American South, in the old Confederate forts of Benning and Bragg, 100,000 acres-plus military fiefdoms allowing full-scale rehearsals for war. Patton's piece of Californian desert had been similarly sized. Here in England they could hardly organize a live fire exercise for fear of hitting postmen and parsons cycling by on lanes they lacked the jurisdiction to close. Marching men got into arguments with farmers about rights of way. Transport columns got into traffic jams, obstructed by chugging tractors on narrow roads bound by high hedges that made navigation by sight impossible.

The on-duty circumstances were a matter of almost constant exasperation. Then when you got your twenty-four-hour or forty-eight-hour leave pass, it was worse. Social opportunities off base were limited to two hick towns called Bideford and Barnstaple. Compton didn't fully appreciate the GI joke about putting the piss back in the horse until he tried his first pint of English beer one evening at a Bideford pub. A fifteen-mile training march had given him a thirst, marching being one of the few martial pursuits they could practise without enraging local people. Or putting the natives' lives at risk with stray ordnance. But even fifteen hard miles under a full pack over sandy country left the beverage sadly wanting. He tried cider, a concoction that smelled of vomit and tasted so sour it made him wince, but at least brought the benefit of feeling like a drink when it had crept into your blood.

The womanhood of Bideford and Barnstaple were sadly lacking too. They did not appear to possess what Johnny Compton believed to be a woman's principal charm. They could not be bought. In his lieutenant's uniform, at the wheel of his jeep, he attracted the initial interest of no end of friendly and inquisitive English females. But sex to him occurred ideally as a cash transaction. He had neither the inclination, nor more particularly the skills, for socializing with women. The lack of the one had precluded the other all his adult life.

Misreading the signs one night in Barnstaple, he managed to insult a pretty girl in a pretty dress in the railway hotel bar by suggesting a pleasurable way in which she could earn herself a five-dollar bill. She left so incensed that when she returned it was predictably with her angry beau in tow. Johnny Compton took a measured sip of his cider and waited for his dick to detumesce as he weighed the fellow up. He was country ruddy, the boyfriend, strong-backed he supposed from digging and baling, hands hammerheads of meat and bone on the ends of vein-trestled arms. Denied a fuck, Compton would ordinarily have welcomed a compensatory fight. But you had to be careful on foreign ground, in well-lit public places, bristling as they tended to be with the eyes and ears of potential witnesses. Past misdemeanours involving ATC personnel and locals meant that the twin towns were thick now with stick-happy MPs to whom rank meant little. Little anyway once they discovered the fighting knife concealed down one of Compton's spats. So he smiled and fulsomely apologized as he memorized the fellow's indignant features for future reference. Forgetting such a slight would have been contrary to his nature. He was a man who always paid out on debts.

London, of course, was much more to his inclination. Length of service alone had earned him his grudging commission. But the army didn't discriminate in the allocating of leave between vets like himself and the smart young men made lieutenant as soon as their basic training was completed. In the time he had been in England, he had enjoyed two spells of leave in the blacked-out capital. Once there, he had taken full advantage of the peculiar and liberating circumstances. His departure on the most recent visit, from a basement flat in Paddington just after four in the morning, had been necessarily swift. But he hadn't had far to walk in the groping blackness to the railway terminus. And he'd had sufficient time to clean up in a lavatory on the concourse prior to catching his return train.

As a child, with his mother dead and his father mostly

away, Johnny Compton had been obliged to learn to feed himself or starve. He'd learned to hunt game with snares and nooses at night. He soon discovered that the best prey lived in burrows on private land. Too many poor scavenged on the common scrub for the pickings to be anything but thin. To get at the most tender morsels of meat, young Johnny was forced to trespass. His fingers still remembered the thump of a rabbit's heart, the swift, panicky pulse under feathers of a game bird caught. He'd got the same exhilarated thrill from doing this that he rediscovered during his night exploits in London. He'd never have thought to feel nostalgic for the clandestine pursuits of his hungry Southern boyhood. But somehow that was how London at night in the war made him feel.

He first heard the rumour in late September 1943, after six months and a lifetime of drills and marches and small arms practice in their little pocket of belligerent rehearsal for the fight some of the men had begun to complain openly was never actually going to come. He heard it in the canteen from a major from Kentucky whose information almost always contained a hard core of fact. The bad news was that it was still going to be Devon. The good news was that it was an area much larger than the one they currently shared with its indigenous civilians. The brass were pressing to implement DF 51, the Defence Regulation that could clear land entirely for military use. They'd tried to apply it to areas of Dartmoor and Salisbury Plain, but had been blocked by the British military. The word was that this time they were going to succeed. The area under discussion was, by British standards, huge. It would need to be. They would be preparing there for the seaborne assault on occupied Europe.

Johnny Compton pressed for a place name. He was a punctilious soldier and had by now learned pretty much by heart the map of the island he was on, because that was what a soldier surely did. Start Bay, he was told in an urgent whisper by the indiscreet major from Kentucky. The South Hams. Pack your bucket and spade, boy. We're going to a place called Slapton Sands.

THREE

Canterbury, June 1976

She awoke alone in David's bed. The next day she was supposed to take the train from Paddington to Totnes. Where was he? She eased across the bed to doze in the warmth his body had left and felt the first wallowing shudders of the cormorant dream coming to claim her before the disturbance of David's return saved her from sleep.

'Where did you go?'

'Roadwork.'

She blinked. He was wearing a towel around his waist and drying his wet hair with another. The bathroom was pretty gross. She figured he must have a stash of laundry hidden where his housemates couldn't find it. 'Excuse me?'

'Roadwork.' He sat on the bed. The skin of his stomach was taut over muscle, even when he sat. There was one tiny ridge of creased skin above his navel. She felt an urge to pinch it, gently. To roll it between forefinger and thumb. She resisted the temptation.

'You mean running.'

'I mean roadwork.'

'But it's running, isn't it? I mean, that's what it amounts to, fundamentally.'

'It's called roadwork. That's what we call it.'

'Right,' she said, nodding. She was glad she had not dreamed the cormorant dream. She hated it, dreaded the way it could lurch into areas of gruesome new detail, hated the helpless fatalism that afflicted her on each nightmare voyage. She had today and tonight with David before her departure. The cormorant dream always left her shaken, struggling to mask the assaulting shock it inflicted. If it followed her to Slapton, she would deal with it there. But she was glad it wasn't going to spoil today.

'I thought we could drive up to London,' David said. 'Splash out on a place to stay tonight. Have dinner, some drinks somewhere. Maybe go up early this afternoon and see a couple of the sights first. Have you done the galleries?'

'Ollie won't mind you taking his car?'

'Not if I fill it with petrol and put some air in the tyres. Ollie gets garage paranoia.'

'Garage paranoia,' Alice said. She was naked under the bedclothes. Acutely conscious, now, of the fact. 'Don't tell me, it's a public school thing.'

'I think it's more of a drug thing. He can't cope with forecourts and pumps. He says the men in the little glass kiosks who take your money look at him in a funny way. The long and the short of it is, he'll lend us the car.'

The long and the short of it. That was an old army saying,

wasn't it? The long and the short and the tall. She could go to the Imperial War Museum. It wasn't far from some of the other sights, from the river, from Westminster Bridge and the Houses of Parliament and the Abbey. 'Haven't you got lectures? Seminars?'

'I have. And I've got a couple of dives to try to get in, too, if I'm going to come over as anything other than a total novice when I get to Bembridge and the fort.'

'I thought you were an experienced diver.'

'I am. Just not recently. You have to go through the drills, the procedures. I need at least a couple of dives.'

His gear was in a large canvas holdall in the hallway of the house. She'd seen the rubber strap of a flipper or a face mask protruding from it when they came through the front door after the drive from Whitstable the night before. It had been black and salt-rimed against the teeth of the bag's heavy metal zipper. She felt very uneasy at the thought of David working under water. There was no particular reason for this. She supposed it had to do with how recent, if brief, had been the visitation of her dream.

'It's the last week of term,' David said. 'It's a question of priorities, Alice. In twenty-four hours, you'll be gone.'

They went up to the university, where Alice sorted the post from her pigeonhole and left a note with the college porter with the telephone number and address of where she would be staying in Strete. Then they were off on the straight, pale road to London, heat ripple and patches of spilled oil the only thing to break the monotony, the road flat and flanked by banks of scrubby yellow grass and the occasional defeated tree. Heat was starting to liberate smells in the car that must have lain discouraged and dormant during its stay in the car park beneath Elliot College. Even with the windows open, the back of the car smelled funky, slightly ripe.

'I know. A forensic scientist would have a ball back there,' David said, putting a cassette into the tape player, guessing her thoughts.

'Somebody's already had a ball back there,' Alice said.

The tape was Van Morrison. Mention of forensics made her think of Sally Emerson. There had been a note from DS Emerson in her pigeonhole, asking for a contact number where she could be reached when she got to south Devon. That had surprised Alice. For reasons different from his, she shared Professor Champion's view that there was no point in continuing to investigate what had happened at her flat in Whitstable. Nobody was going to be caught or punished for what had occurred. Nobody but herself would ever be held to account.

Traffic was light on the London road, and even with the windows open and the faulty exhaust the music sounded great through the cassette player's shrill little speakers. The song was 'Domino'.

'Van Morrison. Safe ground.'

'More like hallowed ground.' David laughed. He sounded happy. 'Have you any idea how unusual it is to wake up every day in this country to weather like this?'

She couldn't believe it. They were going to have a weather conversation. She had read that it was chief among those subjects about which the British conversed most passionately. In fact, no conversation was considered complete, she'd been led to believe before her arrival, without a ritual mention of meteorology. She laughed herself, feeling their speed, the sun, the rhythmic thrill of the music they were listening to. She sensed already that this day would be one she would remember vividly, perfectly, for the rest of whatever time remained of her life.

They drove through New Cross and Lewisham and Camberwell to get to Kennington and the Imperial War Museum. It was the first time Alice had seen these areas of inner London. She saw half-cleared terraces of slums and burned-out cars and violent, skinhead graffiti daubed on the walls of blocks of flats and public buildings. She saw poor people for the first time in any concentration since she had been in England. They gathered in clusters outside pubs and betting shops. They queued outside a post office, outside telephone kiosks and at bus stops. Gaudy displays of public art in painted friezes on lending library façades and gable ends portrayed a happy utopia grotesquely at odds with the general picture of decay, the mood of sullen animosity. Dub reggae thumped from the open maws of second-hand record shops. Shabby cars crawled in thick traffic under the heat. They had their names scrolled in rust-mottled chrome on their boots. Capri, Granada, Cortina. What did English car designers have against Italy and Spain?

The architecture through which they passed was an alienating mix of late-Victorian decrepitude and 1960s brutalism.

'You think this is bad, you should see the Elephant,' David said.

Alice nodded. She thought of her Will Hay film, of its cosy certainties and sleepy, monochrome charms. She thought of the ice-cream parlour in Tankerton, with its tabletops of marbled Formica and knickerbocker glory glasses so scratched by the edges of searching spoons that they had become opaque, as though their glass were frosted. She thought of the jukebox anchored in its cosy berth in a corner of the Neptune. England, she was beginning to think, was less a place than a series of assumptions. Its reality was so diverse and contradictory that you could gain no measure of the place. Looking at it in detail was like holding something too close to your eye, the way a child will when subjecting it to scrutiny. The object becomes blurred, abstract. You lose any sense of the size or nature of the thing. No wonder the Americans during the war were kept isolated from this country, kept safely away from its inconsistencies, its paradoxes and dismaying contradictions.

'Is this part of London as dangerous as it looks?'

David shrugged. 'I'm not a native. But Peckham isn't exactly the Bronx. Nobody has guns here.'

'Except in *The Sweeney.*'

'West London, mostly, *The Sweeney,*' he said. 'That's according to Ollie, who's from Wimbledon and claims to know.' He smiled at her. 'Wait until you get to the War Museum. In a previous life, it used to be a lunatic asylum. It was called Bedlam. Thus the origin of the term.'

'Great,' she said. She looked at her wristwatch. It was a quarter to twelve. They'd had only toast and coffee for breakfast, and the hot, fried food smells of south London's street takeaways, through the open car windows, were making her hungry now.

They stopped outside a café called Perdoni's on Kennington Road. The café had a double frontage and bench seats and photographs of the fathers or grandfathers of the present proprietors posed outside the premises in an earlier part of the century. The pictures looked like they had been taken in the decades prior to the Second World War. While David studied a menu card, Alice went over and looked at one of them. A date had been inked into a corner of the border surrounding the print. It read 1929.

They ate spaghetti bolognese with thick slices of crusty bread and drank carbonated mineral water that was cold and slightly salty and delicious after the hot, fume-filled crawl through south London. After, they ordered cherry pie and cream. Most of the other customers were cab drivers, coming in with their brass badges on loops of leather around their necks, adjusting paunches to the familiar, fixed gap between bench padding and table edge, their black cabs glossy with coach paint in sunshine in a static convoy at the kerb. After her food, Alice savoured the best cup of coffee she had drunk since arriving in England.

The sun was at its apex, but there was a shallow awning over the frontage of Perdoni's, so they could look at the burnished street, at the black cabs and passing traffic, at Kennington's mix of hot pedestrians, from the relative cool of the café interior.

'What happened to London's Italians in the war?'

'Interned,' David said.

'That must have been tough.'

'Very, I would have thought. They were sent to Scotland. To internment camps. So there are a lot of Italians in Glasgow and Edinburgh.'

Alice looked around the café. It was almost one o'clock. There was a queue now at the counter, where they sold sandwiches to take away. And the booths were filling up. There was a large, ugly, 1960s police station on the other side of the road more or less opposite the café. Policemen on their break sunned themselves in plastic chairs on a balcony running the length of an upper floor. Alice could hear policemen in the queue at the sandwich counter. They were not in uniform. But cop banter seemed to be recognizable in any language.

'The Perdonis came back,' she said.

'The Perdonis had something to come back to,' David said, nodding at the photographs on the wall.

They paid the waitress and got up and walked out of the café into the bright day. They turned right and walked past a newsagent's and a barber's and a shop selling fruit and vegetables. Alice thought the precinct around the Imperial War Museum a very suburban setting for a building with such a grand title. But London was arbitrary like that, weirdly juxtaposed, a city that seemed to have made itself up as it went along rather than to have been planned. Also, the building they were headed for had once been Bedlam, a home to lunatics, a place of dubious entertainment for the wealthy in the days when mental illness was considered a spectator sport. And then the War Museum became visible, behind tall trees in parkland bound by spiked iron railings.

After their museum visit they walked back along Kennington Road and then turned on to Westminster Bridge Road and progressed until they arrived at the river. Alice looked down at the lapping water over the embankment wall. She looked down on to the great lions' heads set into the stone of the river bank with mooring rings in their mouths. The bronze lions' heads were tarnished green, and a high tide lapped at the rings in their mouths. On the radio bulletins and the television news, there was endless talk of water rationing and drought. In the newspapers there were pictures almost daily of the cracked beds of empty reservoirs. But the Thames today was high, the water close enough almost to stretch down and touch, its surface glittering with fabulous light in the sun, under the blue sky.

Alice looked over at Westminster Bridge, with its bus traffic a vivid procession of painted toys, and, beyond it, through heat ripple, the Houses of Parliament. Soot and exhaust pollution had coated the building in layers of grime. Dark stains streaked the Gothic complications of its masonry. You could only guess at the original colour of the stone as you watched the building undulate and distort like a mirage. It was like that. It was like a mirage. Fabulously strange and strangely familiar in the heat and the light.

They walked past County Hall in the direction of Blackfriars. They crossed Waterloo Bridge and walked along the north side of the river and crossed again over Blackfriars Bridge to head back towards Kennington Road and the car. Crossing Blackfriars Bridge, businessmen in dark suits and hats carrying briefcases and furled umbrellas passed them singly and in twos staring resolutely ahead. Most of them seemed pale despite the summer. Many of them wore three-piece suits in spite of the heat. Alice felt some of their affectations absurd; the watch chains arranged in fine gold links across tight waistcoats, the bowlers and trilbies, the absurdly redundant brollies. She felt a flicker of attention when they got level with her, or sensed it when a head snapped around after they got past. But she was used to this. Men had always looked at her. It had started before it properly should have. She had been thirteen when she had first become aware of the uninvited attention of men.

She looked to her left, at the wharves lining the southerly side of the working stretch of the river, most of them seemingly derelict. Hooks hung on slack chains from cranes outside buildings marked with the neglect of abandonment. A few barges were still moored here and there. But they were rust-streaked, ragged tarpaulins taut over their empty cargo holds in a half-hearted gesture of proper upkeep.

'What are you thinking about?'

He had stopped and was leaning looking out over the bridge parapet. 'About your boyfriend. Wondering what he does. Who he is. Whether the doubts are beginning to nag, three thousand-odd miles away.'

The bank of the river beyond them described neglect. On the pavement and the road at their backs, all was energy and industry and urgent intent. 'I'd imagine he's pretty intuitive,' Alice said. 'It's not a quality I've ever tested in him. Not until now, I don't suppose.'

'Really?'

She took a deep breath. She shook her head.

'How long?'

'Eighteen months.'

David was quiet. Then he looked at her. 'Poor bugger.'

'He'll survive.'

'You'll tell him?'

'I'll have to,' Alice said. She took a step towards David. He reached a hand out for hers.

They got the car and drove over Waterloo Bridge and along Kingsway and Southampton Row, north towards Euston.

"Where are we staying tonight?'

'Bloomsbury,' he said.

'Wow.'

'Nothing special. A mansion block in Coptic Street. Grand once, I suppose. But the big rooms have all been partitioned off. It's just upmarket bed-and-breakfast accommodation now. I stayed there for a week over the Easter vacation when I needed the British Museum.'

'Couldn't you have stayed with the Apache?'

'Ollie's parents barely tolerate him, let alone his mates. Besides, his claim that Wimbledon is the hub of the universe is only true for two weeks of the year.'

'When it's home to Jimmy Connors?'

'Jimmy Connors. And his implausible socks.'

They were headed for Hampstead Heath. Alice had requested a walk on the Heath, a look at the view. It was six o'clock by the time they got there and they climbed to the parched heights and she looked down on the city, through England's haze of familiar heat, able to pick out Centre-Point, the Post Office Tower, St Paul's.

'It looks . . .'

'What?'

'Fabled,' she said.

'Jesus,' he said. 'And we haven't even had a drink. You should have maybe worn a hat in this sun, Alice.'

They bought ice creams from a van parked on the Heath and sat on a bench and ate them. They heard and then saw Concorde on its steep descent to Heathrow. Alice thought about Pennsylvania, about Easton and Allentown and the little town of Emmaus, sitting on the edge of Amish country, where they had found her father at the side of a barn, bound by his own handcuffs and shot with his own gun through the side of his head.

'Tell me about your dad.'

'I'd rather not.'

'I was honest with you. I was, you know, on Blackfriars Bridge.' They were more or less alone. They shared their high part of the Heath with only the odd dog walker. Alice was dry in the mouth from eating ice cream. She could feel ice cream and chocolate flake swelling in her stomach. Sugar had parched her tongue and made her teeth dry and squeaky against its tip.

They could still hear Concorde. The aircraft had begun its supersonic flights earlier in the year, its fanfare muted by all the noise-conscious nations which had banned it from their airports on the grounds of noise pollution. It was a beautiful aeroplane, Alice thought. It was also incredibly, preposterously loud. How had they thought they'd ever get away with it?

Alice bent over and spat on the grass between her feet.

'I don't believe you did that.'

'Come on. Give me a break.'

'You've got the manners of a hillbilly.'

Alice nodded. She felt like putting her head in his lap. She slid up the bench and did so. He stroked her hair.

'We should go.'

She wanted to go to Chelsea, to the King's Road and a pub where they played live music. They left the Apache's minivan parked outside their hotel in Coptic Street and walked to Russell Square underground station. Walking towards the tube along Southampton Row with David, Alice was aware of how much this area must have changed since the days of the literary Bloomsbury of preconception and myth.

Myth was the problem. Time encouraged distortion. Now, litter flapped and idled in the gutters of the city, drinks cans and discarded newspapers and sweet wrappers and cigarette ends left there by London's apathetic, strike-happy street cleaners. If you read the newspapers, London was in the grip of uncertainty, the mood militant among its public-sector workers and uneasy among a police force still fearful of a metropolitan bombing campaign similar to that the IRA had so bloodily inflicted on Birmingham. The government was moribund, the culture bankrupt, only the weather a cause of constant, predictable surprise as the freakish heatwave and subsequent drought threatened economic catastrophe. In theory, London was the grim capital of a country on its knees. Maybe it was best viewed from a distance, from the dreamy, arcadian heights of Hampstead Heath.

On the way to the underground, they diverted at David's insistence to a pub called the Sun Tavern in Lamb's Conduit Street. It was quaint. She hadn't wanted quaint. Quaint she could get by the hatful in Canterbury. Quaint could be had by the country mile in Bleen, in Tankerton and around. But he'd asked her to try the cider in the Sun Tavern. The pub had high, decorated windows. Their glass was elaborately engraved. The images were stylized and pagan, to do with druids and the worship of the sun. Late light poured in refracted beams through the glass. The pub had bare floorboards, and the scrumpy was drawn from large hooped barrels behind the bar. There was no jukebox. But music was coming from somewhere. It was Fairport Convention, *Liege and Lief*, Sandy Denny singing 'Tam Lin'. Singing about lust, woods, malevolent faeries and their spiteful spells.

'Scrumpy,' David said, handing her a half-pint glass. 'You won't get this in Pennsylvania.'

It looked like horse piss and smelled like vomit to Alice. But it felt like a drink, after a couple of mouthfuls, when it got into her blood.

'How would you sum up London?'

'I wouldn't,' David said. 'I'm not a native.'

'Come on. You're an Englishman.'

'OK,' he said. 'In what terms?'

'I don't know,' she said. She could feel the scrumpy in the heat thrumming through her. The stuff was strong. 'In boxing terms.'

David thought for a moment. 'A heavyweight having a bad round,' he said. 'A great heavyweight, shipping too much punishment.' He winked at her. 'But the fight's only halfway through.'

Cultured Italians and culture-starved Americans made up most of the pedestrian traffic Alice saw as they resumed their walk. The thing was she could easily see these streets rain-drenched, winter-sodden, a homesick Katherine Mansfield chain-smoking Woodbines in the window seat of a tearoom watching T.S. Eliot ride by on an old sit-up-and-beg in bicycle clips. And they had been only the bit-part players. The principals shifted like heavy ghosts behind windows opaque with grime and faded nets. Bloomsbury in 1976 was an incongruous movie set. It smelled of street trash and Aramis aftershave and contraband Monte Christos smoked by affluent tourists from Chicago and Milan. It should have smelled of horse leather and books and brilliantine. Wouldn't you know, she thought. The scrumpy had made her imaginative. She thought she was probably drunk on the stuff.

The King's Road pub, when they got there, was hot and chaotic. Alice had endured an awful lot of what the natives happily described as pub rock since her arrival in England. Pub bands aped Bad Company, Thin Lizzie, Led Zeppelin, of course, and sometimes American offenders like Lynryd Skynryd and the Allman Brothers. Amplification substituted for talent, dry ice for stage presence. It was appallingly depressing and disappointing, given that the Brits had fashioned the rock template. But she'd heard alarmed rumours of something original and new coming out of west London.

Alice didn't think that rock'n'roll was going to save the world. She had no time at all for distant millionaires performing before vast audiences, regardless of how badly they trashed their equipment on stage, or how introspective their lyrics could sound. She loved the English word, 'wanker'. And she thought it wonderfully applicable to someone like Pete Townsend of the Who, smashing a Gibson guitar worth hundreds of pounds into a stack of Marshal amps before an audience of paying customers who earned less than the guitar was worth in a year. She thought it equally descriptive of Bob Dylan, whose appetite for protest songs had not stopped him indulging his wife's architecture hobby to the tune of two million dollars over some domed garden folly. Or maybe it was doomed garden folly, because his wife had divorced him anyway.

Alice held opinions about music not popular in the student world, where people like the Apache believed Jim Morrison the closest thing to a deity since Jesus Christ. Morrison had actually died masturbating in the bathtub. If that didn't make you a wanker . . . She was in a country in which well-educated teenagers sprayed graffiti slogans claiming Clapton is God, apparently believing it. No wonder the object of their adoration had turned to heroin. She lived in a century in which it was very hard to believe at all in the possibility of God. If there was one, he wasn't a white blues guitarist from the home counties. Clapton wasn't a wanker. On the other hand, though, neither was he J.J. Cale. Music wasn't significant, to Alice. She believed that anyone who claimed it was in print was self-serving, Professor Champion included.

But she did like to be entertained. A twenty-three-year-old in a foreign country, she wanted a bit of musical exhilaration. There was an atmosphere in this pub, that night, suggesting she might get it. This was London, after all. This was London.

'There's a bloke in trews over there,' David said.

'In what?'

'Tartan trousers. What the Scots Highlanders dress up in when they have the misfortune not to be in kilts.'

Alice looked. There were about half a dozen of them, with short, spiked hair dyed orange, or bleached. The girls wore black mascara and bright lipstick. One of them was wearing a baggy, shiny black top that reminded Alice a bit of a brief fashion she remembered from her adolescence, when she'd started reading glossy magazines. It had been called the Wet Look.

'Christ Almighty,' David said. 'There's a girl over there wearing a bin bag.'

The girl in the trash sack and her friends were ignoring the band, a threesome with a singer in a white flared suit and a shirt striped like a deck chair. Then the band went off and there was a brief commotion as a glass was thrown at the stage and someone from behind the bar came out and wagged a finger at the small bin bag and trews contingent. Although small, their number was growing. A boy came in and joined them; he had a little brass padlock securing a chain around his neck. The girl with him wore a leather jacket, its sleeves fringed with dozens and dozens of what looked to Alice like diaper pins. They all seemed to know one another. Plump girls in fishnets, skinny boys with acned, amphetamine skin. Then, with a squall of guitar static, there was a band on the stage, four black-haired, emaciated boys in tight drainpipe trousers and torn slogan T-shirts. The noise they made was immediate, unbearably loud with accelerating beat and no discernible rhythm. It was a song, in the sense that the one band member with no instrument to play was bawling words into a microphone. But it wasn't a tune. It was a gathering avalanche of noise. The bin bag contingent rushed towards the small stage and started leaping up and down.

A patrol car delivered them back to Coptic Street at about two a.m. It felt later than that to Alice, or maybe she meant earlier. It looked like dawn was intruding in a corner of the sky above a dark terrace of Georgian houses. Bloomsbury, she thought. Katherine Mansfield puffing away in a café window seat. Eliot in a charcoal three-piece, tall in the saddle. Getting out of the back seat, it occurred to Alice that she had not intended to become anything like this well acquainted with the British police. It was the second time she had been ferried about in a Ford Escort belonging to the force. On this occasion, they'd been much less polite.

'I'm really sorry,' David said, as the car pulled away from the kerb.

'So you say. You shouldn't have hit him, though.'

'Fucker shouldn't have spat at me.'

'You've got a thing about spitting, haven't you?'

'He gobbed in my face, Alice.'

'He was aiming at the band.' She laughed. 'You were a civilian casualty. The victim of a stray shot.'

'It's not funny. He could have a disease.'

'Spit, cannibal lobsters. You're way too fastidious, Davey Boy. You need to lighten up.'

There was a deep cut above David's eye. He'd decked the spitter with a punch so fast she hadn't really seen it and then tried successfully to dodge a pint mug thrown by one of the spitter's friends. A hail of pub glassware had followed the first missile, though, and a heavy ashtray had caught him above the eye, splitting the eyebrow, opening a deep cut he'd had stitched in the casualty department at the Chelsea and Westminster Hospital while the police questioned him and decided, reluctantly Alice thought, not to charge him with assault. The spitter had revived in an observation ward in the same hospital, chipper according to the staff nurse who relieved them with the news that he wasn't dead, feeling no wish to press charges.

On the pavement, Alice looked at her watch. Her ears were still raw, her head thick with the volume of the band in the Chelsea pub. She hadn't enjoyed the music. Had anyone? It wasn't there to be enjoyed. Enjoyment hadn't seemed to her to be the point of it at all. She wouldn't be looking out for singles or an album by the band. But she had enjoyed the experience of seeing them, of being briefly part of something alien and new. She touched the wounded place above David's eye and he winced. She kissed her fingers and touched the wound again, this time very tenderly.

'Thanks,' he said.

'Let's go to bed,' she said to him.

When finally they drifted off, she dreamed the cormorant dream. Her belly in the dream was bilious with cider. She was positioned near the rear of the craft, and when it dipped into the yaw of a swell she recognized its shape, made sense of it, realized with a ragged intake of salt breath that, of course, she was aboard a Higgins boat. A wave slapped foam over her, and she wriggled her toes in her boots to distract her mind from the clutch of nausea. A training run over the dunes in full kit had left blisters on three of her toes. The flare of pain, wriggling them now, gave her the discipline to swallow back the bile her mouth was secreting. She would not puke. No sir. Bile burned her throat. The boat pitched and shuddered. Her swollen toes pushed against ridges of roan leather. She didn't puke. Then a shadow descended and talons, leathery and horned, gripped the gunwale as the great bird settled a few inches from her face.

They got to Paddington Station about ten minutes before the scheduled departure of her train. London was stained and austere in the crawl through heat from Bloomsbury along the Euston Road. The heatwave had enervated working London, its brassy light all wrong-seeming for buildings mournful with age and decay. Marylebone was a pretty, picturesque interlude of well-tended flower boxes and fishmongers' and grocers' shops florid with fruit and vegetable displays and quaint booksellers and almost-rustic pubs. Then they were in Paddington, a place made mean, dispirited, by decades of transience, of washed-up, perished hopes. After Marylebone, Paddington seemed almost furtive with squalor. At a set of traffic lights, Alice looked out of the window up the side of a white-tiled tenement. Age gave the building a decayed and tainted look. Rust-coloured pipes ran about it in varicose bunches. By one high window, torn net over panes opaque with filth, water gushed and dribbled in arterial spurts that had spread a reddish stain all the way down to the pavement. She jumped suddenly, and the lights changed from red; David stalled and a horn honked behind the Apache's car.

'What's wrong?'

'That horn. Must've startled me.'

The car with the impatient driver was level with them now, Bob Marley singing 'No Woman, No Cry' on the radio audible through its wound-down windows.

'He honked because I stalled. I stalled because you nearly leaped out of your skin. Which is covered in goose bumps, by the way. Try again, Alice.'

'I thought I saw a face back there, at an upper window in that white-tiled building on the corner. It startled me.'

David adjusted his driver's mirror and squinted at the receding view. 'White is an exaggeration,' he said. 'And the building looks derelict to me.'

She'd seen what she'd seen. David was looking at her, now, in the driver's mirror. 'A squatter,' he said. And Alice nodded.

She took her single case and her bookbag out of the back of the car and carried them on to the concourse, refusing David's offer of help with the bag with a smile and a shake of her head. She caught sight of her own reflection in the glass of the booth where she collected her pre-paid ticket and was shocked at how pale she looked. David went off to fetch her coffee. She put her bookbag over her shoulder to give herself a free hand. There were announcements over the Tannoy, made indecipherable by the age of the equipment and the way the sound reverberated around the stone station walls and floor. She looked up. The station roof was a high, shallow arch of glass, supported by a framework of iron. The glass was opaque with pigeonshit and rust stains. Some of the panes were cracked and others missing. The roof did not look to Alice especially safe.

She had read that all the major London stations had been bombed in the Blitz. But Paddington didn't look restored; it looked authentic. It was amazing how much of its Victorian architecture had survived the bombing. There would have been tea wagons staffed by volunteers on the concourse. Child refugees in overcoats carrying gas masks. Soldiers in patient, marshalled lines awaiting troop trains to take them to the spaces of the West of England. The air would have been pungent with cigarette smoke and tense in the anticipation of an air-raid siren.

Now, David returned, carrying her coffee in a brown plastic cup that looked as though it was burning his fingers. They were really crappy, these English plastic cups. Either you were scalded or you doubled up on the cup and dribbled the drink down your chin. You had to take the good with the bad, she thought. The English had not discovered styrofoam. But they didn't have McDonald's here, either.

'Thanks,' she said.

He looked at her.

'What?'

'You talked in your sleep last night.'

She laughed, without mirth. 'I hope I was literate, at least. In Bloomsbury.'

'You sounded scared.'

She sipped her coffee. She blew at a stray strand of hair from the corner of her mouth, but it didn't shift. Her eyes avoided his. He brushed the errant strand away from her face, behind her ear, and cupped the side of her head in his hand.

'I'm worried about you.'

'That's romantic.'

'I am, though.'

'Watch out for yourself in the Solent, David. There's sharks in English waters now, with this weather. There were sharks swimming under Brighton Pier last week. I saw the picture in a newspaper.'

He just looked at her. 'Sharks,' he said.

163

'Well,' she said. 'I've a train to catch.'

He took his hand away from her face and it dropped to his side. She saw him wince as he tried to frown and the stitches stretched across his wounded eye. He'd been spat at and he'd punched the spitter out. There'd been no hesitation at all between the act and his retaliation. She remembered what his black friend Clifford Lee had said about him. David was mean, Clifford had said, his expression rueful.

Alice said: 'Were you hit as a child, David? Did your father used to hit you?'

He smiled, the smile as constrained as the earlier frown had been by the neat line of suture mending his face. 'I'll watch out for the sharks, Alice Bourne. I promise,' he said. He kissed her. Then he turned and walked back across the concourse and out of the station.

On her train, she brooded on the events at the War Museum of the previous afternoon. She'd left David to look at the picture gallery there to see an exhibition they had staged for the summer, celebrating the Western Front poets Siegfried Sassoon and Wilfred Owen. While he did that, she took a tour. It was immediately obvious to her that the Great War was the martial event that dominated the museum. Fifty-eight years since its conclusion, the conflict was being re-fought here in display cases full of decommissioned ordnance, tunics heavy with the ribbon and braid distinction of rank, models of dreadnoughts and German battlecruisers and everywhere in the sad, battered human paraphernalia of the struggle in the trenches. Alice didn't have to read the faded letters on display to sense the epic sadness of this war. It was there in a wind-up Vitriola gramophone player and the pile of shellac recordings next to it. In someone's neatly cared-for little sewing and mending kit. In one of the wooden football rattles the pickets had carried to warn the huddled men in the line of a mustard gas attack.

It was understandable that a museum concerning itself with the subject of imperial war should feature most prominently the war in which the British Empire chiefly and most expensively fought. Museum staff, exclusively male, stole about the place in blazers and regimental ties, all of them of an age suggesting that they could personally reminisce about the period 1914 to 1918 should a visitor so require. If the Great War was your subject, it was a fabulous place. It was a fantastic resource. They had maps and charts and battle stratagems. They had artefacts from the assassination in Sarajevo and the service revolver belonging to General Haig. A case full of weapons improvised for trench raids was testimony to the spiteful ingenuity of the Canadians on the Ypres salient. That, or their gleeful wish to render the conflict medieval.

Looking at glass cases full of lovingly crafted knuckle-dusters and home-made fighting knives made war seem like madness on a domestic scale. It reminded Alice that the gloomy corridors and dark halls she walked had once been home to lunatics, manacled to the walls of public wards.

But the museum didn't have the air of an asylum. It didn't possess the energy. It wasn't a place of learning, either, at its heart. It seemed to Alice mostly to function as an eloquent commemoration of courage and loss and sacrifice. Bronze soldiers and sailors cast by the sculptor Charles Sargeant Jagger stood here and there in stoic tribute to the fallen. Principally, this building was a memorial and not a museum at all. Its custodians, the ones not made of bronze, patrolled the place with a sort of ghostly dignity, the expressions on their faces those of men privileged, or condemned, to remember daily what to most of the living was something unimaginable.

She was leaving yet another gallery room devoted to photographs of the Western Front when a particular image arrested her eye. A company of American soldiers, dough-boys, rested at the side of a cornfield in what the caption claimed was the summer of 1918. The war had another four months. It held the horrible surprise of the Hindenburg Offensive still to come the way of these men before its carnage would be complete. The Americans in the picture were easily identifiable by their flat-brimmed hats and britches worn with high puttees. They had discarded their packs and were eating at the roadside and smiling for the camera, standing easy. Only their sergeant, of the soldiers, didn't look relaxed. He was a tall, spare man, half his head cast into shadow by the angle of the sun behind the flat brim of his hat. His jaw was visible in a clenched line as he stared into the camera lens.

'I've seen you before,' Alice said to herself. She went to tap the picture frame with an extended finger, but something stopped her doing it. She fancied she was being observed, and looked around, expecting one of the blazered buffers in a regimental tie to lift an eyebrow in benign disapproval. But there was no one there. 'I've seen you before,' she said to the tense, thin infantry sergeant squinting out from a picture taken fifty-eight years earlier to the month. 'Now where could I have seen you?'

It was there again, the feeling of not being alone in the gallery. The quiet there had suddenly become intimidating and Alice could feel the hair prickle on the nape of her neck. It was cold, damp almost. She looked once more at the photograph. At the summer corn caught in mid-ripple and the men gathered at its edge, smiling in a sane moment of wartime calm. Except for their scowling sergeant. 'I know you,' she said to his picture. She shivered and touched the back of her neck and walked out and on to the next room.

They'd treated the Second World War as an afterthought. There were no displays concerning Blitzkrieg. There was nothing about the Holocaust. There was nothing about the Allied invasion of France or the battle for Berlin; only a few bits and pieces about rationing in England, the London Blitz, convoys, U-boats and the escape of the BEF from Dunkirk. It was almost as if the museum curators were embarrassed that the War to End Wars hadn't done its promised job.

There was nothing about America's contribution to the war; no mention of lend-lease, the war in the Pacific, the three million Americans under arms who had lived and eaten and slept and trained in England in the period prior to the Normandy landings. They were a well-kept secret then, those men. But now? She felt indignant about the museum's exclusion of the American effort in the war. It had been decisive, after all. To omit it entirely from the museum's account of the war struck her not just as jingoistic but as a perverse distortion of history.

Agitated by this, she followed enamel signs pointing the way to the museum tearoom to wait for David and to complain to him about it. The tearoom was cramped, but it had a nice view of yellow lawns and high trees through its single window. The trees were so full of foliage that the shaded areas underneath them still held the deep-green colour of undamaged grass. A ceiling fan turned slowly, agitating tearoom smells.

There was a large tea urn on the counter and behind it, to Alice's surprise, the spreadeagle wings of an Italian Gaggia machine. She ordered a cup of coffee from a woman behind the counter who looked like the kind of volunteer who could have been there at least since Chamberlain's reluctant martial response to the invasion of Poland. She smiled with the sweet smile of someone you could trust to keep the home fires burning.

Alice looked at her watch. London was David's treat. It was David's surprise. She could hardly castigate him for bad timekeeping. Anyway, he was only a couple of minutes late. English boys were subjected to Wilfred Owen in their adolescence, much in the way that Boston Catholics were subjected to the catechism at the age of six. The sweet melancholy of the verse never left them, much as the terror of hellfire never subsequently left the poor Catholic Boston boys. He'd be up there now, rereading 'Anthem for Doomed Youth' and sniffling into Kleenex. Or since he was English, more likely into his shirtsleeve.

'Hello, dear.'

Alice looked away from the window, startled. She'd been enjoying her spiteful little reverie, and the interruption had come as a shock. The tea lady slid a cup and saucer on to the tabletop and sat down in the chair Alice had been waiting for David to occupy.

'I've come to cheer you up,' the tea lady said. She'd brought her bag with her to the table and rummaged in it now and put a packet of Players Navy Cut cigarettes and a Zippo lighter on the tabletop. She offered Alice the pack and then lit up, inhaling deeply and then blowing smoke in a dissipating jet towards the ceiling fan. She was slender, bottle blonde, her hair pulled back in a too-youthful ponytail. Her eyes were a startling green and they watched Alice slyly.

'You're an American, aren't you.' It was a verdict, not a question.

'The accent so obvious?'

The tea lady inhaled again and shook her head. 'I'd have known anyway. The jaw, the teeth. The length of your limbs. You're like a thoroughbred filly.'

'Thanks.'

'Like that singer.'

'Please don't say Joni Mitchell.'

'Joni Mitchell's a Canadian, dearie. I was thinking of that nice American girl, the one who sings, "You're so Vain".'

Alice nodded. She took a sip of her coffee, which was very good. She said as much.

The tea lady smiled. She said: 'What is it that's got you all of a bother?'

'Please don't take this as an insult. But I came here expecting to learn more about America's contribution to World War Two.'

'That makes a change. Most people are brought here by Wilfred Owen.'

'I don't mean stuff about Bikini Beach and Iwo Jima,' Alice said.

'I know what you mean, dear. You mean the bomber crews in East Anglia. Or you mean the infantry in the South-West of England.'

Alice felt her heart start to accelerate. It could have been the coffee. 'That's exactly what I mean.'

The tea lady let out a throaty chuckle. It was a sound rich in tobacco and innuendo. 'I was born in Kennington,' she said. 'But I was a land girl in the war. I met my share of Yanks. More than my share.'

'Where were you a land girl?'

'Not far from Totnes.'

'Not far from Slapton Sands, then.'

The older woman appraised her. She didn't look like a tea lady any more. Any vestige of the servile manner she'd amused herself by adopting with Alice had vanished now. Alice could feel the excitement swell in her chest. It was for moments like this that she studied history. The woman looked at the electric clock on the wall and raised an eyebrow. 'It's my break, for half an hour, any time from now until five that I choose to take it. And there's a pub over the road serves an excellent gin and tonic. Join me for half an hour. I'll tell you what I know about Slapton Sands.'

David came into the tearoom just as they were leaving for the pub. Alice didn't explain what she was doing, where she was going, but asked him if he could while away another half-hour in the museum. He agreed readily enough.

It was almost an hour before she returned and located him, waiting for her in the main foyer and pacing. He said: 'What did that woman say to you?'

'That you were a real looker,' Alice said, grinning. 'But no more, honestly, than a girl like me deserves.' It was the truth. It wasn't the whole truth, but neither was it a lie.

Alice Bourne's train journey to Totnes proved Champion right in one regard at least. England was burning. Scorched fields smouldered between the ancient boundaries of ditches that were empty trenches now. She saw the dry beds of streams and ponds that were patches of blistered yellow mud. Ferns atrophied by sunlight and lack of moisture blazed bright yellow between trunks of trees that were still green and reluctant to ignite. But they smoked and were charred, bark burning on them in the smoke, in the unrelenting storm of the summer heat. The scent of wood-smoke, now bitter, now sweet, infiltrated the carriages of the long express. It was an InterCity train. Its final destination was Plymouth. Alice decided to walk its swaying gangways to the buffet car. She didn't crave British Rail tea or, worse – she'd been warned – the culinary horror of an InterCity sandwich. But she wanted a point of comparison. Thirty-odd years ago Americans in uniform had travelled the same route by the same means of transportation. They'd have had thicker heads, after a night in the West End of London, most of them, than that which cider and lack of sleep had given her. Tea and home-grown apples, or maybe rock cakes, would have comprised any refreshment available at the end only of a long and probably uncomplaining queue. They had come from the land of plenty to the home of shortage, where there was no sugar to sweeten the beverage you queued for and metal was in such short supply that the spoon to stir your tea with hung from a chain on the counter in case it was stolen. One GI had written home about a consignment of bananas he'd somehow seen liberate its way from the black market into the hands of some hungry English children. They hadn't known how to eat the fruit. They'd started chewing at their bananas with the skin still unpeeled.

Jesus, Alice thought to herself, making her way through the undulating train. They'd have passed through stations deliberately deprived of names to confuse an invader. And the ruse had succeeded, except that this invader came from Michigan and Maryland, and not from Prussia and Bavaria. He brought with him not the bayonet and the firing squad, but chocolate and hope. And generosity, Alice thought. And when it counted, he brought with him the determination and the courage to fight.

In the pub opposite the War Museum, Rachel Vine, who would never in the memory of Alice Bourne be reduced again to the status of a mere tea lady, had asked Alice some questions about herself. 'What prompts your interest in this stuff, dearie?'

'Something that shouldn't have happened there. The men who died deserve an explanation.'

'It won't do them any good now, will it?'

The pub was ornate, late Victorian, full of heavily carved wood and pious shadows. In another life, the bar itself could have formed the pulpit of a church. It felt comparatively cool in the dark corner they occupied, but nowhere was true sanctuary from the heat in England that summer. Ice tinkled and melted in bluish shards in the gin in front of Rachel Vine. There was no other sound. The few other customers were sunning themselves on the pavement on the seats outside. So they had the place to themselves.

'Was your father a soldier?'

Alice shook her head. 'Born in 1925. Too young for the draft. He was a cop. A police officer.'

The look on Rachel Vine's face suggested that the use of the past tense was not lost on her. She sipped her gin.

'He died, was killed, in the line of duty,' Alice said. 'My brother was a soldier, killed in the line of duty also.'

'May I ask where?'

'Khe Sanh.'

Nothing. Then: 'Oh, love.'

The windows in the pub were narrow arches of decorated glass. Light flared through the few pellucid fragments and burned gold patches on to the hardwood floor. A service would not have been out of place, Alice thought. She could imagine the staff of the War Museum sitting in august rows amid solemn incantations and the swirl of incense, commemorating something. It was only over the road. But they would come, delivered in a charabanc. Their dignity would demand it.

Rachel Vine lit a cigarette. 'Vietnam was a catastrophe whichever way you look at it. I'm not qualified to argue the rights and wrongs of a foreign war. But you only had to watch the news and read the papers to see that your soldiers were badly led. They were encouraged to underrate their enemy. And they were never really clear about what they were fighting for.'

It had been snowing at Arlington when they lowered her brother into the earth. Washington had been bitterly cold that day. Snow gathered in clumps on the jackhammer and picks they had used to break the frozen ground at the graveside. Falling snow made the grave tools look like ancient relics as it blurred and covered them.

'How different was it in your war?'

Rachel Vine snorted and flicked her peroxide head towards the door. 'You won't see or read anything about it in Bedlam. That place is more of a mausoleum than it is a museum. But the Yanks I met knew bloody well what they were fighting for. They trained to the point of exhaustion. And they had bloody good commanders. As subsequent events demonstrated.'

Alice rose out of her seat. 'Will you have another, Rachel?'

'I will, dearie.'

'What were they fighting for?'

Rachel Vine drained her glass and held it out for Alice to refill. Alcohol had coloured her face under the thick foundation on her cheeks. She had strong facial bones, and the skin over her cheeks was still taut, but glowing rosier now. 'Victory,' she said. Then she said: 'You've come a bloody long way, love, to look for America.'

If you faced its destination, the land burned only to the right of the route of the train. Its rails followed the coast. To the left, salt marsh and sand defeated the threat of fire.

England's island character sat moored and beached and aground through the windows on the left of the journeying train, in hundreds of small, stalwart boats. Pugnacious craft, most of them were, Alice thought. Shrimpers and fishing smacks and dredgers and salvage boats. There were dinghies of the sort that Boy Scouts learned to sail in. She saw the odd pleasure cruiser, but nothing that could have been described as a gin palace. A scrumpy palace, maybe, she thought, seeing one dilapidated craft. It listed at anchor, white paint peeling like scrofulous skin from its bow.

She sipped her British Rail tea in the buffet, rocked rhythmically by the rails, watching the view of the coast go by through the window. The window in her own carriage was filthy and she wanted to see as much of the country as she could. The buffet was quiet because few people were travelling on the train. She sipped her tea and looked at the horrible beige and brown British Rail logos and the horrible white, modular, Formica-covered fittings, and she wondered how the Apache had the nerve to go on about Naugahyde so.

She shared the train with occasional men in suits who sat with attaché cases and pink copies of the *Financial Times* and sometimes calculating machines in front of them. Rank among the businessmen seemed to her signalled by the width of stripes on Bengal business shirts and florid fishtail ties. There were a few pimply boys on the train, too, with shorn hair, dressed in jeans and denim jackets. They all had their things in green duffel bags hoisted on to the luggage racks. David had told her to expect what he called squaddies on the train. To and from their barracks, they always used British Rail, he said. They'd been ordered to wear civilian clothes to travel in since the IRA shot one of them on a suburban railway platform in the autumn of the previous year. But the duffel bags gave them away, didn't they? And they showed the ticket collector a travel pass that wasn't punched, the way her ticket had been punched.

Alice smiled to herself at the realization that her home-sickness had entirely gone. She was excited about Slapton Sands.

She very much intended to see David Lucas again. Coming from where he did, he'd had every right to exact revenge on the spitter in the leather jacket, with its painted-on anarchy symbol and its diaper pin fringe. It hadn't been the English equivalent of redneck bigotry, sneering at differences you didn't understand and lashing out at what you felt in some uneasy way was a threat to you. He seemed a very easy-going character, quite happy to have the piss ripped out of him by his friends, occasionally by her. He'd been brought up rough. If he was mean, as his boxing friend had claimed he was, she thought it probably a retaliatory meanness. She didn't get the impression that he'd pulled the legs off spiders as a child, or torn the wings from flies.

Alice had seen her share of institutional callousness, of casual sorority bullying. She'd heard a fair bit, too, about violence, eavesdropping on the conversations at her father's cop poker vigils. She was honest enough to ask herself the question: what would David have done if the guy had stayed on his feet? And she knew the answer was: hit him again. It was an intimate thing, to have someone hawk and spit the mucus from their lungs or sinuses into your face. It was a violation. Alice felt she had learned a thing or two about violation in her own recent experience. In a way, she envied David his opportunity for swift and clean-cut retribution. She envied him even more his talent for it.

He had reacted in the Chelsea pub in a way he'd always wanted but not always been able to do. His cute black friend with the Peter Tosh dreads was right: David *was* mean. But only to people who were trying to be mean to him. He'd had the shit kicked out of him as a child, she was sure. And she was equally sure he had been in no position to hit back. Which meant that a grown man had done it to him. And Alice Bourne, sipping her tea on the Plymouth-bound train, would have bet money that that man had been his father.

Her mind recollected the short conversation they'd had on Blackfriars Bridge. John would have to be told, if she were going to see David again. So there it was. John would have to be told. She felt pretty bad about that, because loneliness had impelled the relationship more than passion had, and John had done everything he could to erase her reluctant feelings of guilt about using him and to stir a passion she'd never truly felt. David Lucas was younger than she was. He was vain. He was closed. He was stubbornly loyal to ridiculous friends. He was from a background unlikely to provide him with a convertible Jaguar and a Bang & Olufsen stereo system like those among John's many other coveted accoutrements. He was damaged, let alone closed. He had tragic taste in television drama. But the fact was that she could barely remember any more what John looked like. And when she allowed it, David Lucas could fill her with his scent, with the insistent strength and grace of his touch. Was it a crush? The idea of a crush was demeaning. Surely nobody suffered their first crush at the age of twenty-three?

Two men tried to chat her up on the train. David had warned her that this would happen. She'd been incredulous, because the Plymouth express was scheduled to arrive at Totnes at one p.m.

'They get horny without booze?'

'I did. With you. Yesterday afternoon.'

'With strangers?'

'Wait and see. Anyway, there'll be booze. It's an InterCity express.'

She got to the buffet just as its shutter was being unrolled at ten-thirty by a man with 'Steward' Letrasetted on to a red waistcoat. She was fourth, she saw, in a thirsty but stoical queue. The three queue members in front of her ordered beer.

'The trick is to get it while it's cold,' the man who was fifth in line confided from behind her. 'They don't have a cold shelf on the train.'

'Hi, steward,' she said, when it came to her turn. He was

from Liverpool and his name was Jimmy. He didn't dwell on the misapprehension. She didn't draw his attention to the pun.

The first picker-up was a squaddie, a teenager sharing his small features with so much acne that it was impossible for her to concentrate on any one area of his face without fear of causing offence. He kept talking about some assault course and asking her to punch him in the abdomen.

The second suitor only displaced the squaddie because the squaddie assumed they were a couple. Such was the Bengal Lancer's air of assumed intimacy that the squaddie actually apologized to him. And he had the smooth presence of mind to accept. The stripes on his shirt were of a lavish, almost plenipotentiary width. The slopes of its collar rose steeply from the lapels of his chalk-stripe suit. It was hot on the train, probably hotter than it was outside, except in the heat of the burning fields. But he wore his tie knot garrotte-tight around his shaven neck. He talked about the weather, the stock market and America – once having heard her accent. He had been to the Everglades on holiday and had seen Sinatra perform in Vegas. He was urbane and witty and incredibly boring. Alice would not have lain naked with him for all the stock on Wall Street. Behind him, squinting, the squaddie hovered in easy sniping range. Her tea was long finished. She decided it was time to make her way back down the shifting aisle through the long, connecting carriages to her seat.

When she got there, she saw that her bookbag had gone.

She had placed it on the table between the bank of four seats on her side of the aisle. She'd had the four seats to herself. Nobody, at least at Paddington, had got on and sat down in the seats. They were empty still. Fighting panic, she looked quickly along the parallel luggage racks on either side of her compartment. Her bookbag wasn't there. There was luggage space between some of the seat backs, she remembered. David had briefed her on British Rail luggage culture, doing so in the event of a full train. But the spaces were empty.

What the fuck: what the fuck. Everything was in that bookbag. All her text sources, her notes, her photocopies, outline – everything. Warned to go home, she'd defied the warning. And then she had acted with criminal carelessness. Her work had been thrown from a train window as she endured unwanted sexual approaches in the beige purgatory of an InterCity buffet bar. It was singeing, now, on some burning embankment.

She looked at the sign at the end of the carriage for the lavatory. The sign said VACANT. She opened the lavatory door expecting to see her work torn up, dumped in its waterlogged pan. It wasn't there. It wasn't in the lavatory opposite, either. Pale with panic now, she went back to her seat. Had she missed something? She forced herself to sit down. Images from the past days inventoried themselves in her mind.

Public art, painting lies across the Peckham badlands. The rings in the lions' mouths. The House of Commons, undulant in heat. London, burnished in afternoon light from the heights of Hampstead. David's body, toiling in dawn light in a Bloomsbury bed. Doughboys on the march to Ypres, with the man from the cathedral. Rachel Vine, cigarette smoke roiling around her like incense in the pub with a pulpit bar.

She felt a tap on her shoulder. It was the ticket collector. He beamed hotly. He was a man with whom Will Hay's stationmaster could happily have bantered. They were cut from the same cloth. They were soul mates. And he had her bookbag in his hand.

'Can't be too careful, miss,' he said. He waved the bag. He brandished it, more accurately. She could not believe it was real, intact and whole, swinging from his bright fist.

The cathedral man. The cathedral man?

'Thank you,' she said.

Her father had taught her to do it. You've got the basics, he had told her. You've got better than twenty-twenty vision, alert hearing, the intelligence to discipline yourself into remembering only the significant. The meat and potatoes, her old man had called it. Forget the rest of the stuff. The salt and pepper, the relish, the ketchup and mustard are all fine and useful in their way. But the meat and potatoes is the meal. You don't have them, honey, you don't have no dinner.

Her father was an indifferent grammarian, but an excellent cop and a patient and diligent teacher. On top of which, his daughter was an alpha-plus student keen to impress him with her cleverness in a way he would finally, fully appreciate. So she learned afresh from him a skill that she already thought she possessed. She learned to look and to remember, to break down a situation into its component parts to gather disciplined and accurate detail. Significant detail. Or, as he always impressed on her, every significant detail. Alice distinguished herself in this study. After the course was completed, she always got her meat and potatoes. It became ingrained, like instinct, to do it. She was good at it, too. She'd never gone unfed.

The War Museum picture had been posed, as all photographs had needed to be back then because of the limitations of relatively primitive camera and film technology. It had been a sunny summer's day, so the light had been good. That had helped clarify the resulting image, of course. A superior lens and the slow shutter speed had given the picture a surprising depth of field. The photographer had used a tripod. She could tell this not just from the absence of camera shake but also from the angle relative to height from which the picture had been taken. The subjects had tried for a look of jolly spontaneity, probably at the coaxing of the photographer. It would have been a pooled picture, Alice assumed, taken for the American dailies. They had then, they still had now, no national newspapers in America. The photograph would have appeared on an agreed date in the *New York Times* and the *Chicago Tribune* and the *Kansas City Star*. It was a propaganda picture in essence, a morale-booster. There would have been a bullish caption printed underneath along the lines of 'Our Brave Boys in Good Cheer on the Way to Join the Fight'. It would have been read with sardonic smiles in barbershops and on shoeshine thrones by men equally cheery they weren't joining the fight.

One person had not remained obediently still for the full length of the exposure. The platoon sergeant had shifted, his movement probably compulsive rather than some militant gesture of non-cooperation. The resemblance was partially in that captured elusiveness. He'd hidden his hands, curled them into his tunic cuffs. Most of his features had been hidden in the picture by the flat brim of his hat and the shadow cast by that brim. But the thin mouth and lantern jaw were familiar to her. So was the cold reproach of the one seen eye. Mostly, though, and ironically, it was the reluctance of that thin, angular body to remain still, scrutinized, that cemented the link.

The sergeant leading his doughboy company in one of Bedlam's warren of Great War picture galleries was as close in appearance to the cathedral man as would have been a twin. And the man at the cathedral had been watching her. He hadn't been a tourist at all. She'd known it at the time, really. She definitely knew it now. She thought about this for a moment. Then Alice took a deep breath of air. The air aboard her train smelled of stale upholstery and burning fields. Was she going mad? No, she thought. Her bookbag, intact, sat on the table in front of her. No. She didn't think she was going mad at all.

★

'I saw a Will Hay film,' she'd said to Rachel Vine.

Rachel Vine had blinked and stared at her. 'Don't they have laws in America to protect juveniles from that sort of thing?'

'I saw it a couple of days ago. Here. Is that what you used to watch? George Formby? Gracie Fields?'

'You're forgetting Old Mother Riley,' Rachel Vine said. 'And Arthur Askey. Musn't forget Big-Hearted Arthur.'

Alice nodded. Champion had mentioned Old Mother Riley. But he hadn't mentioned Askey. Perhaps her professor was unfamiliar with the Askey oeuvre.

'Personally, I preferred Frank Sinatra to George Formby,' Rachel Vine said. 'Truth be told, I never really warmed to the ukulele. Athough it was all downhill for Sinatra – wasn't it? – once he parted company with Tommy Dorsey and his orchestra.'

Alice sat back against her seat. 'You're not quite who you pretend to be, are you, Mrs Vine?'

The woman opposite turned her Zippo lighter between nimble, nicotined fingers with her wrist cocked on the pub table between them. When she spoke, she'd dropped the cod cockney altogether. 'I was born in Kennington. My father was a Member of Parliament and bought a house in Walcot Square. It's within the sound of the Division Bell.'

Alice nodded. She knew about the Division Bell.

'I really was a land girl, too. I've still got the callouses. Based near Totnes, also true. I did encounter the GIs. I was there the night in a Totnes pub when a seriously pissed ranger became so incensed by our licensing laws that he offered to buy the entire liquor stock at closing time just so he could carry on drinking. When that ploy failed, he got together with three buddies at the bar and made a bid for the pub. The offer was accepted. They woke up on the floor the following day, in an eighteenth-century coach-house to which they now owned the deeds.'

'What were they like?'

'Hideously hungover, I should imagine. Poorer, too.'

'The GIs generally. What were they like?'

'That's a question unworthy of you, dearie. And you don't look like Carly Simon, by the way.'

'Why do you persist with this "dearie" shit, Rachel?'

'It goes down very well with most of the punters at Bedlam. They like characters. And I like the job. Without it, I fear I'd gather dust, like the leaves on those potted plants over there.' She nodded.

Alice looked at the potted plants. The pots were brass. The plants were the sort you saw in the vicinity of christening fonts. 'What were they like?'

'Very randy, most of them. They were young men, deprived of the company of women, who had never been fitter in their lives. They may not have been as obsessed by sex as they were reputed to be, but they weren't far off it, in what free time they were given. They liked to drink. Not even the taste of English beer could dull their enthusiasm for alcohol. God, they were thirsty. They tended to be courteous and cheerful. They were a terribly soft touch, most of them, around kids. Most of them weren't much more than kids themselves.'

'They sound like the troops from Disneyland.'

Rachel Vine lit another cigarette. 'All sweetness and light?' She exhaled at the ceiling. 'Not entirely. The segregation was pretty shocking to us even back then. Separate but equal, I believe was the phrase. The blacks were paid the same and wore the same uniform, but they were kept apart. There were some really vile bigots, not all of them from the South. And there were a few out-and-out psychopaths. Every army has a few of those.'

Alice looked at her watch. They had been there half an hour. The pub might have an ecclesiastical feel, but the time passed a lot quicker here than she'd ever known it to in church.

'What can you tell me about Slapton Sands?'

Rachel Vine squinted at her through smoke. Her eyes were quite small, feline and glittery in the thin beams of sunlight through the window. She'd been a head-turner in her time, Alice could tell. It was pretty obvious, removed as she now was from stacks of crockery and her cash register and cake display. Divested of her period pinny, her scarf. She'd been what David and his friends would call a stunner. Now she said: 'The deaths occurred in April of 1944. No details ever reached the public domain. But corpses are difficult things to keep secret when they start washing up all along the coast. I've no proof to offer you concerning any of this. All I can tell you is how I heard several hundred of those soldiers met their end.'

In the spring of 1944, Rachel Vine was twenty-seven. The man she was dating was a thirty-three-year-old American infantry colonel called Richard Fitzpatrick. Fitzpatrick had a wife and two young children at home in Rhode Island. Rachel knew all about them. The colonel kept a family picture in his wallet. And she didn't particularly approve of what she was doing. Her previous boyfriend had been in the RAF. He'd flown a Blenheim until the night when it set out over the North Sea on a bombing mission to Germany from which the aircraft never returned. Rachel justified her affair with Pat by telling herself she was on the rebound. That was what she called him. Everyone called him Pat. He, in turn, justified his infidelity by saying that if he was going to be killed, he wanted to live until he died. Put to the pin of their collars, it was something similar to what all the adulterous Americans said.

Pat was training men at Slapton Sands. It was an open secret in the towns and villages of south Devon that the Yanks were training there for invasion. The big questions were where and when. Pat could make the same educated guess as anyone. But only the chiefs of staff really knew. The possibilities were so widespread that Field Marshal Rommel had been obliged to fortify the entire Atlantic coast of France. Wherever they landed, the assault would be costly. The Germans were expert and well-equipped fighters. Everyone was aware of the casualties suffered by the Canadian commandos in the abortive raid on Dieppe. All the Americans could do was rehearse and rehearse again in the hope that they were as well prepared as possible when the real thing finally came.

Pat didn't discuss the detail much with Rachel. At first she put this down, cynically, to an adulterer's talent for discretion. Then she wondered if he wasn't trying to glorify the importance of what he did by pretending it was more secret than it was. There were plenty of braggarts in the pubs, cryptically claiming to do hush-hush work for this ministry or that. But after a few weeks of seeing him, Rachel realized that Pat was largely silent on the subject of what went on at Slapton Sands out of professionalism. 'You have a saying here,' he told her with a smile. '"Careless talk costs lives."'

She nodded. She was familiar enough with the posters. Everyone was.

'It's as simple as that, honey. I don't want to turn a slogan into a prophesy.'

Rachel thought that two things helped the American military maintain their secrets better than the British were able to do. The first was the fact that they were in a foreign country. No matter how welcome they were made to feel, participating in choral societies and harvest festivals and whist drives and village sports days, they were guests confronted by a culture so alien to them that it couldn't do other than remind them at every baffling turn of the reason why they were actually there.

The other consideration was their stubbornly insisted-on autonomy. Yes, they pedalled out on their bicycles to win hearts and minds in Britain's rural heartland. Their endurance marches often concluded at convenient wayside inns. They baked cakes for school Christmas parties. But they lived on their own bases, guarded by their own sentries, eating rations shipped from Australia. Unlike the Anzacs, they were never billeted with British families. Even if they committed a crime in England, and some were caught doing so, they were tried and punished under American military jurisdiction. The worst case involved a GI who shot to death his English girlfriend in full view of the owner of the tailor's shop in the Midlands where she worked as a cutter. More typical was the case of two GIs stealing a car at gunpoint. They'd been drunk, lost and footsore, and they'd needed to get back to their base.

Rachel Vine learned the details of both these cases from Pat, who took an interest because in civilian life he'd worked as a lawyer in the state prosecutor's office in New York. In both the cases he told Rachel about, the victims had been British. Both crimes had been committed on British soil. But the offenders were tried, found guilty and punished by American military courts. The shooter would have gone back to the USA and got the chair, Pat told Rachel, if he hadn't put the gun under his own chin after killing his footloose sweetheart. The GI highwaymen were properly found guilty. Their jail sentences were served in the United States.

America's citizen army was in but not of Britain, just as its soldiers were in but not of the army itself. They were training for a job. They'd do the training, do the job and then go home. And in the meantime they'd keep the secrets they were supposed to. Maybe Pat would have cracked under Gestapo thumbscrews, the threat of a dawn firing squad. But seduction, as Rachel Vine discovered, left her ex-lawyer tight-lipped about what he did during the daytime.

Of course, she told Alice, there were other ways of knowing what went on at Slapton Sands.

Rory Carnegie was a Scottish trawlerman forced south by some scandal involving an unsafe boat that sank with all hands in a squall off Aberdeen. The tragedy taught Rory a bitter lesson about maritime safety. But the lesson came too late as far as the licensing authority for fishing out of his home port was concerned. Exiled south, he tried fishing first out of Penzance, but fell foul of a Cornish cartel of boat owners who slashed his nets and put sugar into the fuel tanks of two of his craft as they sat at anchor. What was left of his little fleet limped along the Devon coast as far as Dartmouth. Here, Rory was greeted grudgingly. But at least his boats were not vandalized in the night.

His Aberdeen mishap had cost eleven lives. He remained a careful man with a pound note. He was a Scot, after all. But he sent his boats out after Aberdeen alert to every safety requirement. They had life rafts, gimbals compasses, distress flares and, if they were of a tonnage expected to fish beyond coastal waters, two-way radios.

The radios were top notch. But this was a happy fluke. Rory bought them as a job lot from a Liverpool shipping agent who sidelined in bankrupt stock. The wireless sets were American. A manufacturer in Chicago had been pitching them to the German military, on the point of signing a deal when the Japanese attacked Pearl Harbor.

The Americans in the South Hams claimed not just land but a substantial square mileage of sea. Putting all that water out of bounds to fishermen did two things: it put the trawlermen's backs up, and it quickly enriched the fishing stock.

Rory Carnegie fished the forbidden Devon waters with impunity. He fished Start Bay, his boats the only ones to do so. The Americans were often on the water. But Rory was never caught. He listened to the American boats giving their positions, communicating orders and instructions on an open frequency, able thus to steer well clear of them. Incredibly, they didn't bother to encode or scramble their radio transmissions. Rory eavesdropped on them. And so, one disastrous day in April 1944, did the German navy.

'How did you know him?' Alice asked.

'Black market,' Rachel Vine said. 'Grey market, really. It wasn't a case of spivs selling nylons and contraband whisky on street corners. It was strictly perishables, foodstuffs with toff appeal and a short lifespan. And no lineage, if you get my drift.'

'You were a war profiteer?'

Rachel Vine squinted at Alice through smoke. Her eyes were misted, squinting emeralds. 'I organized a lunch every Sunday for the disadvantaged children of Totnes, most of them evacuees. We're talking about a time in England of rickets, of polio, of plain old malnutrition. Lots of protein in fish, love. Lots of goodness in Rory Carnegie's cod and whiting.'

'Oh God. I'm sorry.'

'He was partial to truffles and asparagus. Lordly appetites for a Scot. And he had a sweet tooth. Most of them do, apparently. Sugar beet. Couldn't get enough of it.'

"I'm so sorry, Rachel.'

'We'd go for a drink, after the trade. And he'd tell me what the Yanks were up to off the coast.'

A war profiteer. Alice couldn't believe she'd said it. She felt mortified.

'Don't worry, love,' Rachel said, patting her hand. 'You had to be there. And you should thank God, really, that you weren't.'

A gold Cortina headed the rank of minicabs at Totnes Station. It formed a convoy of one by a painted sign saying 'Rank'. The cab's interior smelled of leatherette and, stalely, of cigarettes. There were quick splotches of Shake 'n' Vac on the corduroy carpet in Alice's footwell. The driver was sitting in a raised bucket seat, wearing a four-part seat belt that organized itself around a circular disc in the middle of his chest. He looked a bit like a picture of a Red Arrows pilot Alice had seen in a photo essay in one of the glossy magazines that came with the Sunday newspapers. Except that his wrap-around sunglasses made him look like a Red Arrows pilot with the head of a grinning fly. Status Quo were playing on his cassette player. Judging by the acoustics, the speakers had been positioned beneath the rear seats. The Fly drove as fast as the Cortina allowed along empty, winding roads. The engine had been race-tuned, souped-up; you could hear the whine of its pistons even over the Quo. She cluched her bookbag, trying to distract herself from the obvious danger she was in by looking at a view mostly obscured by tall, tangled hedgerows. She felt a thrum of excitement in her stomach that had nothing to do with the speed of the car or the percussive thump of the music. She was here. She could imagine Jeeps and Sherman tanks and columns of marching men on these roads. The topography was the same. The roads had not been widened, painted with white central lines, punctuated by the reflective Catseyes that rippled under tyres on most of the English roads outside the cities. The South Hams seemed unchanged and unchanging. Surely, she would find here what it was she was looking for.

Her room in Strete was the upper room in a small cottage facing the sea. She was admitted and shown around by a neighbour of the woman who owned the cottage. 'Neighbour' was a loose term, since the cottage was isolated, the only building on that section of the bay. But the cottage owner had been called away to deal with some emergency concerning her daughter in London. Positioned under the eaves, the room had a cosy quality better suited to winter than to summer. But its double window opened on sand, sea, horizon and sky. There was no heat ripple to impede the view. Looking out over the water, Alice felt it was the most space she had seen since her arrival in England. At the margin of water and land, the sea gathered in long, undulant, foam-crested waves. They rippled shorewards, dense with strength and momentum, each different, each its own elemental proposition of force and teeming consequence.

David Lucas had been right: it was nothing like the coast at Whitstable, where the sea was constrained by the bulk of Sheppey and the shingle beach ordered by its neat rows of equidistant groynes. Whitstable bustled and crowed on the edge of the water. It cultivated oyster beds. Its snug harbour and nautical pubs and sailors' cottages somehow domesticated the sea. Here, by forbidding contrast, all was exposure. The sea was ragged and the sand desolate. The sea was blue, of course, under its blameless blue sky, which was different from her dreaming of it. In her dreams, the sea at Slapton was coloured a treacherous green. Despite the weird, enduring stillness imposed all over England by the heatwave, there seemed the suggestion on Start Bay of a breeze. It did nothing, really, to cool the air, but it delivered a faint, untameable tang of salt.

*

Rory Carnegie had laughed, over his black market drinks with Rachel Vine, about the Higgins boats, the landing craft that the American strike troops came ashore in when they practised their seaborne assaults at Slapton Sands. Flat-bottomed, constructed of wood, they had the handling capabilities, he said, of a fruit crate with the lid removed. They were high-sided, not to provide their human cargo with armour, but simply to prevent them from being swamped. But they were notoriously difficult to manoeuvre. They steered badly and tended to broadside a swell of their own accord, regardless of what the steersman did with the tiller. Underpowered and heavily burdened, they didn't have the speed or mass to respond to what an uncertain sea was doing. And the Americans were learning on the job. Rory would watch through his binoculars, his nets dragged bulging to either side of his own wash, as the Higgins boats were delivered into the sea off an American cruiser and were buoyed this way and that in the unhappy chaos of a stranded flotilla, two or three out of a dozen of them making for their target of the shore with anything approaching certainty as the rest pitched and wallowed on the swell.

But the mirth dried on his lips fairly soon. Even Rory had to admit that the Americans were ferociously quick learners. They lost a few of their landing craft. They must have lost a few men with them, because the fruit crates sank with alarming swiftness and he never saw any rescue craft. But in weeks their handling of the Higgins boats became dexterous and confident. They'd be dropped in a heavy sea and chug in a relentless, disciplined formation for the shore. Rory's crews began to see odd, fugitive lights flickering when they fished at night, and the Scotsman realized that the Yanks were practising moonlight assaults. Soon they were moonless assaults. Not long after, Rory stopped joking at the expense of the Slapton Sands Yanks altogether. It was the Americans, after all, who had constructed his excellent radio sets. They mean business, he said to Rachel Vine with a shrug. Rory Carnegie was not just grudging in his acknowledgement of others' accomplishments. He was a king among begrudgers. But she could tell he was increasingly impressed by what it was he spied on.

There was a note from her landlady on the bureau in Alice Bourne's room. It outlined the idiosyncracies of the plumbing and told her where her key was hidden. The neighbour had let her in. The note said that there was a bicycle she could gladly use leaning against the potting shed at the rear of the cottage. Under the note was a small map, detailing local amenities. These were scant, unless she chose to cycle to Dartmouth or Totnes. Hence the dimensions of the map. There was a pub at the northern end of Slapton Sands that served reasonable food. She would find tea, a jar of instant coffee, sugar and powdered milk along with a kettle in her room.

And someone had telephoned her here yesterday. A woman called Emerson seemed most anxious that Alice return her call at the earliest opportunity. The landlady had written a number down. There was a payphone in the pub, she added helpfully. There was a phone in the cottage, too. Alice had seen it on its dedicated table under a directory on a chain in the cottage entrance hallway. But the English were peculiar, she knew, about the use of their phones.

Alice looked at her watch. It was two o'clock. She was hungry and she felt dirty from the train. But there was something she needed to do that did not immediately involve plumbing, a bicycle ride or Sally Emerson. She needed to walk along the coast road to Slapton Sands. She needed to look landwards at the coast there from the limit of the sea.

The coast road was a straightish, narrow strip of asphalt edged on both sides by tussocks of razor grass. Small avalanches of sand had trickled here and there down the banks on to the asphalt. At intervals, she saw grey ruins of reinforced concrete half-buried in sand and grass. She supposed these were the sangars and pillboxes built by the Americans as mock fortifications. Except that there was nothing mock about them, really. They had been built to the same specifications as the real thing and then defended with grim obstinacy by men using live rounds in their guise as the German defenders of conquered French territory. The concrete had weathered in salt and wind exposure, and the ribbed steel reinforcing rods showed here and there amid stains and trickles of red-brown rust. The fortifications were pitted in clusters and rows with craters gouged by high-velocity rounds. If they had been defended stubbornly, they had been attacked with the fury of an invading force that faced extinction if it was driven back from its beachhead into the sea. She had read that they had trained and drilled with such exhaustive relentlessness that their war games became indistinguishable from actual combat. The citizen army resented their chickenshit tasks, the kitchen fatigues, the endless saluting of officers for whom they had scant personal regard. But they didn't mind so much the field practices designed to keep them from becoming disaffected and bored. And so they became highly efficient. And so when the real thing came, it was thought, they would do it by rote, performing their murderous, terrifying task with no greater fear or forethought than they would give to yet another drill.

The bay extended to the left of the road she was on. If she stepped up on to the grass bank she could see the width of flat sand descending to the sea. The sand was vast and largely featureless. There were strands of fleshy seaweed and some bits of beach debris, indistinguishable from this distance, down there on the tide line above the foam-edged breakers. But there was nothing suggestive of violence or tragedy. To her right, scrub and thorns clung to sandy soil. The small shrubs and trees were stunted and deformed by wind. They grew withered, tenacious. There were wild blackberry bushes and dune pines in little clusters. Behind them, the land had begun to rise. On the road itself, she encountered no people, no traffic. Birds coloured the bushes, singing, industrious. And there were gulls flapping and shrieking above the flotsam and weed on the tide line.

There was no sign announcing Slapton Sands. It was a place that had existed for so long at the forefront of the mind of Alice Bourne that she had half-expected to see some physical commemoration of the fact of the place at its boundary. Not one of those illuminated signs erected out of civic pride to announce some hick town in America, but something ancient and English. She'd seen such a sign at St George's Circus in London near where they'd parked the Apache's minivan for the visit to the War Museum. Solemn and time-battered, its face bore the chiselled legend: 'Westminster lies one mile to the west of this Monument.' Information about the cartographic fact of Slapton would surely have been just as valid. The Slapton signpost would be stone, cracked, canted. It occurred to her, as she looked for it in vain, that there may very well have been just such a post. But it would have been plucked from the ground when England faced the threat of invasion before American soldiers had ever arrived here. It gathered moss on the bed of the gravel lagoon at Slapton Leys. It had been re-rooted in the garden of a Devon village pub for morris men to dance around at Midsummer's Eve as they travestied some ancient pagan rite.

It didn't matter. She knew she had reached the place. Alice left the road and walked out on a diagonal line towards the edge of the water. The sand was firm under her feet, and the approaching sea began to roar like a dull, rhythmic reckoning. She'd brought a small shoulder bag with her, and she stopped now and took off her shoes and rolled her jeans up above her calf muscles and put flipflops from the shoulder bag on her feet. The breeze was faint when she stood again, but it was noticeable, a sensation of freshness on her face and in her hair. And salt. Not the rank malevolence of the salt smell oozing through wallpaper and linoleum in her Whitstable flat, but a clean suggestion of the sea. She had reached the water's edge before she turned back to look at the land.

They would have dipped and plunged shorewards in their Higgins boats, heavy with hampering kit. Then the ramps would have splashed down into the waves, and with their rifles raised over their heads they would have leaped, racing, into the surf and, gulping with cold and the weight of waterlogged pack and clothing, seen what it was she was looking at now. From a soldier's perspective, the beach was a vast and featureless killing ground. Infantry landing here would be fired down on from the sangars and slit trenches and pillboxes, which were now the partially bulldozed ruins she'd seen from the coast road. There was no natural cover at all. Even without such obstacles as mines and coils of defensive wire, the beach was a suicidal location for an assault. Seeing Slapton for real, she realized instantly what she had not from her conversation with the Colorado veteran, from her reading on infantry tactics and from her scrupulous study of the detailed aerial photographs she had located in the library and mounted on the epidiascope at

Kent. The soldiers who practised for Normandy here could master the mechanics of their landing craft until they were able to embark, beach and disembark in their sleep. But the only way for them and their commanders to know whether their battle plan would work would be to try it out for real. They would have to land tanks to provide cover for an infantry advance. They would need to pulverize the beach defences using the heavy guns aboard their battlecruisers. They would need fighter-bomber support to strafe and harry defending units. Without all of these, the result would be obvious. It would be butchery. It would be a massacre.

Alice turned around to face the sea. Rory Carnegie's secret lay somewhere on its bottom, if Rachel Vine had told her the truth in a pub in Lambeth which had felt towards the end of their conversation as hushed and sanctified as a confessional. Well, the sea would tell her nothing. But Rory Carnegie might, if she could locate the man and persuade him to talk to her. Rachel hadn't known if Rory was alive still or dead. He'd be about seventy years old, she calculated. Fishing has always been a deadly profession, but he was a canny fisherman. And he took pretty good care of himself off the water. For a Scot.

She turned her back on the sea and studied the land again. Not this time in the disciplined way a soldier might, but as someone would seeing it the way she did, as an American, as a visitor seeing a foreign landscape properly from this perspective for the first time. Beyond the ridge of the coast road and the undistinguished scrub to its rear, the land must have gathered soil and mineral richness, rising as steep green hills with patches of verdant woodland. The trees were a mix of cedar, sycamore, elm and larch. There was no precise element to this vista of grass and tall trees and gentle hills that defined it specifically as English. At least, there was no element she could identify, unless it was the soft light and crepuscular shadows. But the indefinable, defining something, was there nevertheless. The scene was English in the same unmistakable way as would be churning milkmaids, maypoles, a girning fool in a smock on a country stile. And you may as well include the green man, she thought to herself. And those damned morris dancers.

She was filled, looking at the hills and the dark shapes of gathered woodland, all at once with a feeling she always associated with English twilights. It usually crept up on her in that silence when the singing of birds became suddenly more audible, with the sun sinking and the sky starting to flush pink in the west and objects gaining a gloamy, summery luminescence, as though they were not real, those pub benches, those tables and table umbrellas and garden walls. As though they were pretend objects cut from crepe paper, from the intense fabric of stage or film props. Usually, there would be music, something recently familiar but fundamentally strange. She recalled Sandy Denny, her voice ululant and sad, singing 'The Banks of the Nile', on a cassette player at a Canterbury garden party. At first, she had mistaken this mood for melancholy. And then, because it felt vaguely sad, with homesickness. But what it was, she realized now, was alienation. It was the feeling of being somewhere, somehow strange, and being unable to escape your surroundings and return to the familiar, to the recognizably safe, to the effortlessly known and understood. It was a childlike sentiment. She felt it at twilight because the coming of darkness signalled to her instinct that she was spending another night away from home. She felt it now because it must have been what those boys had felt thirty-odd years ago approaching this inalienable English landscape from the sea.

What would they have made of the south Devon hills, those boys from the wheatfields of Nebraska, from Iowa and the flat, arid earth of west Texas? Would their collective hearts have sunk each time they rehearsed their landing at the sheer, remote-from-home strangeness of where they fetched up?

Perhaps they did. But Alice Bourne believed that Americans were tougher, too, back then. They were far less given to indulgent sentiment. They were still a pioneering people. Childhood was a swift rite of passage, not a coddling America's youth felt any collective reluctance to leave behind. Sure, they were boys. But they were tough boys, in it together. They had their army buddies; they had what their German enemies called camaraderie. She could hear the sea behind her. It seemed to shudder and hiss against the shingle and sand. The sea. The encroaching, whispering, assaulting waves of the sea. Each of those boys was alone in death, though, she thought. Camaraderie compensates only the living.

Alice went back to the cottage in Strete and took a bath. She got the sit-up-and-beg from the lean-to behind the cottage. She cycled to the post office on her landlady's map that doubled as a provisions store. She bought a bottle of lemonade and cream crackers and triangles of processed cheese wrapped in foil in a wheel-shaped, compressed-paper box. She put her purchases in the basket mounted between the handlebars of the bike and cycled back and ate a picnic on the beach. I could be right out of an Agatha Christie story, she thought, chewing. Except that I'm too messy an eater. And I haven't a smooth but sinister vicar with me to move along the plot. She was beat when finally she got back to the cottage. She read for a while and then hit the sack. The phone rang twice after she went to sleep. The second time it rang and rang before it finally stopped. Either her landlady had persistent friends, Alice thought, snug under the eaves and the covers. Or she owes someone urgent money.

It was the following morning before she saw her landlady's note and remembered she was supposed to call DS Emerson. By the time she saw the note, she was on her way out of the door with her camera loaded with film and her notebook in her bag. She looked at the telephone in the hallway. It was pink, this instrument, the precise colour of cheap nail varnish. The note was in her hand. Should she call Emerson now? The English were funny about their phones. Thirty miles was considered long distance and the cost of a trunk call astronomical. The only place she'd seen the phone profligately used was in episodes of *The Sweeney*. She wouldn't do it, she decided. The very fact of the phone put her in a position of trust she wasn't about to abuse. It was eight o'clock that evening and she was in the pub on the northern end of Slapton seafront when she finally fished the number from her bag and returned DS Emerson's call.

'Sally Emerson.'

This surprised Alice. She'd expected to have to leave a message. She was momentarily silent, coins in her fingers over the slit in the metal box you pushed them through.

'Is that Alice Bourne?'

'Yes. It's me. Hi.'

Nothing. Then: 'We got a match on that latent. The print we took from the note in your room where it was pressed over the gum?'

'I know what a latent is.'

'We've vastly improved our whole forensic database,' Emerson said. 'After the Black Panther case?'

The detective sounded nervous. Alice said: 'The match for the print?'

'A Paddington prostitute was roughed up by a punter. Her pimp arrived and confronted the punter, armed with a knife. Your partial matches a print on the knife handle left by the punter after he'd taken the knife from the pimp and cut him up with it.' Emerson sounded odd. 'And cut the girl.'

Pips interrupted, and Alice shoved coins into the slot. 'So what's the connection? Apart from the print.'

'The crime I'm talking about was committed early in 1944,' Emerson said. 'The man who committed it was an American soldier based at Slapton Sands.'

Breathing was a function Alice Bourne was unaware of normally. Now it came so laboured that it threatened her capacity to speak.

'What was his name?'

'Johnny Compton.'

'Where is he now?'

'Not where he's supposed to be. He's dead, Miss Bourne. According to his record, Compton died at Slapton Sands.'

'You've got his army file in front of you?'

'Not exactly,' Emerson said. 'I did a course with a chap who works at the American embassy. I asked him to get whatever he could on Compton, released and telexed to me.'

'OK. OK.' The breathing was already marginally better. It was a relief, what she was hearing, in a way. 'What did Compton's father do?'

'Why do you want to know?'

'Do you have that information?'

'Compton was from a military family, it seems. His father fought with distinction in the First World War.'

'He was an infantryman,' Alice said. 'He was a doughboy sergeant. He fought at Ypres.'

'I think you ought to come back to Canterbury,' Emerson said. Her tone now was measured, neutral.

'I saw Johnny Compton three days ago. In Canterbury, near the Cathedral Gate.'

There was a silence. Then: 'He'd be a man in his early sixties now.'

Alice laughed.

'I think you ought to come back here.'

'What for?' Alice said. She was thinking about the rusty, arterial gush of water down the side of a Paddington tenement. Of a grey visage behind grey nets and filthy glass. 'You don't believe in ghosts.'

'There's something else. David Lucas was hurt yesterday in a diving accident.'

'Oh Jesus.'

'He's OK,' Emerson said. 'He spent the night under observation. But he's absolutely fine.'

'Would you tell me how the accident happened?'

'I think you should come back to Canterbury, Miss Bourne.'

After Alice hung up, she thought about what Champion had said at his supper gathering about Sally Emerson, about how her talent would take her to Scotland Yard, where she would gain no further promotion and eventually become disillusioned. This case at least, would provide her with no collar. It would do nothing for her detective's reputation. From inside the pub, the jukebox was loud when customers, mostly young men, opened the swing doors to the lavatories and a row of coathooks over a bench where the phone had been installed. Someone was singing on the jukebox about how he must have been through about a million girls. It was Elvin Bishop, the song 'Fooled around and Fell in Love'. A ploughman's lunch had provided her dinner, cheddar cheese and pickled onions eaten to the same cock-happy soundtrack. Thin Lizzie swaggering on about the boys being back in town. Or Bad Company, Paul Rodgers crooning mightily about some easy sexual conquest. Why didn't they fucking grow up, all of them? She could think of several things she would like to do with Messrs Bishop, Lynott and Rodgers. None of them involved a bed. The pickled onions had been shallots really, and they had given her heartburn. Or maybe the music had. Or the pint of cider she'd drunk, eating her bread and cheese. Except that it wasn't heartburn, was it? She was sick with dread at what Emerson had told her about Johnny Compton. She was sick with guilt and foreboding about David Lucas. She looked at the phone, wishing she could call someone. Wishing she could call her dad, truth be told, hear once again the comfort and resolution in her father's voice. She went back into the pub, where at least she wasn't bothered. Not bothered, anyway, by the living.

In the bar, Alice fought the emotions threatening to overwhelm her at that moment by thinking of salient facts. It was a new discipline, this. One she was quickly having to learn. Alice knew, because her father had told her, that fingerprinting was the gold standard of criminal forensics. The police forces of England and Wales had pioneered its use, adopting the Henry classification as long ago as 1901. Fingerprints, friction ridges dermatologically, were individual. Characterized by loops, whirls, arches and tents, no two people on the planet possessed an identical set.

Alice knew, because Sally Emerson had told her, that the Fingerprint Bureau at Scotland Yard used civilian scene-of-crime officers. They weren't cops, but they underwent five years of training before they qualified to work on actual cases. Their fingerprint cards, until this year, had been held in manually maintained files. Now, following the mistakes made in this Black Panther case, they had introduced a computerized database. Maybe the computers had enabled the match to be made quicker. But the old card-index system worked just fine back home, where the FBI held around a hundred million sets of prints, yet Depression gangster John Dillinger had been so concerned about being nailed by his that he burned the pads off his fingers with acid. It hadn't worked.

Dillinger's prints had grown back. Everyone's did, apparently. It was as though there was a fingerprint template, her dad had told Alice, burdened on a felon's soul.

A Frenchman called Edmund Locard had devised a twelve-point comparison proof for fingerprint identification in 1918. But you didn't need twelve. Not really, you didn't, unless you were showboating in front of a particularly stupid judge and jury.

Alice rubbed her eyes and swallowed gas, aware of ghostly shallots in pickling vinegar and ancient cider apples. She groaned to herself, alone.

David had driven straight back to Canterbury, arriving soon after midday. He'd taken the boat out at around five in the afternoon for a routine dive in about three fathoms of water off Reculver. He'd been accompanied by a friend.

'You're not supposed to dive alone,' Emerson said. 'Divers have this thing called the buddy system. If a diver gets into trouble, or suffers equipment failure, his buddy knows what to do. But Lucas dived solo.'

'Who was in the boat?'

Emerson was silent for a moment. Alice sensed that the detective was furious about all of this: about Compton, about David Lucas, about her.

'What are you like on multiple choice, Alice?' she said. 'If it had been the flatulent public school moron, or the tramp he knocks about with, he'd be dead, wouldn't he? It was the half-caste boy. It was Clifford Lee who saved his life.'

Clifford had been wearing David's watch. It was a ten-minute dive. David was roped around one ankle to a rowlock on the boat. After ten minutes, Clifford tugged on the rope. After twelve, he tugged again. And nothing happened.

211

'Lucas had at least had the sense to bring along a spare face mask,' Emerson said. 'Lee put it on, went in and pulled his way down along the rope. He managed to get Lucas's weight belt and air tank off and hauled him back up.'

'What had gone wrong?'

Emerson laughed. 'Depends on who you ask,' she said. 'Lucas is convinced he got snagged in seaweed. His air mix could have been wrong. In this weather, in a full wetsuit, it could have been the heat. Divers can become disorientated and confused, even at relatively shallow depths. It's why they have this buddy procedure. Whatever, he was unconscious by the time he came up.'

'What does Clifford say?'

Emerson laughed again. Her laugh was bitter over the phone with lack of mirth. 'I don't think Mr Lee thinks much of the police. Made some remark about blacks being poor swimmers on account of their small lungs. I think he was being ironic. But he was adamant about one thing.'

'Yes?'

'Seaweed. There wasn't any.'

Salient facts, Alice thought to herself, her fingers drumming an absent tattoo on the side of her glass. Salient facts.

The US army had introduced fingerprinting as early as 1905. She hadn't known that until poor, bright Sally Emerson had told her so over the phone. But she hadn't needed to, had she? It was Compton's latent. They'd find others, if they went to a room near the top of a Paddington tenement clad in white tiles like rotting tooth enamel and did some dusting there. It was Johnny Compton, and wasn't 'latent' a terrible threat of a word?

He'd been a vicious individual in life, possessed of the same shiftless malice embodied in his father's photograph on the wall in the War Museum. Meanness had been born and bred in him. Alice could pretty much guess at the facts contained in the file from which Sally Emerson had been permitted her extracts. There'd be a catalogue of thinly detailed misdemeanours. Pilfering, drunkenness, incidences of paid-for sex where the bargain struck was not kept to the payee's satisfaction. Joining America's small, shabby peace-time army was what men like Johnny Compton did to avoid Depression breadlines and to stay out of jail. She could hear his crackerbarrel accent, the voice pitched on the bitter ground between a quarrel and a complaint. He'd have had that sinewy strength a jackal has. He'd be reptile quick in a fight. Her wonder was what such a soldier would have done at Slapton Sands. After the draft and the army reforms, they rooted out and replaced all the feeble-minded and degenerate timeservers not up to the rigours of fighting a war. The process had been as ruthless as it had been comprehensive. So how had a recidivist like Compton survived the cull? More important, what was he doing right now, interfering from death with the living? What was this uneasy spirit trying to scare her away from finding out?

The answer to these questions might be contained in his file. But Alice doubted it. The army files she'd been allowed to see in the past had always been remarkable for how little significant detail they contained.

When finally she walked outside the pub, she shivered, though it wasn't cold. There hadn't been a single jacket or pullover hung on the hooks by the pub payphone. How many English summers could have boasted that? There was shingle, gritty under the soles of her shoes and the tide must have been out, out there in the blackness, because there was a subtle odour of salt decay.

It had to be coincidence, what had happened to David Lucas. Diving was dangerous, and he had said himself that he was out of practice at it. The ghost of Johnny Compton couldn't harm people in the physical world. She was fairly confident of that. If he could, he would have harmed her by now. He'd been a man in life with an appetite for hurting women. But she had dreamed too often lately of drowning. And she couldn't help thinking of David Lucas, who'd got up from a hospital bed and gone home and packed and left for the Isle of Wight and Bembridge. She couldn't help seeing David dead on the bottom of a dim sea, swaying in the current, his precious life spent on the promise of a few hundred pounds.

FOUR

The South Hams, 1944

A brass hat called Clark had coined the phrase that voiced the obvious. Clark was a two-star memo specialist who had somehow weaselled his way into General Marshall's little black book of officer preferment. Some soldiers thought the black book a myth fostered by Marshall himself to encourage efficiency and openness among officers discussing the art and mechanics of war. Johnny Compton, however, knew this to be horseshit. Openness worked only if your opinions on military matters were voiced in the right accent, in sentences securely bolted by grammar gained as the privilege of a paid-for education. And Marshall's little black book of preferment was no myth. He'd seen the general take it out and make entries in it twice, once in manoeuvres at Benning and, again, in George Patton's army kingdom in California.

Clark was no doubt some servile, self-seeking jerk. In a moment of revelation, however, he'd opined that 'A soldier is always green unless he's been under fire'. To Compton's knowledge, the general had never in his service life fought anything more lethal than a cold. But his words, with his reputation, had since gained the currency of gold.

At least, that was the comfort Johnny Compton clung to as he waited to see Colonel Fitzpatrick under the canvas awning of the camp's administration block. He was flanked by two MPs. They were big guys, and they'd strip-searched him after the English police had delivered him into their custody. He didn't look or feel his best. He'd struggled with the English cops who'd tried to arrest him at Paddington. He'd known that English cops went unarmed and bet heavily on his chances of escape. The cops were old, all the young English guys abroad, fighting, or down the coal mines or in factories, combat exempted. So the cops had been older guys, maybe in their forties. He'd decked three of them but then got cornered in an alley. They hadn't taken kindly to seeing their own, unconscious and bleeding in a street gutter. A skilled beating had followed in the cells under Paddington police station. A really tough old limey cop had delivered it with his fists and knees and a hardwood truncheon. Johnny thought he'd be lucky if he stopped pissing blood after a week. He also thought that if the guys with the white armbands had not come for him as promptly as they had, he would now be occupying a mortuary drawer.

He turned his hat in his hands. Rain beat and withered on shuddering canvas. The MPs stood like burly statues on either side of him. He hated the weather in this fucking country. He would have paid for the smell of jasmine and julep, now, in the English night. But he got kerosene smoke and damp, mildewing canvas. It was a rotten fucking place. He hurt everyfuckingwhere.

He concentrated on what it was he knew about Richard Fitzpatrick. Fitzpatrick was a proper lawyer, at least. That was the one perverse benefit of this amateur, vastly inflated army he had found himself in. You could get a proper haircut and expert dentistry. Real musicians performed at the concerts that real impresarios organized on behalf of their fellow brothers in arms. Real cooks dished out the chow. And Fitzpatrick would tell him exactly what chance he had of escaping a sentence served in an English prison cell.

The pimp hadn't even looked English, when he came to think about it. He was some kind of spic from one of those little British Empire places. Maltese, maybe. And the spic had been the one who upped the stakes by pulling the knife.

Rain dripped and canvas shuddered like cold flesh. If he looked to right or left – and his facial swellings just allowed it – Compton saw disdainful fury on the faces of the MPs flanking him. In truth, he was ashamed. His own father would have felt the same shame, he knew, chastising himself with that unshirkable fact. He'd let matters get messy, out of hand. He'd been caught. And you did not get caught. It was his own first principle, the rule by which he judged himself. His daddy would have expected no different. He had a standard to maintain, a proud tradition. You absolutely did not get caught. But he had; he'd been caught. It was no consolation that he'd got clean away from similar scrapes on a dozen occasions. He'd have to deal with the failure and with the shame of it eventually. Now, though, he had to think about Fitzpatrick.

He had to forget that the colonel was a wartime colonel, and not a colonel of note. He had to forget the Irish name, with its privileged reek of Boston Catholicism. He had to remember his own value, in which regard he could give sincere and grateful thanks to General Mark Clark. And he had to remember to identify Fitzpatrick's weaknesses.

It was hard, though. They had brought him back manacled, lying on his stomach on the boards of a flat-bed truck. He felt like he needed desperately to pee, thanks to the attention paid his kidneys by the big limey cop. He hadn't smoked a cigarette in better than thirteen hours and his craving for a Lucky now was even greater discomfort to him than his bruises, his abrasions, his bone-weary fatigue. He didn't even have the consolation of a stick of gum. And he wasn't going to get one from the white hats guarding him. They tended to cosy up to the British police, to foster good relations. Didn't matter to them that he was a trained officer who had dedicated his professional life to the service of his country. Cops were cops in any language, in any uniform you chose to clothe them in. They'd pronounced their own verdict on the man in their charge. It was a harsh and unhappy one.

Rain pattered and squalled in big, gusty drops against the

canvas roof. It really knew how to fucking rain in England. And it was damp all the time. The waterproof hadn't been invented that could keep this miserable climate from seeping into your clothes and your flesh and, eventually, into your bones. There were lots of things he liked about England, able to consider it in a more convivial mood. The booze. The women. The blackout. But the weather was awful. The climate was defeating. And they said that in France the weather was even worse. Compton wondered, seriously, if he would now ever get to see France. His father had fought with distinction in France. What a sorry fucking mess he was in. He tried to look at his watch, out of habit, but they'd taken it from his wrist and, anyway, the crystal had been smashed in the first part of his long night of London trouble, when he had wrestled the knife from the grip of that greasy fucking pimp before giving him what he had coming.

Fitzpatrick, Fitzpatrick. He must know something about the colonel. In the sorry condition he was in, it was hard enough to think straight, let alone to remember or plan. But he couldn't go in there naked, unarmed. There had to be something. Maybe it would come to him when he saw the man.

He could smell bacon cooking on the long iron skillets in the kitchen block. He could smell hot bacon fat and eggs frying in the fat left on the skillets from the soft rinds of tender hogs. He could hear the banter of the Negro cooks, growing more cheerful as they snaffled themselves a morsel

219

of pork belly and their senses wakened and stirred to the hot rhythms of a busy kitchen shift. In truth, though, they sounded more subdued than usual. Or maybe that was just him. He could smell bread and coffee, too, as the camp stirred into life long before the reluctant coming of another miserable English dawn. And he could hear an approaching column of marching men, weariness evident in the trudge of their boots and the creak of leather and canvas under rain capes as they laboured home after a field exercise. It was breakfast and then bed for those troops, the snug and blissful reward well earned for the hard routine of bivouacs and field rations high up on Dartmoor. They'd have been up there for seventy-two hours, lying low in the day and fighting at night. Learning by touch the contours of unfamiliar territory. Making the hostile terrain their friend, their advantage. They were becoming soldiers. Christ, who was he kidding? They had become soldiers, hadn't they?

Compton turned his hat in his hands, racked by the craving for a smoke. A Lucky and a cup of hot, strong coffee. What would he not give for that blissful combination of humble comforts? He was no glutton. He was hardly one for the soft life at all. His childhood had taught him how to go hungry for days. But now, he panged inside his sore body for the simple pleasures he would continue to be denied for he didn't know how long. Who was this damned Fitzpatrick? He'd discover soon enough. They were pulling back the canvas entry flap to the army lawyer's office, grabbing his manacled arms, bustling him under-prepared into his unhappy audience with the citizen army brass.

Fitzpatrick's office was fuggy with cigarette smoke. Smoke hung in a sour haze to about halfway up the height of the room. The big zinc ashtray on the colonel's desk carried maybe a pack and a half of butts. There was a bottle of Benzedrine on the colonel's desk. Compton couldn't tell how many pills had gone from the bottle. And he had no way of knowing how recently they'd gone. But the foil seal on the bottle neck was broken and the bottle was nowhere close to full. The colonel had his elbows on the desk and his head behind his hands. His telephone, one of his telephones – Compton saw that there were two – began to ring. The colonel ignored it.

'Unshackle him.'

The white hats hesitated.

'Do it!'

They unlocked the chains constraining his elbows and wrists.

'Thank you. Dismiss,' the colonel said.

And the white hats were gone.

'You can salute, soldier,' Colonel Fitzpatrick said to Compton. 'At least, you should be able to. The Brits claim they didn't break any bones.'

He saluted stiffly.

The desk telephone was still ringing. It was an insistent, insinuating sound. It was an itchy sound this early in the morning, Compton thought. If you carried the rank, you'd throw the fucking thing out of the window.

Then it stopped.

And Fitzpatrick took his hands away from his face.

Compton knew him. They all did, every soldier in the camp, by his nickname, which was Hollywood. He had that look about him, of Gable and Flynn. Except that Fitzpatrick didn't have his Hollywood face on now. He'd aged, or something. He didn't look right. He looked emptied out, angry and all emptied out. In the run of routine, he was a man so dazzlingly handsome you couldn't even get angry about it. Jesus, you half-wanted to fuck him yourself. But not now. Now, Colonel Hollywood looked ill, cancerous.

'Cops printed you, right?'

'Yes, sir.'

'Christ.'

'Didn't do nothing, sir.'

'Save the bullshit, soldier.'

The phone rang, the other one on his desk, a different tone, the same insistent plea to answer it. This time it worked. Fitzpatrick listened, said 'yes' and 'no' and 'uh-uh' from time to time, contributing nothing. Compton remained at attention. Day was coming into the colonel's quarters now, subdued and English. The dawn in these parts didn't announce itself. It was a sly insinuation of apologetic light.

'Stand easy, Compton.'

Compton did. 'Sir?'

'Compton?'

'You look terrible, sir. Sir, you look worse than me.'

'You're a disgrace to your rank, lieutenant,' Fitzpatrick said. 'You're an affront to that uniform. If I had my way you'd be in the brig, now, wearing a full set of irons on a homeward-bound rust bucket out of Liverpool. Any justice, a U-boat would put your miserable ass on the bottom of the Atlantic. Otherwise, you'd be on your way back home to break stones with your ankles chained.'

Back at attention, Compton said nothing.

'You have a major exercise, what? Tomorrow?'

'The day after,' Compton said. 'In front of the generals.'

Fitzpatrick sat and seemed to consider something other than what they were there for. His insults, his threats, had been half-hearted, the rhetoric of a man going through the motions. Whatever was on his mind, it didn't have much to do with a cut-up pimp or a hooker carrying a brand-new scar.

'Do it right, in front of the brass,' Fitzpatrick said eventually. 'Do it right. Forget about Paddington.'

'I have, sir,' Compton said. Which would soon enough become the truth.

It was raining when Johnny Compton left the colonel's tent. There was no wind, and the air tasted rank with diesel from a column of tanks and troop carriers churning mud and making slow progress leaving the maintenance yard where they assembled for a metalled road and another day of manoeuvres. Already there was the crack of small arms

223

fire from one of the ranges. The sound was shrill and sustained, the sound you got with high-velocity rounds. It was the snipers. The snipers were out there, concealed and patient on the range. Compton walked between the cook-houses and the neat rows of Nissen huts, the barrelled accommodation blocks glistening in the rain and that weird, greenish light you got off the sea when cloud and rain obscured the sun. Jeeps were firing up and a party of Negro soldiers were pitchforking hay from bales on the back of a truck to give tyres purchase on tracks churned to mud by their vehicles and the persistent English weather.

He still wanted a cigarette and a cup of strong coffee. He wanted to curl under a blanket and have warmth and comfort tender to his wounds. He wanted to understand just exactly why they had let him get away without appropriate punishment for what he'd done. But he'd go down to the shore, first, before addressing any of that. Some forgotten thing nagged at the mind of Johnny Compton. So he went down to the shore to try to remember, amid the relative seclusion of the tripwires and the tank traps and the beached Higgins boats, exactly what it was that had eluded him.

FIVE

Dartmouth, 1976

Alice Bourne travelled to Dartmouth early on the morning of her fourth full day in Devon. She spent the previous three making observations and notes, taking photographs and talking to residents, mostly elderly, who had been mature adults in December 1943 at the time of the enforced evacuations. She had arranged to do this in the weeks prior to her arrival by corresponding with two helpful parsons with a parish each in Strete and Chillington. She'd embarked on the plan expecting tortuous negotiations with various church bodies and diocese. That is what would have happened at home, she knew, before access to individual interviewees could even have been considered in principle, let alone organized. It was part of the fallout, the trickle-down, from Watergate. Even the most innocent Americans were paranoid about talking openly to strangers armed with tape machines and notebooks. In the country for which the term 'open society' had been coined, it was a sad irony.

In England it was very different. Both priests, or strictly speaking one priest and one vicar, were happy to put her

225

request informally to their flocks without referral to a higher counsel. More than half a dozen parishioners said they'd be happy to speak to the American historian. So Alice spent two afternoons consuming tea and biscuits and cake and listening. And trying not to think of the fort at Bembridge, of the weed manacles trailing from foundations thick with the promise of entombment and rot.

She didn't learn much of significance that she hadn't already known or guessed. But the sheer scale of the Slapton operation began to become clearer to her. The evacuees tended not to have been evacuated very far. Most took lodgings with friends or relatives within tantalizing closeness to their old, forbidden homes. They spoke of skies over the south Devon coast dark with American aircraft in massed formations. Windows would buzz and dogs howl in their kennels with the dense, vibrating volume of their engines.

'It used to set my teeth on edge,' one woman told Alice, who nodded and sipped from a china cup. 'Mind, I still had my own teeth then.'

Troop lorries and armoured convoys would block every road approaching the clandestine base in vast traffic snarls of strutted canvas and caterpillar tracks and shouting, purposeful men. Searchlights in powerful clusters carved silver beams above Start Bay in the dead of night. The boom of heavy guns from American battleships anchored off the coast would peal like persistent thunder as the white lightning of their muzzle flashes jittered through the sky.

Men were in and out all the time, every American combat soldier stationed in Britain seemingly schooled, in the months and weeks before Normandy, in what the Slapton operation had to teach them about their daunting, clandestine task.

'How the Germans didn't know they were there beggars belief,' a retired postmaster said to Alice. 'But they landed nearly half a million men in two days on the Normandy beaches. Can't do that sort of thing without practice. It's a bit like eggs, isn't it?'

Alice sipped her tea. 'Like eggs?'

'Can't make an omelette, dear. Not without breaking them.'

The vast acreage of land occupied for all this preparation should have made security a challenge, if not an impossibility, Alice thought. But one of her interviewees begged to differ.

A resident named Jane Cartwright went back to her cottage in Chillington to retrieve a keepsake forgotten in the original haste of the move. She didn't think the Americans would patrol a particular area of the perimeter where they had built a formidable fence. At least, it looked formidable. But part of its course ran parallel with a dried-up ditch where Mrs Cartwright sometimes took her dog to crap when she walked it. And her dog had discovered a collapsed foxhole in one bank of the ditch that now provided a shallow tunnel under the fence. The keepsake was a moonstone ring given to her by her husband at the conclusion of his most recent leave. They'd spent their final evening before his departure at a country fair. He'd won the ring shooting targets with an air rifle at a sharpshooting gallery there. Mrs Cartwright's husband was a soldier serving in Italy with the Royal Engineers. And one night she had a few drinks in a pub with two of her friends and, geed on by them, emboldened by alcohol, set off on her quest of sentimental retrieval.

'It was a huge place to attempt to patrol,' Mrs Cartwright said to Alice. 'I knew the terrain like the back of my hand. I knew the Americans were billeted in Nissen huts and had promised to stay out of our abandoned villages. I thought it would be a cakewalk, quite honestly. I'd have attempted it sober, I'm embarrassed to say.'

She was challenged about fifty yards in by a perimeter guard. He had a pistol, pointed at her, in one hand. The other held a torch, also pointed at her. 'He was about six feet four and had an accent from somewhere like Arkansas. He was extremely, and I mean extremely, pissed off.'

Alice must have looked shocked.

Mrs Cartwright smiled. 'I'm sorry, dear, but he was. I could hear approaching guard dogs, barking. Other sentry voices. So could he, thank God. Because he was very close in those moments to shooting me.'

Alice looked around. She was listening to this anecdote in a Chillington vicarage. She could smell beeswax polish lovingly applied to burred walnut and oak. There were freshly cut flowers in several vases around the room. These churchmen always had a direct route to devout house-keepers. A tall clock with a pendulum and weights visible through a glass panel ticked audibly on the wall. Glassware on occasional tables and window ledges threw dancing, sun-suffused shadows.

'They took me to a captain, who questioned me. Then they searched me, thoroughly, and took away my wrist-watch and my cigarette case and lighter and – oh yes – my shoelaces.'

Alice sipped her tea, which she could no longer taste.

'They locked me in a room with no furniture or light. It smelled so heavily of disinfectant that I thought the fumes might make me suffocate. It was there to get rid of the other smells. Urine, faeces, vomit, you know. Vomit in particular has a smell that's hard to conceal. Very acidic. It's the stomach enzymes, apparently.'

'How long did they leave you there?'

'Could have been twenty minutes. Could have been an hour or even two. I'd no way of knowing. Certainly it was long enough to sober up.'

'And then?'

'I was taken to a car containing a chief inspector from the Devon Constabulary. I don't think the chief inspector ever left the vehicle. I don't think the protocol allowed him to set foot on their base. His driver drove me in handcuffs to Totnes, where I was strip-searched and interrogated for several hours by a chap and a girl from Special Branch. The girl was very keen to know what languages I spoke. They gave me something that made me puke so hard the retching burst blood vessels in my eyes. They gave me a half-pint glass of black molasses and a bedpan. If I had been hiding anything in my body, they would have found it. They held me for forty-eight hours while they corroborated my story. So the irony was that the Americans retrieved my ring. And they very magnanimously saw to it that I got it back.'

Alice saw that Mrs Cartwright was fingering the ring now, on the third finger of her right hand. She was a neat woman, pertly figured, smartly dressed. Her hair was fine and frosted blue. Frosted probably, Alice thought, touched by the gesture, for this very encounter. Mrs Cartwright looked at her full in the face. 'I've never told anybody any of this before. I can assure you it's all quite true.'

'Were you indignant about your treatment? This was England, Mrs Cartwright.'

'Yes, it was, dear. And it still is.' She patted the embroidered wings of the chair she sat in. 'And that pretty much answers your question, doesn't it?'

Alice heard the ticktock of time slipping by on the vicarage wall.

> *Stands the church clock at ten to three?*
> *And is there honey still for tea?*

Wrong war, she thought confusedly. That was David Lucas, all that marmoreal, doomed youth and poppy field stuff. She hoped with all her heart for David's safety, then, amid watery hazard, under his fort. Her own, poor brother had been doomed. His loss in youth had inspired no ardent verses, though. What was wrong with her? She'd drunk too much of what the Apache always called Rosie Lee. Or it was it just too much sun?

'There's one more thing,' Mrs Cartwright said brightly. And Alice knew that everything so far had been the mere preamble to this.

'You had further dealings with them?'

'Not intentionally.'

'Go on,' Alice said. 'Please.'

'It was one morning in the cottage hospital at Kingsbridge. I was doing all that dig for victory stuff and had got a septic finger for my pains. While I was waiting to be treated, two Americans came into the vestibule of the building, demanding to see a doctor. There was no doctor present, and they got the duty nurse. They screamed at her for blood plasma. And I do mean screamed. There wasn't any, I think. It was only a cottage hospital. Their stocks pretty much ran to milk powder for new mothers who found they couldn't breast-feed. Emergency blankets for the parish poor in very cold spells. They cleaned cuts and applied dressings to abrasions and burns.'

'Did the soldiers say anything about burns?'

Mrs Cartwright paused, as if trying to remember. Alice thought she remembered perfectly well. 'No. They didn't say anything about anything. They were rushing greatly and they were deeply distressed. They left with boxes of lint and bandages. Ampoules of morphine. A big bottle of ether. And a case filled with bottles of TCP. No blood plasma, I remember that.'

'When was this?'

'I'm pretty sure it was April of 1944.'

Pretty sure.

'Date?'

'I think around the twenty-ninth.'

Alice nodded. Birds were singing in the vicarage garden. It was a gorgeous afternoon. Weren't they all, in England just now?

'There was some catastrophe, wasn't there?' Mrs Cartwright said.

'I think so,' Alice said. 'Yes, I think there was.'

Mrs Cartwright nodded. In sunlight, you could see her scalp through her hair, see where the dye had congealed and gathered at the withering roots. This summer, Alice thought. It's relentless and entirely without remorse.

Alice took photographs of the beach at Slapton from various elevations. She was using a black and white film originated by Agfa for medical photography. Ordinarily it wouldn't have been any good for landscape work in England. There wouldn't have been sufficient ambient light. But it would work perfectly in this weather, she was told. The specific qualities of the film were subtle graduations of contour and astonishing detail over a considerable depth of field. She had borrowed the Leica camera and the lenses from the university photography club, and its secretary had advised her to buy the Agfa stock, after asking what she wanted the camera for. She made sketches and she wrote notes. She was gathering impressions, really. Her visit to Slapton Sands had never been about uncovering conclusive evidence. That lay, if anywhere, in a confidential report gathering dust in a file probably in Washington. She was here because the something covered up had happened here. She was neither a psychic nor a cop. She was a historian. She was here for the simple reason that however barren it proved in providing her with finished material, this place, this location, was her primary source.

On her third day she called Professor Champion, using the telephone to do so in the cottage. Her landlady had still not returned, and in Alice's mind she was by now assuming the status of rumour or myth. Champion had requested she call him once a week in his capacity as her course supervisor. He'd said to reverse the charges, which she did. He was still on campus, guest lecturing at the lucrative summer school they ran. Alice made the call at five-fifteen, still within campus office hours. The college switchboard must have closed for the long vacation, though. It didn't respond. Alice eventually reached the professor directly on his office number.

'The police are looking for you.'

Well, she thought. That's the niceties dispensed with. 'They found me. I spoke to your former protégé.'

'You did what?'

'Sally Emerson. The maths teacher in waiting. I spoke to her two days ago.'

She heard his desk lighter click and hiss. There was a pause while he breathed in smoke and breathed it out again. 'I'm not talking about the Kent Constabulary. This chap was based in Lambeth. In Kennington.'

Alice was pretty sure that David had parked the Apache's car legally. Of course, the Apache, spiritual heir to the Lizard King, was not the type to worry about things like those tax discs they displayed on windscreens in England. But there was nothing to connect the car to her. They'd had a later brush with the law. But nothing of consequence. And not in Kennington.

'You used your student card to validate access to some microfiche files in the Imperial War Museum.'

'I did. They were a waste of time.'

'After your departure it was noticed that a photograph had been removed from the wall of one of the galleries.'

'I don't have it,' Alice said. But she knew which one it was.

'Give them a call,' Champion said. 'As a courtesy. Put suspicious minds at rest.' He gave her the number and the name of a policeman who worked the day shift on the front desk. She didn't even bother to copy the number down. 'How are things otherwise?'

'Curiouser and curiouser, professor,' she said.

But her words did not reflect her feelings. The pun was

anything but funny. Alice had the sense that she was being driven towards a discovery she was being deliberately and systematically scared away from making. She didn't know which was more alarming. The malign spirit of Johnny Compton had almost disabled her with fear, on those occasions in which it had manifested itself. But she had the strong intimation that each lead she uncovered led her along a predetermined path. And that was just as unnerving. It called into question whether she acted out of free will. It made her feel like a child following planted clues in the pages of a story hurtling towards its dreadful conclusion.

Alice figured that two catastrophes, not one, had claimed the lives of the soldiers killed in such appalling numbers at Slapton Sands. Both, she concluded, had taken place in April 1944, just a few weeks before the date set for D-day. She strongly believed that the second tragedy had taken place not so much despite the first but in some perverse way because of it. And the second event was the one the US army were determined to keep a secret.

Something had happened at sea. American bodies had washed up, for weeks, all along a large stretch of coastline. But whatever her Colorado vet had almost been a party to had happened not at sea but on the beach. It was smooth, he had said, free of shell holes, of corpses, of the chaotic litter of battle. But talking to him had left Alice convinced that something had happened. Craters and corpses could be bulldozed into sand. Some industrious subterfuge had taken place that April night, something her vet had been prevented at gunpoint from witnessing. What price a mass grave full of young Americans under the sand at Slapton? Listen to your hunches, her dad had told Alice. She was increasingly sure that some awful event had taken place on the beach.

There was always the possibility that the first incident could be independently corroborated, proven, even, with evidence the American military establishment would be unable to refute. So they would continue to deny that anything went wrong. And then, if given no alternative by incontrovertible proof, they would admit to the first of these covered-up, costly events. But they would never admit to the second. They would insist that a single, regrettable incident had claimed all the casualties.

If what she suspected about the first incident were true, there would have been no need of blood plasma and morphine supplies. But then, if what she believed about the first incident were true, how in God's name had the second tragedy been allowed to occur? And what part had Johnny Compton played in it that so shamed his ghost now? Jesus, the man had mutilated a prostitute. He'd been a scumbag in life, so what could he conceivably want to scare her away from finding out about that sordid life in death?

Compton's role had to concern the second incident, Alice believed. He was an infantry officer. His only possible part in the first Slapton tragedy would be as victim. Or witness. That was her supposition, anyway. Tomorrow, she hoped to establish at least that much as fact.

Now, though, she was unnerved by the disappearance of the picture from the Imperial War Museum. She wished there was someone she could sit down and talk to. She needed the simple assurance of good and trusted company. It would be so comforting to walk down to the pub at the far end of Slapton Sands from the cottage and meet Rachel Vine there, puffing on a Players Navy Cut, scowling at the volume of the jukebox, sipping a gin and tonic at a corner table. Or Mrs Cartwright. Mrs Cartwright would do, blue-rinsed Jane Cartwright, composure unruffled by the scrutiny of the Special Branch, happy to talk about church fêtes and gardening prizes and the purgative power of black molasses. Except that Jane Cartwright's pub excursions had very probably ended in 1945, with the return from the war of her husband.

Who else was there? Who else would she be happy to share a drink with in the pub? Clifford Lee was an interesting guy. Metric Larry had called Clifford a Hardy man. She enjoyed Thomas Hardy herself. They could discuss English literature over a pint, the way students were traditionally supposed to do. According to Metric Larry, he liked her. She'd like to buy him a drink, get to know him better, thank him for saving David's life. As if he'd have done anything different than go into the water. As though she had any right to the presumption.

Who else? Who was she kidding? There was nobody else. She had liked Sally Emerson. The woman was a compelling mix of physical allure and blade-keen intelligence. But she would always associate Emerson with the disturbed, disturbing circumstances that had led her to meet the woman in the first place. Professor Champion? Champion was clever, but he considered a failure any social encounter with a woman that didn't end with you lying underneath him nailed naked to a bed.

Which, of course, left David Lucas.

From the age of eight, Alice had never shared a classroom with the children of parents who weren't rich. Her isolation had made her independent, given her an objectivity beyond her years. Insular, disdainful, arrogant, remote: those had been the words used to describe her by her school contemporaries, and Alice had been happy to consider each a sort of accolade. Her attitude got her through. She was self-contained. She valued self-possession. When what her father drove or where her family vacationed provoked cruel adolescent mirth among her schoolmates, Alice genuinely didn't care. You had to respect someone's opinion before it had the power to hurt your feelings. If you didn't depend on other people, they couldn't let you down. It was her and her dad and her brother, not against the world exactly, but sort of, in a way that had suited her very well.

Except that now it was only her. And unnerved by Johnny Compton's thieving ghost, she craved company as she never had in her life. And the company she particularly craved was that of David Lucas. He'd be under the fort at Bembridge now, groping through kelp and gloom in a wetsuit, dragging breaths from a cylinder strapped to his back, a belt full of lead countering his body's buoyancy, keeping him close to the bottom.

'Be wary, David,' Alice said. 'Be wary of the sharks.' She could not believe how much she missed and feared for him then. 'Be safe, David,' she said, comforted for a moment just by the small intimacy of saying his name out loud.

She took a long breath and looked at her watch. It was seven o'clock. It was evening, though you'd barely guess it from the quality of light. They hadn't yet got to the English longest day. Alice intended to go to a town for that particular event. She'd drink scrumpy in a beer garden and try to avoid wisecracking about John Barleycorn and the green man and the inevitable troupe of fucking morris men. Assuming, of course, that she could find the companions to avoid wisecracking about these things with.

She had retreated to her room after the phone conversation with Champion. One of the necessary disciplines of her isolation was the rationing of fear. She had known the thing that now had a name, the Johnny Compton thing, would follow her here. So she had imposed certain disciplines on her thinking to deal with that contingency. Except that contingency was the wrong word. Because Johnny Compton's pursuit of her was a creeping inevitability. She was being haunted, properly haunted, by an unquiet, angry ghost. She could sense it now, in her cottage room under the eaves, as the cosy room grew thick with the forbidding odour of the sea. As the air grew heavy and portentous, dread settled on her and made her shiver and clutch at herself, bizarrely, watching heat ripple on the oozing, glossy asphalt melting in brilliant puddles on the coast road outside her window. She felt the thick breath of him, the tar from his tobacco-heavy lungs. He lived in her, revolting, dead.

'Bitch,' he said.

She felt the coarse texture of his tongue, licking her ear. Light had bled and perished from the room. She was enfeebled by darkness, trapped and reeling under the salt ooze of decay, corruption.

'Go home, bitch.'

And it was gone.

When she was able to, she walked out of the cottage and across the coast road and sat on a hillock of razor grass and cried. She cried with terror and eventually with relief. She stopped crying only because shock had exhausted her beyond the point where she could continue. When you were unpractised at crying, it seemed to require a sapping energy. Alice sat on her hillock of razor grass and rubbed rawness and salt from her eyes. No one had passed her. Nobody had come along the road. She ran finger and thumb down a ragged edge of grass. Blood bloomed from her thumb. The blood pulsed out of her in droplets and dripped with the accelerated thump of her heart. She looked back to the cottage. It seemed out of shape, contorted and leering like a carnival funhouse. But it was just a cottage, she knew. It was just a cottage on a quiet and picturesque part of the English coast. There were pretty seashells picked from the shore on its window ledges. There were sentimental Victorian prints to do with boats and harbours on its walls. A guest book by the door was filled with happy testimonials. It was only a bed-and-breakfast cottage. And a ghost lurked there, corrupted and rancorous.

'I'm going nowhere until I've nailed you,' Alice said. But she said it to herself. Because it was not an announcement. Nor did she mean it as defiant rhetoric. She felt the threat would be heard and understood without it needing to be voiced. Grief had taught Alice Bourne a forlorn economy when it came to the shedding of tears. She didn't easily let them go. She was angry now, at having been frightened into crying. In life, Johnny Compton had evidently hated women. In death, Alice now determined she would be one he would be made to fear. He would hear words, would Johnny Compton. He would sense the determination in her threat.

He had already. It was why he was here.

That night, for what was to be the last time, Alice dreamed the cormorant dream. She was aboard the same uneasy, flimsy-bottomed shudder of a boat. Its course was the same bewildering slough through peaks and troughs of emerald sea. She felt the familiar lurch of panic as it lost sight of shore. And the great bird seemed more prehistoric than ever, fish scales oozing through reptile talons as it settled on the gunwale and it fixed her with its glare. The bird shifted, but did not take flight when she began to climb

241

up the side of the hull. She gripped the gunwale next to where the cormorant perched and gained purchase with the toes of her boots on the tails of the unfinished bolt screws that held the hull plates together. She slipped feet first into the water, aware of the height of the swell and the cold shock of it as the Higgins boat swayed from her reach and the instant weight of water in her clothing and boots and ammunition belt and pack dragged her under. Salt burned her nose in the water, filling her throat and lungs. She opened her eyes and saw a trail of small bubbles rise towards the opaque light receding above her. She didn't know if they were from her body or her clothing. She sank, steadily, and the receding light diminished into dark. She remembered no last thoughts when she awoke. Just an absence, growing colder and colder in her, with diminishing light.

Her father had told her that most men were creatures of habit. The worst of them became criminals. Most of the criminals were caught and convicted eventually for their crimes. They were given long, harsh sentences in maximum-security prisons. On occasions, some of them managed to escape. And it didn't matter how brutal or desperate the means of escape, or how long and desperately they ran to evade recapture. Men were creatures of habit, and eventually they went home. Wait long enough, her dad told her, and you'll find them there. You'll discover them sleeping in their own bed or reclining on their own porch.

The staying away hurts them more than the thought of recapture. They return to their loved ones and the routine they knew. To the smells and sanctity of home. It's what they escaped to find again. It's the thing they missed. It's the great and enduring paradox of the absconded criminal. They spend years plotting escapes of breathtaking ingenuity, only to go back in the rare event they succeed to the one place they know we're guaranteed to go looking for them.

Dartmouth was a welcome contrast to the emptiness of Start Bay. The harbour itself was an open rectangle of old stone, a drop of twenty feet to the crowds and clusters of boats berthed in mud and silt below, with the tide out. The stones from which the harbour walls were constructed were big, dank things plugged by the rings of mooring chains and pitted where others had broken free in violent weather. Sea moss hung from the stone in dripping green beards. Under the strengthening sun, the harbour smelled of mussels and seaweed and oozes in the mud of escaping outboard and engine fuel. To the rear of the harbour, shops and hotels formed a handsome, higgledy-piggledy terrace Alice thought was probably mostly Georgian. There were tourists in Dartmouth, absent in their droves from Slapton Sands. They were English tourists. Or more accurately they were British. Leaning against the painted iron rail around the harbour, Alice heard voices from Scotland and Wales and the harsh accent of Ulster. It was an odd accent to hear in play, hearing it as she had, always venting hatred and indignation on the English television and radio news.

They were not affluent tourists, these. Their shoes and their clothes were cheap, and there were lots of elderly people and family groups. A number of the older tourists limped, the legacy of childhood rickets or polio epidemics. The visitors here reminded her a bit of her summer vacations with Bobby and her dad to Atlantic City. The same cheap sandals and sunglasses. The same awkward sunburns from the beach. The same air of privileged anticipation. Christ, he'd been a good father, her dad. He'd been the best. The best. How the missing of him burned in her still.

She heard passing cricket commentaries on little transistor radios clutched to the ears of liver-spotted men. Some of the youths carried huge cassette players on shoulder straps. In the Georgian huddle of Dartmouth, her ears were assaulted by Queen and Rod Stewart and the Quo. They were the aural equivalent of tribal banners, these cassette players, she thought. It was a conclusion reached when a boy in a wedge cut limped by under his colossal burden of tape player and the batteries needed to power the thing into life, playing the new Bowie single, 'Golden Years'.

Rory Carnegie was easy to find. He was one of her father's creatures of habit. But he was not an escaped felon. He had no requirement here of a disguise. And he looked much the way Rachel Vine had described him. He wore a tam-o'shanter, as he always did, to protect his bald head from the sun. A thick, full moustache covered his top lip. He'd been something in rugby called a prop forward in his youth, and his nose had been flattened, compressed. It looked like a boxer's nose to Alice, and gave Rory Carnegie's face a pugnacious cast. He sat on a bench at the side of the harbour with a sea rod extending over the top rail from between his feet. He showed the interest in the rod a spear-carrying extra might in his weapon on a movie set in a lull between scenes. The clincher was the tattoos visible on his crossed arms. The ink had faded over time, but they were high-class work and deeply and confidently etched. Alice could see the coil of a mermaid's tail, make out the scales and tailfin shape on the left arm, the one nearest her. He turned his head and looked at her. His eyes were very blue, very pale in the ruddy tan of his face.

'I'd guess you're not looking for the time, lass,' Rory Carnegie said. His voice sounded as though its owner had never departed Aberdeen. Men are creatures of habit, Alice reminded herself. He never would have left Aberdeen if he hadn't been exiled by the other trawlermen. He'd fetched up here before the outbreak of war, after a false start in Penzance. And here he'd stayed.

'Have you caught anything?'

'What do you think.'

'I don't think you're trying.'

'They're not biting. You're nibbling, though. Why?'

'I want to know what happened at Slapton Sands.'

Carnegie didn't blink. The nerve that had allowed him to net fish in forbidden waters in wartime had neither diminished nor deserted him. There was a large watch on a metal bracelet on his wrist. It was a Rolex, like the watch David had been sent by his father. Only this one had seen a lot less wear. Time had been kind to Rory Carnegie.

'You should play poker,' Alice said. 'You'd have a lot more success than you do with that rod.'

He looked around. He had the bench to himself. Nobody was particularly near them. No one was paying them undue attention. He's acting like a spy in a movie, Alice thought.

'How did you find me?'

'Rachel Vine.'

Carnegie let out a long breath between clenched teeth. He looked at Alice again. His eyes were an astonishing colour, almost turquoise, like the Iroquois jewellery Joni Mitchell and the like wore when their brief bouts of social conscience forced the real, Tiffany's stuff from off their wrists, from around their gilded throats.

'You know,' Carnegie said, 'you look a little bit like that singer.' He unfolded his arms and lifted a hand, flicking the fingers close to his cheek, thoughtful.

'You remember Rachel Vine?'

'Not so bonnie as you are,' Carnegie said, still in apparent thought. 'Though I doubt a more seductive creature ever drew breath.'

'Can we talk?'

He stood. He was burly, but fat hung nowhere on him. He extended his hand. 'Rory Carnegie.'

Alice shook hands with him. His palm felt like heavy wood roughed with sandpaper. 'Alice Bourne.'

'We'll go somewhere quiet. My house is in walking distance, or there's a hotel with secluded space in its lobby, if you'd prefer. I've been waiting for this encounter for thirty-two years. Though I have to say I'd have bet on its being with a man.'

Alice allowed him to lead her to his house. He was a primary source, after all. She could not gain and might well lose from insisting on neutral ground. It wasn't why she was here, to be timid and cautious. She knew from shaking hands with him that his fingers, strong enough still to crush bone, had only dabbed at the formality of gripping hers in introduction. Rachel Vine had described Carnegie to her as a remorseful man, a man who had learned his lesson in the careless fishing tragedy for which he'd been responsible, before the war, off the Scottish coast. And she trusted Rachel's judgement. There was no warmth, admittedly, in Carnegie's eyes, but she was looking for truth, not consolation.

'How is Rachel?'

Carnegie's house was not what she'd expected. Alice had half-anticipated some nautical mausoleum, a place full of brass and mahogany Jack Tar souvenirs. She'd expected the

Scotsman's home to look a bit like the interior of the Neptune pub. But it didn't. It was devoid of clutter, empty of artefacts. There was nothing here to suggest a shipborne past. Nothing, except the man. The walls were stripped and painted and the furniture low-slung, Scandinavian. He had a reel-to-reel tape machine and floor-standing Wharfdale loudspeakers. The texture and tonality of the room were tasteful and entirely masculine. There was no woman sharing Carnegie's life. A turned wooden bowl of fruit on a tabletop was his sole concession to softness. But the plums and apples and grapes in the bowl were polished spheres remote from bruising or rot.

'The rod is a prop,' he said to her, returning from the kitchen with drinks. 'As you rightly surmised. Cheers.'

'Cheers.'

The room was cool and shaded. It gave no indication of the tormenting heat outside, the wincing brightness. It might even have been air-conditioned, though there was no hum. Rory Carnegie had not yet sat. He coughed. 'This is harder than I thought,' he said. He seemed to waver, then, physically, between two directions, and Alice feared he was about to change his mind, keep his long-claimed secret, show her the door with the ice still clinking in her untouched glass on its coaster on the table. Instead, he dropped to his haunches and opened a drawer in the table and took out a rack of pipes. He began to fill a pipe from a tobacco pouch taken from the drawer.

'The rod is so I won't be taken for a child pervert. It gives me an excuse to sit and ponder with a blameless view of the harbour. And of the sea.'

His pipes all had those twin metal stems that were supposed to cool the tobacco and at the same time channel spit away from the mouthpiece and bowl. Alice was always seeing advertisements for them in the Sunday supplements. They were a clue to his character, like the Grundig reel-to-reel and the Rotel amplifier on the shelf underneath it. Like the Rolex on his wrist and the radio sets he'd had his ocean-going boats fitted with all those years ago out of apparent remorse after some salty tragedy in the waters off the Scottish coast. He was a man attracted by precision. If he'd been at all interested in sea angling, he'd have had a better rod to fish with. A more complicated reel. He'd have had a bait box full of cunning lures and binoculars and all sorts of other shit. Sonar, probably. Sonar for the sharks.

'You're gay, aren't you, Mr Carnegie?'

He was puffing on his over-engineered pipe. Her dad had been an occasional pipe smoker. Carnegie's pipe didn't look like it delivered very much of what the Sunday adverts promised.

'That was why you left Aberdeen. You were indiscreet there. There was some scandal or something. You were ostracized, and you brought your boats south.'

'I wasn't ostracized, girl. I was driven out.'

'You bought those radio sets off the guy in Liverpool because you like high-end stuff. You think it's neat.'

'Neat?'

'You get a buzz out of technology. When it works.'

'Oh it worked all right. It worked too bloody well,' Carnegie said. 'And that makes me queer?'

'No wife. No kids. Being queer gives you the time and money to indulge your interest.'

'You're very perceptive.'

'My dad was a cop.'

'Nevertheless. You're very perceptive.'

She felt sorry for him. It had been better for Rory Carnegie, more acceptable, for deadly negligence rather than sexual inclination to have driven him from his home to seek work elsewhere. And so he'd invented the lie Rachel Vine still propagated. Even now, presumably because he was a single, childless man, he had needed to invent a hapless excuse just to sit and enjoy a vista of the sea. Worse, this pantomime was obliged to be acted out in a town the man had called home for better than thirty years.

'It's why I prefer the term "queer" to "gay",' Carnegie said. 'Yes, Alice Bourne, I can read some of your thoughts.' She nodded.

Puffing at his pipe, he sat down. Whatever barrier had existed had been broken between them now. He coughed again, to clear his throat. 'We should talk about Slapton Sands. More accurately, we should talk about an incident that occurred on the way to Slapton Sands. Have you heard of Operation Tiger?'

Alice shook her head. Her heart was beating with a hard insistence. This was the moment at which truth was delivered into history. She was witnessing history's birth. Better, she was herself delivering it.

Carnegie spoke for about forty-five minutes. He looked tired when he stopped, emptied out, sitting with his hands redundant between his knees on his sofa, his backside perched on its panels of bachelor hide. Real hide, Carnegie's, Alice thought to herself. No call for the fake stuff there, in his otherwise fraudulent life. The sea had been good to him, and he was a man who had spent with fastidious greed the profits of its benefice. Perhaps he was grateful it hadn't killed him as well over the course of its many capricious opportunities. For whatever reason, he payed homage to it daily, there on his harbour bench, with his ornamental fishing rod between his legs.

'What will you do with this information?'

'I think there's more,' Alice said. 'I think this is only the half of it.'

'It was enough for me,' Carnegie said.

'I should go.'

'Aye.'

'Thank you.'

A grunt from the sofa. Alice stood. It felt like a midnight full of stormy imposition. It was two-fifteen in the afternoon. Standing, she said: 'Your fruit looks very fine in that bowl, Mr Carnegie.' She nodded towards it. 'It must be very fresh.'

'It'll always look fine,' Carnegie said, rising. 'And it will never be fresh. My fruit's made of wax. Here, I'll see you to the door.'

His house was on the corner of a terrace on one side of a narrow street. It was more of an alley, really, and when he opened his front door the sun reflected with full force off the whitewashed wall of the building opposite. The light was dazzling, vertiginous, and Alice felt momentarily snow-blind. She recovered and looked at Carnegie. It affected him less. He'd spent much of his working life staring at stretches of ocean, waiting for the telltale stippling on the surface of a populous shoal beneath. He still watched the sea every day. His eyes must long have learned to accommodate all manner and density of light.

With her hand shading her eyes, Alice said: 'You called Rachel Vine the most seductive creature you've ever encountered. Did you fall for her charms?'

Carnegie smiled. 'That's a delicate way for the daughter of a cop to put it. But you've no right to ask the question.'

'I'm sorry,' Alice said. She turned to go.

'The answer is that we did sleep together, Miss Bourne.' Alice turned back to look at him. 'Rachel was having an affair with a colonel based at Slapton Sands. He was killed on Omaha Beach. She took it hard. I tried to comfort her. We ended up in bed, as people tended to then.'

Alice nodded.

'They were peculiar times. War is—' he hesitated. 'Well,' he smiled. She could not see his eyes in the black shadow cast across his face by the light. 'War is war, isn't it?'

Alice Bourne nodded and made to leave. What she heard next, she heard with her back to the exiled fisherman.

'They'd have gone anyway, you know. Didn't matter how many of them died in the preparation. That was the point of the preparation, to get the execution right. That was the reason for all those live-fire exercises. They expected seventy per cent casualties when they got there, Miss Bourne.'

She turned around. She didn't know what had made him so loquacious, now, at their parting.

'Nothing was going to stop them, Miss Bourne,' Carnegie said. 'And if you read your history books, you'll know that nothing did.'

She'd been delivered to Dartmouth by the Fly. The ride had been good-enough value. But he'd averaged speeds of around eighty on roads where SLOW was cautioned in white paint in high letters every few hundred yards. And the volume at which he played his music had left her tolerance for Status Quo, never high, at breaking point. She'd catch a bus that followed the coast on a route south and stop in Strete. She was in no particular hurry to get back, flat now with the feeling of anticlimax where anticipation and the thrill of possibility had been before.

Rory Carnegie was not a Status Quo man. She had looked at the row of reel-to-reel tape boxes on his shelves, filed alphabetically, their titles and artists' details hand-lettered in tiny script on their spines. He listened to Elgar and Vaughan Williams and Britten. There was some Gershwin, some Aaron Copland. He had tapes of Scottish reels and English and Celtic sea shanties. But nothing so vulgar as popular music. She thought he was probably the most fastidious man she had ever met. He had thrived on the subterfuge of war, but its chaos and waste had appalled him. He'd been dishonest and dishonourable, strictly speaking, in his dogged pursuit of profit from the prevailing circumstances. But he had not done anything Alice could sincerely think of as bad. In the truest sense, he was an honest man. She believed absolutely his account of Operation Tiger, its catalogue of errors and its tragic and avoidable cost. She believed he'd heard what he'd heard and seen what he'd seen. There was no question that they were sights and sounds that lived with the man still. Rachel Vine hadn't been the only one of them in need of the warmth and forgetful pleasure of the one night he admitted they'd shared a bed. There'd probably been more than the one tryst. But contingent, fatally compromised, their affair had died of apathy, leaving only a begrudging fondness that had lingered down the years in each of their separate memories. Alice was good on other people's affairs, she thought, shrewd and intuitive. She considered it the gift given in compensation for being so completely useless at dealing with any romance of her own.

She pondered on her audience with Carnegie, on the sweltering bus ride returning her to Strete. The upright part of her seat was covered in some sort of textured plastic and sweat stuck to it from her back through the white-cotton shirt she had chosen to wear for the encounter. The bus jounced on old springs, and the smell of smouldering fields was dense in the air. It was a single-decker. She always travelled on the top deck on double-decker buses, partially for the novelty, mostly to see what she could of England in the limited time she had in the country. The upper decks always stank of stale and more recent cigarette smoke, and their floors were always littered with cigarette ends. And smokers always closed all the windows, as if affronted by the hazard of an encounter with fresh air. But you saw more. On the single-decker to Strete, she saw mostly hedgerows, whatever burned, burning behind their dense and thorny veils.

It struck her as very British, this attitude towards the fire threatening to devour the whole of rural southern England. Either it was discretion or it was stoicism. Either way, it was very different from the way in which they behaved towards similar emergencies at home. There were nightly bulletins about the threatened conflagration on the TV news, excitable presenters standing in the foreground of some smouldering cornfield or wood, bellowing on about it into their microphones. Concern had reached critical levels, at least in the media. But absolutely nothing had been done. There was no provision to fight the fires because, as they said on the news, there was no precedent: 'The last time we had a comparable dry spell, five hundred years ago, we don't know what they did.' The reservoirs were dry. There was no evacuation, no cordoning off, no pre-emptive burning to create firebreaks. Maybe this is what they were like in the war, she thought. Maybe this is what we got so antsy and pissed off about. We'd shipped three million men to Britain and Northern Ireland to prepare for the invasion of Europe, and the domestic population were bumbling along like characters in a Will Hay movie with the view that everything would turn out all right in the end.

On the night she had been subjected to his Lou Reed records, Alice had also been treated, by the Apache, to his Jim Morrison conspiracy theory. The CIA had assassinated Morrison in his bath.

'Nothing to do with morbid obesity and his colossal intake of drugs, then?'

'Coincidence.'

He'd started on about the Salem witch trials. Hadn't gone nearly far enough with their burnings and hangings, according to the Apache. The witch covens of America were still obviously very productive.

Alice asked him why it was that if the Americans were such wankers, all the English rock stars sang in American accents. His stoned expression had given way to a fit of paranoid blinking. Then he'd looked smug. 'Bowie doesn't,' he said.

'Most of them do.'

'Marc Bolan sings in English.'

'The Moody Blues sound American.'

'They're wankers.'

'Rod Stewart?'

'A wanker.'

'Elton John?'

Silence. Elton didn't even merit a retort.

'Mick Jagger,' Alice said. ' "Love in Vain".'

'She's got a point, Ollie,' David said. 'You honestly calling Mick a wanker?'

The Apache had blinked for what had seemed like several minutes. Then he said: 'You really want to know what happened here in the war, Alice? Don't bother with your trip to the seaside. Watch an episode of *Dad's Army*.'

So she had. And she had seen straight away that the humour in the show was based on human nature and therefore in truth. But *Dad's Army* were not the commandos trained in Scotland on Lord Lovat's estate for missions that were always murderous, if they weren't suicidal. *Dad's Army* weren't the British paratroopers sent into Arnhem aboard balsawood gliders, believing they could win against impossible odds.

The English let their country burn when heat and drought combined to prostrate the arid land. Their rock stars strutted the globe wearing borrowed voices. Their cities were baleful places in the grip of strikes and Irish Republican terrorist threats. There was talk of power cuts. People still moaned about the referendum two years earlier that had dumped them into Europe at the expense of their beloved Commonwealth. She'd eavesdropped on Kentish bus conversations in which older people talked about a segregationist called Enoch Powell as though invoking the name of a prophet. The Apache boasted about landing an egg on the lapel of Powell's suit as students lobbied, shouting 'Fascist', in a bid to stop the man from being publicly heard, outside an open meeting in Ramsgate.

Thirty-six years ago, by the autumn of 1940, the British had lost the war. Mainland Europe had fallen, and so had Scandinavia. The British army had been routed in France. The Germans occupied Jersey and Guernsey and London was defencelessly battered by day and night bombing raids. U-boats ruled the Atlantic. There was no fuel for the coming winter. What poor food there was was running out. Lack of fuel meant that the diminishing ration supplies were mostly eaten raw. By any sane assessment, Britain had been defeated. But it never seemed to have occurred to the British people that when you'd lost, you surrendered. As her bus ground and shuddered towards Strete, Alice knew that England was a country far beyond her capacity for understanding.

Her cosy attic room was rank with smoke. The windows had been closed and the curtains drawn. The room was still and goose-flesh cold. She crossed her arms, and her fingers bumped along raised flesh, like Braille. A pile of his smoked-down Luckies occupied an open oyster shell, previously pretty with mother-of-pearl, she'd salvaged from the beach. Something had been written on the dressing table mirror. She had applied lipstick that morning after brushing her hair, wanting to look respectable, not student-like, in the event that she found Rory Carnegie. The words had been written in the lipstick, which she had left out in haste on the dressing table. The lipstick had been Chanel Red. Now the mirror wore it, all of it, in an angry smear. The cylinder sat upright with its contents sheared off, bright as a bullet casing. There would be fingerprints on the lipstick cylinder. They would belong to Johnny Compton, a dead American who had cut a prostitute in Paddington in 1944.

The dead odour of the sea was there, of course. But the cormorant dream had made her so inured to the smell that it no longer shocked or sickened her. What did was the thin, vindictive meanness of him. His malevolence lingered, as acrid and chilly as the smoke in the room. Absurdly, Peter Cushing came into her mind, the Hammer horror actor rumoured to live in Whitstable, the film star she'd never seen there. In her mind, Cushing was attired in the reassuring tweeds that signalled a Hammer gent. He was carrying a doctor's bag and telling a pale, soon-to-be vampire that the dead could rest only if they possessed a soul. Hammer theology. She couldn't put a name to the film containing the scene she'd recalled. But she could almost smile at that phrase, Hammer theology.

Johnny Compton didn't possess a soul. She shuddered. The cold and the dread were almost overwhelming. Her panic was what someone might feel waist-deep in quicksand, far out on a baleful shore, aware of an incoming tide.

Be brave, she told herself. Be brave like Bobby, her dead brother.

Be brave. Like her dad, killed by a carefully sited bullet, the barrel of his own pistol pressed against his head.

Opening the curtains meant walking to the window, which meant passing the dressing table mirror and the message she had not yet dared to read. Downstairs, she heard the front door slam emphatically shut. But that was her imagination. Come on, girl, she said to herself. Come on.

Every spool of film had been destroyed. She had shot five rolls in total. Four left on the dressing table had been stripped and exposed to the light. The fifth, three or four frames short of fully used, had been taken from the camera too. The ruined rolls had been strung across her bed. The camera, though, was intact. It sat innocent on the bedside table, where she had left it.

She saw something else in the room, then.

Rory Carnegie had put a cocktail stick with a sliver of skewered lemon in her glass when he had delivered her a drink. She had eaten the lemon, blunted and frayed the point of the stick, nervously chewing on it.

Now she saw the same type of stick, half-chewed, in the water glass on the table by her bed. It skewered a maggot, dead but lately swollen in its development, blue with the press against pupa of urgent legs.

Alice gave in. She ran down the stairs and vomited hard into the lavatory. She puked and heaved, saliva spooling into the glossy green reaches of the toilet bowl. For a while she just gripped the bowl and groaned. She ran a thumb across her forehead as if to rill beads of nauseous sweat. But there were none. When she stopped retching, she hauled herself up and looked at her face in the mirror above the sink. One of her eyes had become bloodshot.

With her breath still barely under control, she found the note left by her absentee landlady before the woman's helter-skelter flight to some apparent London emergency involving her student daughter. Alice picked up the nail-polish-coloured receiver and rang the number left on the note.

'Hello?'

On the second ring. 'Mrs Chantry?'

Nothing.

'It's Alice Bourne.'

Nothing.

'Why do I think you've been expecting this call?'

'You shouldn't stay there, Miss Bourne.' Stolid, middle-aged, Mrs Chantry's was the already familiar voice of the rural English west.

'Is that why you aren't staying here?'

A silence. 'I've arranged for a service. But the priest has to come all the way from Chichester. There's a presence.'

Alice didn't say anything.

'I'm sensitive.'

So am I, Alice thought, her mouth still sour with puke. She swallowed. 'A service?'

'An exorcism.'

'When did you first notice this presence?'

'The day you confirmed your booking.'

'And you just ran away?'

Silence. Not quite silence: Alice could hear her landlady's breathing. 'It isn't to do with me, is it, Miss Bourne?'

It was warm down here, and bright. The hall carpet had a jaunty, abstract pattern of yellow geometric shapes on blue. Pale wallpaper had been precisely hung. There was a round, stained-glass window set at head height in the wooden front door. St Peter, Christ's fisher of men, was depicted in a halo aboard a boat, hauling in a plump net. Everything was normal, if you ignored the conversation she was having and the clammy legacy of the thing that had been upstairs.

'Mrs Chantry? When will you come home?'

'When it is home, dear. After the priest has come from Chichester and gone again.'

There was a pause, as though the woman intended to say something else. But she replaced her daughter's telephone receiver and Alice got instead the burr of an English dialling tone. She walked back upstairs. The second flight was hard and opening the door to her room harder still. She walked over to the window and pulled back the curtains and struggled with the window catch. Her fingers were slick with sweat on the metal catch and shaking, anyway, so it was difficult. She got the window open and looked through space towards the beach. She expected to see a gaunt, grey-haired figure staring up at her with a look of vacant malice from the sand. But there was nobody. The beach was empty. She breathed in clean salt air and turned back to the room. Her Chanel Red lipstick was crimson across the glass.

Compton had written 'Git Home Bitch' in the hand of someone as poorly schooled at writing as he was at grammar. She wasn't dead. He was. But he was not at rest.

She had taken notes as Rory Carnegie had told her his story. Now she took her notebook and put it with a ring-bound A4 refill pad in her bookbag. She would walk to the pub on the coast road at the far end of Slapton Sands and transcribe the notes she had taken as the old fisherman had murmured his grim recollection of events. She had intended to do it here but could not now stay in this house. She looked at her watch. It was just after five. English licensing laws were still something of a mystery to her, but there was a slate sign by the front porch of the pub saying that in summer they opened at five-thirty. It was certainly summer. It would take her half an hour at least to walk the distance, walking as she intended to on the high, shingle and sand curve of the bay. She would come back tonight and make up a bed in the sitting room and leave on all the house lights like that mawkish drunk, Richard, who married the figure skater in the Joni Mitchell song. Mrs Chantry was hardly in a position to complain. Right now, Alice could not imagine coming back and staying another night here in the darkness. It was brief, the night, in this bright, burning summer. It was light until ten, and dawn broke shortly after four. But it was still in the night, and silent then, and she was alone. The previous night had tested her resolve. The night to come would test it further. She was angry at this series of squalid and destructive violations. She wanted the mystery solved, the ghost put to rest, the objective achieved, the whole project triumphantly vindicated in a blaze of academic glory. But she did not want to stare back into the eyeless sockets of a dead man with no soul, confronted by him in the dark part of the night, come to make good his threat. She dreaded that, almost as much as she dreaded the phone call from Sally Emerson to say that they were dragging Bembridge harbour for a drowned diver's corpse.

Alice wiped the stain from the mirror with Kleenex from her bag until it was just a waxy smear on the glass. She shouldered her bookbag and set off for Slapton Sands.

In the early hours of 28 April 1944, Rory Carnegie, thirty-six years old and already in his own mind too comfortably off for this sort of shite, was drinking coffee laced with a good slug of Johnny Walker whisky in the wheelhouse of the fishing vessel *Skylark*. Rory was not in the best of tempers. He seldom was when obliged to embark at midnight. Setting a skipper's example interfered with his private life. Much of what he did in his recreational time was necessarily clandestine. Fishing forbidden waters was immensely profit-able, but it had to be accomplished while others in civilian occupations were inclined to be either asleep or enjoying themselves. All work and no play, Rory thought.

There was another reason for his foul mood. It was the way Rory masked his growing fear of what they were doing. Capture meant imprisonment, if the crew's story that they were doing this for profit were even believed. The length and conditions of incarceration were determined by the seriousness of the apparent crime. If they were suspected of spying, they could kiss their liberty goodbye for the duration. No alleged traitors were being tried until the war ended. But as war profiteers they would face stiff sentences for flaunting government regulations barring them from this part of the coast. They would be disgraced, ostracized, his small fleet sequestered and sold at public auction with whatever nominal proceeds there were going towards the prosecution of the war.

What really frightened Rory, though, were mines. Defensive mines had been laid along the coast. They were thickly strewn, their positions marked only on charts given to Royal Navy vessels with a specific course that risked encountering them. Rory didn't possess such a chart. Even if he'd managed to appropriate one, the charts were far from foolproof. Heavy weather sheared mines free of their moorings all the time. Many of them were washed up, like giant, featureless porcupines, on Britain's beaches. But many more lurked under the water in snags of kelp and flotsam, awaiting the bump of an unsuspecting hull.

A mine would certainly destroy the *Skylark*. It was a wooden-hulled, Clyde-built forty-footer. Planking and caulk were no barrier to high explosives. If Rory and his crew were unlucky, their mine wouldn't kill them outright. They would go into the sea with burns and blast injuries and bleed to death or die of shock and exposure there, choking on the fuel from their own diesel tanks. When Rory thought about mines, about their lurking surfaces of febrile, explosive spikes, he grew angry at his greedy pursuit of hake and flounder. Fish and profit seemed nowhere near worth the horrible exposure to risk. Such thoughts darkened his mood, so his crew kept away from their scowling, foul-mouthed skipper. And Rory kept the hip flask handy to sweeten both beverage and temperament.

He worried about U-boats slightly less. He fished the westerly English coastal water of Lyme, Babbacombe, Tor and Start Bays. The sea was relatively shallow and the tides notoriously tricky. Submarines risked being stranded on sandbanks, or having to negotiate shallows half-submerged and vulnerable to detection from the air. Exposed U-boats offered patrolling fighter planes wonderful target practice. They were still a concern for Rory and his crews, though. On several trips he had heard the lurking grind of submarine engines. The *Skylark* would be nothing more than a smallish blip on their sonar. But a U-boat, starved of a kill for a week, might consider it a target worth the cost of a torpedo.

In the early hours of this particular April morning, Carnegie had a more immediate concern. The weather was dirty. There was a substantial swell, a chill, fitful wind and drifting fogbanks, some of them heavy. The atmospheric conditions were afflicting the *Skylark*'s radio with squalls and bursts of loud, impenetrable static. Carnegie was listening in, as he always did, to the unscrambled frequency used by the Americans for their ship-to-ship and ship-to-shore communications. And something was very definitely up. The level of their coms traffic was much higher than it should have been. Several craft were communicating in what seemed to be a convoy or flotilla of boats.

After listening intently for about twenty minutes, he heard a position given. Carnegie rolled heavy canvas blinds down over his ship's windows and, by the feeble red bulb of a hooded electric torch, consulted his charts. They were in Lyme Bay, heading towards his own position. There were a dozen nautical miles or so between him and them. The headland of Hope's Nose lay between them. But Carnegie doubted that even the most vigilant lookout would see more than a couple of hundred yards in daylight between fogbanks if this weather kept up. They were on a course, he guessed, for Slapton Sands. The vessels were LSTs (Landing Ships, Tank), and they were moving slowly. They wouldn't reach their destination at their present speed for between four and five hours. It would be more than two hours, even if he dropped anchor and stayed put, before the American flotilla chanced upon the *Skylark*. But in two hours Rory Carnegie and his vessel would be long gone, hold heaving with illicit fish.

Their voyage had been delayed. That was the gist of all the angry traffic he had heard from the flotilla on his radio between bursts of interference. They had waited for an escort that hadn't arrived. A Royal Navy destroyer designated to watch their tail had failed to turn up. Their schedule was urgent and eventually they'd had to leave without any escort at all. They were tank and troop carriers, essentially, unarmed cargo craft. They were sailing, unprotected, towards what Carnegie assumed was to be an exercise on the beach at Slapton. He felt the hair at the nape of his neck prick the wool of his sweater as he considered what was happening. He felt the same dank sense of foreboding he felt when the *Skylark* pitched through floating debris and he allowed himself to speculate that the spikes of a mine might lie bobbing beneath its oil-slick slurry of seaweed and sodden timber fragments.

Rory Carnegie knew what the exercises were for. He was neither spy nor traitor, but the powerful, delicate radio sets aboard his seagoing boats had given him enough solid information for espionage over the months he'd been using the equipment to evade American shipping. The Yanks were preparing for invasion. The flotilla of LSTs would be packed with infantry soldiers and those Higgins boats they lowered from davits on their decks for a beach assault. The men would be fully laden with weaponry, kit-heavy with the pouches of live ammo they always used for their rehearsals. Their heavy-weapons units would be armed with light machine guns. Every man would be hung about with grenades. But the boats themselves, the boats that carried them, were unarmed. And unescorted. 'Jesus,' Carnegie said, in the pitch dark of his shuttered wheelhouse. His coffee mug was still in his hand. He swilled its cold contents and drank. The grounds of his coffee were bitter and the whisky residue did nothing to sweeten the taste. He rolled back the blinds. There was no horizon in the mist, and the foul night was blind to stars. If anything, the swell was increasing. They were four hours away from the breaking of dawn.

'The sea is always dangerous,' Carnegie told Alice Bourne. 'It's powerful, treacherous. Its violence is elemental and vast, and no sailor worthy of the name ever feels fully at home on the water, whatever skills we flatter ourselves we possess. But all that's in peacetime. In war, the sea becomes a truly terrible place.'

Alice knew that most of the men aboard the ships in Carnegie's flotilla would have been seeing salt water for the first time when they embarked from New York for Belfast or Liverpool. They'd have travelled in convoys, harried by chasing U-boats. Some believed the happy fallacy that the quicker troopships, the converted transatlantic liners like the *Queen Mary*, could outrun pursuit. But it wasn't true, because the U-boats hunted in ambushing packs. Their first impression of the sea had been for those Americans a place where they were targets, preyed on and vulnerable. Alice didn't suppose that impression had ever greatly changed. Certainly it would have been no different as they wallowed in darkness and fog, packed in a procession of LSTs, with the invisible Devon coast some miles to the right of where they travelled and the shifting Atlantic wilderness to their left.

The mist had lifted, the flotilla had come around the headland and they were about six miles away when Rory Carnegie saw the first explosion flicker just over the horizon on his port bow. His radio was suddenly alive with snarls of cogent sound amid the static as boat crews tried desperately to coordinate their flight from an attack. Smoke formed a ragged column in the lightning sky as a boat burned. Carnegie's American radio was so good that he could hear a captain giving the calm order to abandon ship, telling the men aboard to go into the water in their Mae West life jackets, telling them there was no time to lower the Higgins boats, telling them to jump and swim clear before the engine room blew.

The second explosion provided a double flash and then a boom that reached the ears of those aboard the *Skylark* across six miles of open water. It wasn't naval guns inflicting the devastation; Carnegie would have heard the scream and whistle of shells over the open channel. It was torpedoes. A torpedo had hit the second boat and detonated something volatile, something like full ammunition boxes or, more likely, crates of mortar or anti-tank shells. There was a plume of smoke now over the horizon. It billowed black and greasy above the sinking wreckage, Carnegie knew, of at least two ships.

He heard a mayday on the radio. The Yanks were under attack from a squadron of German E-Boats. He could hear the brave, pitiful sound of small arms fire as the Yanks aboard the surviving LSTs attempted to fend off the assault.

Evidently Rory Carnegie had not been the only one to hear them give their position as they waited forlornly for their British escort to Slapton Sands. Someone had been alert enough on the French coast to translate what he was monitoring and to realize its significance in time to scramble the E-boat squadron.

The screams of men in the water were clear over the *Skylark*'s radio as a third explosion ripped the sky where it met the sea away over the port bow in a jagged orange streak. Carnegie looked up. It was fully dawn now, and his crew had clustered around the wheelhouse and were listening to what he was.

The E-boats sank two flotilla vessels and badly damaged a third before making a swift retreat from their hit-and-run raid. The American convoy carried doggedly on towards Slapton Sands and whatever part it was still to play in the exercise there.

'The troops aboard the LSTs were 4th Infantry Division,' Carnegie said.

'How do you know?'

'By their insignia. Dead boys washed up all along the coast. There was no word about it, not publicly, but that's who they were. The Division recovered from this particular mishap, obviously.'

Alice nodded. The 4th Infantry Division had performed the successful assault on Omaha Beach. They had landed there six weeks after the events the fisherman was describing.

'Didn't you go and see if you could help?'

'Aye, we did. By the time we got to the spot, the surviving Yank ships were about four miles on. We could have put out, legitimately, from Teignmouth or Brixham and got to the spot by then. It doesn't take a minute to make a lying entry on to an empty page in a ship's log. We had a plausible story. But there was no one around to listen to it.'

'There were no survivors?'

'I later heard there were some injured men aboard the damaged boat. But there were no survivors in the water, no.'

'Had they died of exposure? What? Did they drown?'

Carnegie looked uncomfortable. 'They were carrying a lot of equipment. Packs, two water bottles apiece, entrenching tools. They hadn't had time to take off their ammunition pouches before jumping. I'd estimate they were carrying around eighty pounds of equipment per man. And so they hit the water hard.'

'How did they die, if they didn't drown, Mr Carnegie?'

'They hadn't been drilled in how to use a Mae West. You inflated those life jackets in the water, you see. But they'd put them on and inflated them before jumping. When they hit the water, with the posture forced by the Mae Wests, with the weight of what they had been unable to discard, most of those soldiers broke their necks.'

'Oh Christ,' Alice said.

'You seem very particular on the numbers, Miss Bourne. I'd say there were six or seven hundred corpses in the water. That would be about right for two LSTs sunk. It seems a lot, when you look at all those yellow lifejackets littered about on the green of the sea. It seems a shocking number of dead, all of them moving, none of them living, shifting only with the swell.' Carnegie stopped. He was back there. Alice waited. 'After a while, when you realize none of them are alive, you do stop counting. But I'd say between six and seven hundred were there. Dispersal was slow, just a gentle, onshore current. It was fewer than a thousand. It was less than the number you have suggested to me were lost.'

'It was enough.'

'Aye,' Carnegie said, nodding. 'It was that, all right.'

She sat at a table outside the pub on the Slapton shore and sipped occasionally at a half-pint of cider and wrote up her notes from her own, improvised shorthand. It was eight o'clock by the time she finished. She had written Rory Carnegie's phone number in a diagonal scrawl of pencil across the bottom of her last page of shorthand notes in case another question occurred to her. He was a scrupulous man, was Carnegie, she thought. He was polite as well as fastidious. There was a sea wall on this part of the shore. It was too high to see over sat at her table, but low enough for her to lean on, standing, with her elbows. She walked over to the wall and looked out across the scrabble of stones and sand descending to the waves a few hundred feet away. She wondered what it would be like to exit a Higgins boat in surf like that, loose-bowelled, weighed down by fear and equipment, straight into the withering onslaught of German machine-gun fire.

She wanted to ask Carnegie why it was he was still so mesmerized by the sea. Why did he bother with the silly deceit of the rod and bait box to idle all day at Dartmouth harbour? It was a Joseph Conrad question, wasn't it? One for the old Polish master mariner who rested now, for ever, in a dry grave she had visited herself. Conrad had been buried in Canterbury. She couldn't ask Carnegie that, though. She didn't think he'd be able to articulate an answer. But a couple of hours of intense recollection might have uncovered more pertinent detail in his mind. He'd put together more about the Slapton tragedy than had ever been published in their official histories by either the US army or the US navy. He might have remembered something that could help confirm her own emergent theory. Or quash it.

She used the phone in the pub. 'Mr Carnegie?'

'Lassie.' He'd been drinking. His voice was heavy, his accent thickened. She assumed it was the weight of Scotch. But he didn't sound affronted by her call.

'Rachel Vine told me she never got anything out of Colonel Fitzpatrick.'

She heard Carnegie chuckle. 'I doubt that was strictly true.'

'Nothing pertinent, I mean. I wonder—'

'There's something you should know about Rachel Vine, Miss Bourne.'

'Which is?'

'She died seven years ago.'

'But I met her. I spoke to her.'

'Nevertheless,' Carnegie said.

'You couldn't be mistaken?'

'I attended the funeral. The burial was in Streatham. I saw her coffin lowered into the ground. I stood at the graveside and sprinkled earth on to its lid.'

'How did she die?'

'An overdose. Barbiturates washed down with gin. She had throat cancer, you see.'

'Thank you, Mr Carnegie.'

'Take care, girl.'

Behind her, in the body of the pub, Alice could hear Pink Floyd playing on the jukebox. The song was 'The Great Gig in the Sky'. From its open doorway, she looked into the bar. It was dark against the sunlight, a refuge for the two or three middle-aged men seated on old chairs at wooden tables drinking in its gloom. A row of burnished copper pots adorned the far wall on a shelf flanked by a pair of warming pans. There were pictures, but you couldn't tell what their thick whorls of oil paint portrayed in the prevailing absence of light. There was nobody waiting to serve behind the bar. Probably sneaking a smoke out by the heaped beer kegs and piled bottle crates to the pub's rear. Here and there, thin shafts of sunlight penetrated to provide the bar with odd, gilded highlights. The till provided one of these. She guessed it was Victorian. It was a great curved thing, embellished with plugs and buttons, the symbols for England's old currency still featured in the narrow glass display that topped the machine. Mermaids cavorted in tarnished gilt on its edges and rills, between the shrouds of lost ships, above sea chests half-sunk in silt with their weight of pirate booty.

Alice walked into the bar. She didn't mind Pink Floyd. She didn't think anyone would bother her there. There was something reassuring about the pub. She would wait at the bar until the bored barmaid finished her smoke. Then she would order a fresh drink. She would drink it in here. She didn't want to go back outside. It was almost nine o'clock, and she really felt that she needed a drink.

SIX

The South Hams, 1944

The morning of 29 April broke clear and fine. Compton was up well before dawn. He watched the spring sun come up from the road they had built themselves along the coast. He drank coffee from a flask filled in one of the kitchen blocks and smoked his first Lucky of the day. He felt sober, thorough, businesslike. He inspected the sangar from which he would coordinate the three heavy-weapons companies under his command, once they were deployed for the day's exercise. Everything there was as it should have been. He stopped for a moment, allowing the luxury of warmth to spread through the healing bruises on his back. He could smell spring flowers and early sap in strengthening sunlight from the scrub on the landward side of the road. Honeysuckle, lavender and ferns still heavy with the verdant aroma of dew. Looking up the slope, he could see the grass growing greener in swathes as the minerals got richer in the soil. Trees swayed gently in clusters on the slope of hills rising to the sky. This was a beautiful country, if you let yourself think about it.

Compton realized that he hadn't. Not very much. Not so much as a country boy might have.

Today would be the proving of him. He'd come to a decision, after the beating he'd taken in Paddington. Or more particularly, he'd come to a decision after the inexplicable let-off he'd got from that mick colonel, Fitzpatrick. A man can only ride his luck so far, his old man used to say. And wasn't that the truth?

Fact was, the enlisted men and even the draftees weren't half so bad as he'd thought they'd be. They actually respected his expertise. He'd learned his craft behind the Browning tripod in Mexico and the Philippines and Cuba. He'd scored the highest aggregate ever recorded on the range at Bragg. Any man he schooled could, by the time he'd finished with them, dismantle and put back together a machine gun blindfold in less time than it took them in the cookhouse to boil an egg. He was hard and he was humourless. He was somewhat short on social skills. But no man he tutored would go into battle behind a heavy machine gun less than expertly prepared. He'd grown, he considered, with the advent of war. He'd been experienced in combat and munitions theory before its outbreak. Now he considered himself a proven professional.

If he could keep away from working girls, Johnny figured he had a chance to make something of himself. Maybe when he got to France he could even better the old man's medal tally. That would take some doing. But why not? The fight would be long and arduous enough. And though he felt no personal grudge against the Germans, he didn't fear them either. It was plumb against his scrappy, Southern nature ever to back out of a genuine fight.

He was looking forward to France. He anticipated it would be weeks now, rather than months, before their departure. He had been at Slapton Sands for almost half a year. The camp had gotten so entrenched and enormous, it was hard to imagine it gone. The brass talked about the 'tail' behind the 'teeth' of the fighting infantry, the cooks and transportation and handlers of ammunition and fuel. The ratio of noncombatants to every fighting soldier was something like four to one. So Slapton Sands had become a sort of city, or at least a substantial town. Soon they'd be all gone, though, the place dismantled, the barren earth rectangles under their clusters of hangars and cooking galleys and Nissen huts like the earth they'd churned into makeshift tracks, grown all back over with grass. Maybe in thirty or forty years, Johnny mused, someone would come to this part of the coast picnicking on a summer's day and chance upon a shell casing or a rusting bayonet blade and wonder what on earth could have transpired here.

He'd be glad and sorry to leave England. He found the place congenial enough, excepting Paddington. He'd developed a taste for pubs and for the cider they drank there in this part of the country. But the people were baffling. He found himself smiling, standing by his sangar in the spring sun, at the recollection of one of his very few attempts to integrate. Some of the officers had been pressurized into accepting an invitation to see a movie specially shown for them at a church hall in one of the villages. It had been a double bill. The first film starred an old guy called Will Hay who was funny enough in a dopey, Laurel and Hardy sort of a way. The second film featured some guy called George Formby. George Formby turned out to be just plain fucking weird. He played the ukulele and had teeth like a retard. Some of the guys had laughed, but not in the bits they were supposed to. And there was a trailer for some other comedian called Big-Hearted Arthur Askey. It was Compton's view that a little bit of Big-Hearted Arthur would go an awful long way. Some of the guys, pissed off by too much exposure to George Formby, had thrown candies at the screen. At Big-Hearted Arthur. Where was the British Betty Grable? he'd wondered afterwards. No. The British had been beyond him. He jumped down into the sangar and fingered the binoculars worn around his neck.

According to the United States infantry manual, a heavy-weapons company was always commanded by a captain. It was a rank Lieutenant Compton expected to be offered after today. Each company comprised two sections. Each section was composed of two machine-gun squads, each of those under the immediate command of a squad sergeant. It meant that there were eight guns to a company, which gave Compton's three company command a total of twenty-four.

The weapons under his command were Browning .30 heavy-calibre machine guns. They were fully automatic, recoil-operated and water-cooled. They fired a 175-grain bullet to an effective range of 1,100 yards, from 250-round belts. Including tripod and water, each gun weighed about 93 pounds.

Compton's set-up was necessarily different from what it would have been in the field. He'd drilled hundreds of green troops in the effective disposition of machine guns as weapons of offence, entrenchment and ambush. There was no scenario, no disposition on which he had not schooled the recruits. But today's task was very specific. They were the Germans, today. They were the bad guys defending the coast of occupied France. They would present the field of fire that would greet the assault force arriving in their amphibians. It would, as ever, be a live-fire exercise. It would replicate battle conditions as accurately as was possible. General Clark, safely ensconced in Marshall's little black book of officer preferment, had said the words. 'A soldier is always green unless he's been under fire,' Clark had said. And the words had become gospel. They'd be under fire today, all right. Johnny Compton and the guns under his command would see to it.

According to the manual, each heavy-weapons squad comprised a corporal leader, machine gunner, assistant machine gunner and four ammunition bearers. But today, at Slapton Sands, the squads under Lieutenant Compton were not Americans in the field. Squads of three were sufficient to operate each gun. The guns were in emplacements fanning to either side of the sangar from which he would coordinate and direct his defensive fire power. Two of them were in pillboxes. It was vital that the assault force practised its technique for overrunning prepared German defensive positions. The rest were behind redoubts and berms or dug into foxholes. It was equally vital that the Americans landing in France could quickly identify the source of machine-gun fire and learn to deal with it swiftly and at economical cost.

Now, he could hear the first of his men digging with picks and shovels into the unprepared positions on the landward side of their metalled coast road. He watched the others walking along the road from the base in a straggle of relaxed chatter, under their burdens of equipment. Chatter was OK. Chatter was probably good. He wouldn't have thought so once, but something had broken, or merely become benign in Johnny Compton, especially in the hours since the beating in Paddington that he considered should have killed him. He honestly believed, on this spring morning, that he could make something of his life, of the opportunities he'd been delivered.

It wasn't so much the fights. What soldier didn't occasionally fight? Though the fights, in truth, were unbecoming to an officer. They were bad enough for a lieutenant. For a captain, they'd be worse. He could curtail the fights, though, he was sure. The women would be the bigger test. If he could only keep away from the whores.

Compton saw that one of his squads was struggling to establish a clear field of fire from the position plotted on the preparatory map he'd given them. Four hundred yards to his right, they were attacking unyielding earth with a pick and casting nervous glances in his direction. Johnny smiled to himself. Now would be a good time to demonstrate his quality of leadership, his new-found tolerance, the expertise hard won when he served Uncle Sam's Cinderella army in Guam, in Cuba, and in Texas on the Rio Grande through a jumpy, tequila- and mescal-fuelled posting he didn't care to recall all that closely in precise detail. He waved a salute to the sergeant commanding the hapless squad, smiled, and saw the man's shoulders settle into a posture of relief. He smelled the ripening smells of good country, liberated by the warmth of a spring sun. There was word that Harry Butcher would be observing today. Fitzpatrick had sought Johnny out last night, high on expectation and Benzedrine, and told him so. Butcher was Eisenhower's right-hand man. Butcher had the ear of the supreme commander. Butcher was the key to automatic promotion for a man anyway doing a captain's job.

'There was a fuck-up here while you were away,' Fitzpatrick had confided, in that incontinent way men on Benzedrine had of becoming altogether too pally and garrulous to keep a secret properly, 'so things had better go like clockwork tomorrow.'

Compton had nodded. 'Sir,' he'd said, confining his reply to a single word. But it had been hard not to smile.

Each gun was aimed at its target by a traversing and elevating mechanism, calibrated in millimetres and always referred to by the heavy-weapons squads as the T&E. One millimetre of elevation represented a yard's height or depth differential over a thousand yards of range. Nobody had really addressed the conflict in scales of measurement between the continental and imperial systems. But to Compton that didn't matter. You relied on tables to tell you about angles of fire. And Johnny knew the tables by heart. Many gunners liked to open with a burst ranged low and left of the target and then calibrate their gun accordingly. It was a technique that worked well enough on the target range, if you were parsimonious enough with that first burst to accommodate the quartermaster. But it wouldn't work for Johnny, today, firing over the heads of American boys. His machine-gun bullets needed to be close enough to make them wince, to encourage them into crouching urgency, to make them aware of the zipping pattern of death sewn inches above their heads. But he did not want any of his squads to cut a boatful of them down at the knees, just to find the range.

They were scheduled to hit the beach at nine o'clock. He had studied the tide tables for this part of the coast, as well as the tables governing the angle of their T&E. The range was eight hundred yards, and the initial burst, before they stopped to reload and re-calibrate, would give ground clearance at that range of seven feet. Twenty-four guns, two hundred and fifty rounds in every can. That was a full automatic burst of close to seven thousand rounds. It wasn't quite the welcome Field Marshal Rommel would be planning for them in France. The men coming ashore today in their Higgins boats would not be strafed by fighter patrols or hit by shells from self-propelled guns and waiting tanks. But as they waded ashore and started to pick their way between the percussion caps buried in the sand to simulate landmines, it would certainly do wonders for their concentration.

His squads had been in position for thirty-five minutes when Compton saw the LSTs broach the horizon. Through his binoculars, he saw well-drilled crews swinging them out on davits and then lowering the packed landing craft into the water. The Higgins boats, thirty-five men to a boat, manoeuvred into position on the water and then came shorewards in a row as precise and disciplined as a line of advancing infantry. He whistled and looked at his wrist-watch. He'd been given a new wristwatch from supplies. They were right on time. Damn, it was impressive. He picked up his steel helmet, put it on and adjusted the chinstrap, just as the shells from the naval batteries over the horizon began to shriek their approach, signalling their softening up of the German defences. The shells fell on the sand, short of the road, short of where Compton and his men were snugly dug in. It was a rehearsal, after all. But the series of big explosions ripped craters in the sand and shingle, sending stones zipping and clattering into the granite face of Compton's sangar, filling his eyes with grit and his body with the jerking, percussive reverberation of heavy artillery. Then the bombardment ceased and

Compton looked through the firing slit. The dimensions of the beach looked somehow wrong to him, and a moment of anxiety troubled his mind. Just the bombardment, he thought, dismissing his niggle of doubt. Shakes everything up. Distorts things slightly. Alters the perspective. He didn't need his binoculars now to see the line of Higgins boats. He could see spray churn and spatter off their steel ramps as the craft rose and dipped on the swell towards the shore. He could see the sun glint on helmet edges where the green camouflage paint found no purchase on shiny steel.

The machine-gun fire command was given in six stages. Lieutenant Johnny Compton stood. This was his moment. 'Prepare to fire,' he said, giving the alert. He was glad that his voice sounded strong, full-lunged, with natural authority. 'Front,' he said, giving the direction. In his peripheral vision, he saw the appreciable sight of alert squads hunkered over their guns. 'Amphibious infantry assault,' Compton said, giving the target description. The Higgins boats were almost on the beach. In pure spring light, across shell-cratered sand, he thought they looked very close. 'Range, eight hundred,' he called out. 'Traverse and search,' giving the method of fire. 'Rapid fire,' giving the engagement command. On the beach, the ramps were coming down. Men were wading with rifles at port arms and above their heads in columns five and six abreast into the surf. 'Fire!' Compton said.

And he watched as soldiers began to jig and shudder in the surf and the foam on wavetops turned red with the terrible clatter of bullets leaving muzzles and entering men and killing them. Killing them in a red, tattering swathe, soaking the sea with them. Killing them all, it seemed to Johnny Compton, who had given the last order he would ever utter. Killing them all.

SEVEN

Slapton Sands, 1976

It was still light when Alice left the pub. She didn't really mind going back to the cottage in Strete in the dark. It was the thought of arriving there in darkness that bothered her.

Before leaving the pub, she tried to reach Sally Emerson. Emerson picked up her extension on the first ring.

'You're a workaholic,' Alice said.

'I hope you're calling me long distance. From sunny Pennsylvania.'

'That soldier identified by the partial print?'

'Lieutenant Compton.'

'Did your American embassy friend find out anything about him you haven't told me?'

'He's dead, Alice. He died at Slapton Sands.'

'Anything?' Alice could hear Emerson rifle through papers. The detective coughed to clear her throat.

'There's a comment on his file written by a Colonel Fitzpatrick, dated April 1944. Just says that Compton's antipathy towards prostitutes might be connected to the manner of his father's death. Compton senior died of renal

288

failure, but the cause was syphilis, apparently contracted in France in the final stages of the Great War. Got furlough. Got laid. Got unlucky.'

'Sounds like a direct quote.'

'I'm reading what's written in front of me.'

Alice nodded.

'Compton's father was a hero, by the way. But I told you that, didn't I?'

'You did,' Alice said. 'Thanks.'

'Take care, Alice.'

'Everyone tells me that, lately. Is that, like, a figure of English speech?'

'No. It's a piece of advice.'

She walked back to Strete along the beach. It was late, and the sea and sand wore that luminescent, late light, as though they were being vividly imagined, more than lived, in some dream she was having of them. The tide line was a thick trail of debris and glossy, dark-green weed. Walking it, she could single out artefacts amid the stones and shells and flotsam from boats. She sat on her haunches and picked at something that had caught her eye. It was a small, rust-covered button. It could have been a tunic button from a uniform. But it could have been anything, she thought, discarding it, brushing rust smears from her fingers on the legs of her jeans.

There had been two separate tragedies. The one Rory Carnegie had told her about had happened first. That explained the bodies that Carnegie, her Colorado veteran and other independent sources reported being washed up on the beaches of Devon beyond the military exclusion zone around Slapton Sands.

The second incident had happened on the beach itself. It was the aftermath of this event that her Colorado veteran had almost stumbled on on his hungover return from leave in London. It was this event, or its aftermath, that Jane Cartwright recalled in remembering the two hysterical troops sent to gather what medical supplies they could from a local cottage hospital.

Carnegie had not underestimated the number of bodies in the water. That attack and sinking had claimed about half of the total number of lives she believed to have been lost. You could allocate blame in the convoy attack. The Americans should not have been using an open radio frequency for their communications. The British should have sent the destroyer escort they had promised. The troops aboard the LSTs should have been drilled in the use of their life jackets. But it was the enemy who had attacked. It was an expensive lesson learned and reflected badly on Poon, the American admiral in overall charge of the naval contribution to Operation Tiger. But it did not really amount to a scandal.

So what had happened on the beach? It had to be friendly fire. Alice could only imagine casualties in their hundreds being inflicted by large offshore naval batteries laying a creeping barrage at the wrong time, or in the wrong place. But Johnny Compton had been an infantry soldier and a relatively lowly soldier at that. How could he have been instrumental in the deaths of seven hundred men? What could Compton's ghost be trying to scare her away from finding out?

She was only sure that she would not now find the answer at Slapton Sands. It lay in a file she had failed to access. Armed with a name, she might be able to source fresh information from somewhere. Sally Emerson's old college pal at the American embassy could be a useful contact. She would have that drink with Emerson when she got back to Canterbury and see if there was some way an introduction could be engineered.

Away by the coast road, she could see the small obelisk erected by the US army in tribute to what the people here had endured in having to leave their homes during the war. Even armed with her existing, incomplete knowledge, she thought the British government might erect a very substantial monument to commemorate what the Americans who trained here had done for them in liberating Europe. She walked closer to the stone tribute and looked at it. It was modest, but more dignified for the modest isolation of its size on the ground where it stood. She brushed a hand against the stone, which wore a fine, polished grain against her fingertips. The face of the obelisk, fully shaded from the sun, was almost cool. It cast a shadow, now, in this late part of the day, longer than its height, caught in the descent of the sun.

A friendly-fire catastrophe would have wounded as well

as killed men. The two troopers looking for blood plasma at that cottage hospital had been urgent about the treatment of the living, not about the accommodation of the dead. If there were living witnesses to such a terrible event, why had it not become public knowledge long before now? Partly it would have been because exposure was not the fashion of the day. Public attitudes had changed a lot in thirty-odd years. You only had to look at something like the raid on Dieppe. Nothing could have been so suicidally misconceived. In that single assault, over the space of a few hours, six thousand Canadian commandos were killed and wounded. The raid had been Mountbatten's idea, but he had kept his job and reputation. The Queen's uncle, admiral and lord, had been promoted beyond his abilities by the fiercely royalist Churchill. But no blame had attached to him either. Men died in war and in the preparation for war. It was to be expected. And the men expected to fight were stoical about the fact. Certainly none of the commandos who survived it complained about what met them at Dieppe.

But there was another reason, too, Alice felt.

She had crept down from bed to the door, once, one night when Bobby was back from 'Nam on leave and drinking with her dad in his dad's den. Dad was relaxing on his Naugahyde recliner. Except that he wasn't really relaxing. He had his arms and ankles crossed and the veins were big and blue and knotted with tension in his big, cop arms, below his rolled-up shirtsleeves. Alice had felt terribly sorry at that moment for her father and had been too young then to know why. She knew now, though. She knew how desperately afraid that Bobby would lose his life her dad had been. His posture had been that of a father curtailing fatherly instinct only by agonized effort of will. His instinct, he told his daughter later, all the time Bobby was home, was to gather his son in his arms and carry him to his room and secure him there with locks and bars and nails, hammered through the doorframe.

'Just a boy,' her dad kept saying, the afternoon he told her this, in a Washington coffee shop a half-mile from Arlington after they had put her brother in the ground. He kept clenching and unclenching his fist on the counter, looking at it. 'I felt all the time he was home his life was like sand, or water, Allie. Slipping through my fingers.'

But she didn't know that on the night she crept down the stairs to the door of the den. She remembered registering shock at the fact that her brother was holding a beer. He was nineteen, not yet old enough legally to drink, and he seemed slightly self-conscious, sipping occasionally from the bottle in front of his dad. But their father must have given it to him. Bobby wouldn't have helped himself to beer from the fridge.

Alice remembered that the lights were dimmed and that Simon and Garfunkel were playing on the stereo. Her dad liked Oscar Peterson, that kind of thing. Bobby liked Hendrix and the Doors. Simon and Garfunkel was the middle ground between them. The den had been built on to the back of the house and had a glass roof. Alice remembered the insistent drumming of heavy rain on the roof. They were playing the stereo with the volume very low. The two of them weren't saying anything. But that was normal. Sometimes they would fish together for hours side by side on the bank of a stream and swap barely a grunt. It was more contentment than reticence. They took great pleasure, her father and brother, in one another's company. At least, they did when her father wasn't wrestling against the strength of the fear and foreboding he felt for his son.

Then Bobby said: 'How's the war going, Dad?'

And her father sighed. 'Don't you know?'

'I know what I read in *Stars and Stripes*,' Bobby said. 'None of us believes it, though. It's all chaos on the ground. You get into a firefight, you might be aware of the two or three guys closest to you. Anything else is just confusion and chaos.'

'Not like John Wayne, then,' her father said.

And Bobby laughed. 'No, Dad. Definitely not like John Wayne.'

And that was how it was when men came under fire. It was chaos and confusion. It was why generals stood on the high ground to the rear of the action. If there had been a friendly-fire incident on the beach Alice now walked, none of the men who survived it would have known its true extent or reason. Only a very few people would have been aware of the complete picture. And in desperate times, with the invasion for which they were rehearsing only weeks away, they had done everything in their power to conceal it.

★

Alice was dreaming of exorcism, of swinging incense burners and hooded figures murmuring incantations, when she was awoken by hammering at the cottage door. In the dream she had been dressed as some sort of neophyte, standing at an altar in a chapel resembling the pub opposite the Imperial War Museum in which she had talked with the ghost of Rachel Vine. Rachel Vine was in the dream, robed in black, her powdered face grotesque in candlelight under a halo of platinum hair. But the knocking was real. It crashed with ominous insistence through the dream's shaky logic and woke her from her sleep on the sofa of the cottage sitting room. From here, she could see the front door. And she saw a substantial shadow moving this way and that through the stained-glass circle in the door as the knocker was hammered at again.

'Let me in.'

Sweet Christ, Alice thought.

'Let me in, Alice.'

And she recognized the voice.

'Hang on.'

He looked dirty and dishevelled and tired. There were grease stains smearing his cheeks and chin and his hair was pale with dust. He had on an old, open motorcycle jacket, and there was a gleam of sweat from the sitting room light in the cleft where his neck met his chest.

'Fucking hell, David!' He recoiled. 'Have you the remotest fucking idea of the time?'

'Hello, Alice,' he said.

She tried to hold him, to gather him in her arms. He slid the motorcycle jacket from his shoulders and held her tightly. His hair was smoky with the smell of burning fields, and the muscles jumped under his skin with fatigue.

'It seems a long time,' he said.

'Years,' she said. 'It seems like years.'

She made him some coffee from a jar of instant she found in the kitchen.

'Is there any milk?'

She looked. The fridge was empty. 'No.'

'Alice Bourne. Homebuilder.' He found a can of Marvel on a shelf and spooned some of it into his cup. He seemed distracted. 'Why are you sleeping downstairs?'

'How did you find me?'

'You said you were staying in a cottage on the coast at Strete. This is the only building fitting the description. The lights were on. I thought you were up, working. Or playing cards with an insomniac landlady. Where is the landlady, by the way? I should really rent a room.'

'Where's your watch?' There was a circle around the wrist of his left arm paler than his otherwise tanned skin.

'I sold it. Bought a bike with the money. The rear tyre punctured about three miles back. I didn't intend just to turn up like this in the middle of the night. I'd brought a sleeping bag. I tried to bed down in an old concrete shelter on the side of the coast road back there. But I really got the creeps. Funny. I've never been frightened of the dark.'

'Why are you here, David?'

'I'm going on a trip. It's why I bought the bike. I wanted to see you before I went. I haven't been able to stop thinking about you.'

'Have you wanted to?'

He smiled. 'No,' he said. 'Not remotely.'

He had been detained by police as he went through Portsmouth and tried to board the Isle of Wight ferry. They didn't arrest him or charge him with anything. They just made it very plain that he would be wiser to cooperate than to make unnecessary fuss. It had been David's past experience with the police that the Perry Mason stuff only worked on television. So he went obediently with them. He surrendered his student ID. He submitted to fingerprinting and, when questioned, admitted to a series of juvenile misdemeanours he presumed they had learned of from the force in Merseyside. He did not think two incidents of adolescent shoplifting and a nightclub fracas involving hair-trigger doormen deserving of this kind of fuss. Then he remembered the King's Road pub fight and wondered if the spitter he'd hit had been more badly damaged than had been realized at the time. He hoped not. He very much regretted the incident. He'd thought himself a tosser and a bully for throwing the punch, once he'd considered it soberly.

He was left in a locked room, with plenty of opportunity to dwell on his possible crime, deprived of his watch and belt and bootlaces. There was nothing to read, no clock on the wall. He sat on a plastic modular chair, facing a Formica-topped table separating an identical, opposing chair from his. As unrecorded moments slipped by, David started to wish there was something to occupy him there. He'd have welcomed even the diversion of one of those magazines from which he'd learned the intimate details of poor Peter Cushing's grief-afflicted life.

The woman entered the room unescorted. She sat without ceremony and questioned him. She knew a lot about him and wanted to know more.

'What did she look like?' Alice asked. But she didn't need to ask.

'Slim,' David said. 'Green eyes. Sexy. Smokes too much.'

'Exactly as I described her to you.'

'No,' David said. 'You described her as sympathetic. She wasn't sympathetic. She was scary. And she was extremely angry.'

He was allowed to leave, to collect and gather his things, after Emerson was summoned from the room to take a telephone call.

'I could have told you the prints weren't mine,' David said to her, as she passed afterwards in the corridor and he threaded the laces back into his boots.

'You could,' she said, her back to him, walking away. 'You could have told me anything, or nothing at all.' But she'd seemed ruffled, shaken. One hand played distractedly with her hair where the weight of it sat bright between the shoulder blades on her retreating back.

It didn't matter that David was late turning up at Bembridge. The fort dive was headed by a Frenchman called Robert Artaud. Artaud had worked on and off with David's father. The two men were old friends. It was how David had got the job. Artaud smiled wryly when he saw the Rolex fastened to David's wrist.

And he seemed to take to David. The clear skies and calm of the heatwave made the job more straightforward than it otherwise might have been. Perhaps because he hated doing it, David was a thorough and scrupulous diver. He operated at a level of professionalism well above the student wage he was being paid. Rig divers had a deserved reputation for playing hard, and Robert Artaud did his best to live up to this, even given the limited opportunities presented to his crew on the Isle of Wight. There were no clubs or casinos on the island and he moaned loudly about the lack of them. But there were plenty of pubs. On their fourth evening, pretty hammered in a pub in Cowes, David noticed that Robert was looking at him in a way he didn't really understand. He put it down to drink. But it persisted. Eventually he was too uncomfortable with the scrutiny to let it pass any longer without comment.

'Chip off the old block?'

'He's dying, David. Your father is dying. It's not for me to say you should be reconciled. I don't think he would say it himself. But I do know he loves you.'

Artaud had given David an address in Aberdeen. He'd got two hundred and fifty pounds for the watch and spent a hundred of it on the bike. He'd ridden from Portsmouth to Slapton Sands, where he had punctured. In the morning he would repair the puncture and ride on to Scotland and the seamen's mission in Aberdeen where his father waited for death.

'I'm so sorry, David.' Alice was beside him now, on the sofa in the cottage.

His shoulders shifted and his eyes searched the room. 'Tell me how things are going with you, Alice. Are you on the way to solving your mystery? Is sleeping down here part of some cunning academic strategy?' He tried to smile, but in his struggle with incipient grief the smile was overcome.

'Will you go back to the sea fort?'

'No, I'm finished with diving. I can get a job with Ollie on a firm that puts the guest tents up at Wimbledon. Or so he says.'

'Connors will be there,' Alice said. 'With his implausible socks.'

'Several pairs, I should think,' David said. 'He could be there for the entire fortnight. He's the favourite to win it.'

Seven matches. You had to win seven matches to win a Grand Prix tournament. She thought of the racket she'd won in a college tournament, rotting with her mildew-spotted clothes in the wardrobe of her abandoned Whitstable flat. Jimmy Connors played with a steel racket that flashed and glittered in the sun. She was reminded of the record player at Professor Champion's summer party, metal glittering in sunshine on a tabletop as Joni Mitchell sang a song about sprinklers watering the velvet lawns of affluence. In her mind, the summer party seemed an ancient, mythic event, like a ritual practised by some vanished tribe. It had taken place less than a fortnight ago. It was the occasion on which she and David had first met.

'Why won't you dive again? Were you spooked?'

'No,' he said. 'Not spooked. Not the way I was tonight.'

'Last night,' Alice said, looking at her watch. 'It was last night.'

David nodded. He was weary and troubled and dirty from the road. But he was here. He was here and she thought him safe.

'Lie with me until it gets light,' she said. 'Let me hold you.'

At dawn they went back together to retrieve David's bike. The bike lay where he had left it, under the cowl of his unzipped sleeping bag by the side of the road. It was an old army bike, a BSA Bantam, a criminally underpowered machine, it looked to Alice, for any task involving couriers conveying orders and intelligence which measured life and death. It had a sprung saddle and was still painted matt army green. The embossed BSA badge affixed to the fuel tank reminded her of a heraldic device from Professor Champion's obscure and much-beloved era of jousting knights.

'Puny little thing,' she said.

'Me? Or the bike?'

'Guess.'

'Steve McQueen rode one of these in *The Great Escape*.'

'Probably why he didn't get away.'

God, it felt good to see him again. She had become so isolated since their parting at Paddington Station. She had felt alienated. She had genuinely tried, and sincerely failed, really to understand what England was about. And she'd been under siege, haunted. The sour, vindictive soul of Johnny Compton had haunted her.

'Do you believe in ghosts, David?'

'Only revenants.'

'Only what?'

He had his back to her. He was on his haunches at the side of the coast road struggling with his motorcycle. It was only just after dawn, and there was no real heat in the day yet. But she could smell oil from the cylinder head and petrol leaking from the choke. She was coming round to the belief that the guy who'd sold David the bike had really seen him coming.

'My nan was a psychic,' he said. 'She was genuine, gifted. She did it reluctantly, had to be cajoled, but she could discourse with the dead.'

Alice nodded. A month ago. A month ago, this stuff would have had her laughing out loud.

'But you never see the dead. It's only revenants hang about, apparently. They're suicides and restless on account of it. Like uninvited guests who can't get into the party.'

'So they do what? Loiter outside?'

'Pretty much.'

He took off the rear wheel of the motorbike with tools from the bike's toolkit and stripped out the inner tube to repair the puncture. All the while he kept glancing towards a pile of cement debris and reinforcing rods topping a man-made excavation at the side of the road. Alice walked across to the construction. It was a sangar. Further down the road, to right and left of the sangar, she could see evidence of pillboxes, also the objects of untidy and half-hearted attempts at demolition and clearance. His claustrophobia, of course. David's claustrophobia had put him under the stars last night, in the sangar, rather than in the ruins of one of the pillboxes, with their enveloping roofs and imaginary risk of entombment. She stood on its lip.

'It stank like rotten fish down there last night,' David said, nodding. 'And it was freezing. Jesus, it was like the grave.'

Alice climbed down. The smell was there, rotten and rancorous, familiar to her but fading now, with the advent of the sunshine, of the day.

She found Compton's note in a cheap metal cigarette case under an inch of sand beneath one of the stones that still remained from the paved sangar floor. His Zippo lighter lay next to the case. He had written his note by the flame from his lighter and then buried them and slipped aboard a Higgins boat for the short voyage that would terminate his life. He apologized to whoever found the note. And he apologized for what he had done. He had not known about the surge tides they experienced in the spring on this section of coast. The surge tide had delivered his targets closer in and so higher up the beach than he had calculated. So his machine-gun companies had fired full belts from twenty-four guns into, rather than over the heads of, the assault troops on the beach. It was an appallingly easy mistake. Someone like Rory Carnegie could have pointed his error out to Johnny Compton long before it was allowed its terrible consequences. But Johnny Compton had never met anyone like Rory Carnegie. He had never been allowed to.

The note was heavily scored in its folds where time had further creased and scarred the cheap paper. It looked like the kind of document an eighth-grade student might have produced after much painstaking toil. Alice felt no sense of vindication or triumph holding her proof in her hand, only a deep and abiding sadness for the fate of so many determined young men. She knew she would never dream the cormorant dream again. She felt glad, at least, of that. Everything the dead machine gunner had done to her had been done to prevent her from achieving this moment of revelation. Yet she felt equally sure that the discovery had been predetermined. She had dreamed the slipping over the side of the craft into cold oblivion. But the detail would have continued to accrue, wouldn't it? The dream could go back as well as forth in its enaction of events. The cormorant dream could advance and recede much as the tide did. Eventually she would have dreamed the note and its careful burial, too. But what did the note say, really? What did it say of true and authentic significance?

Rory Carnegie, without knowing he was doing so, had probably summed it up best. Outside the careful mausoleum he called a home, in blinding, abstract sunshine, he'd grown garrulous following his recollection of the unacknowledged, floating dead. They were always going to go, Carnegie said. Whatever the mistakes and mishaps encountered in the preparation, *the Yanks were always going to go*. By her own, now fully informed estimate, they had lost around fifteen hundred men at Slapton Sands over the course of a couple of days. But those days had been six weeks before D-day, and the urgency of the schedule had demanded that they simply absorb the losses and whatever fatal lessons they could learn from them.

General Bradley had lost two thousand men on Omaha Beach. He'd lost a further forty thousand over the following eight days as his infantry learned the hard way how to fight the Germans in the hedgerows of Normandy. But he had not faltered, had he? Bradley had not so much as paused.

What Alice had discovered at Slapton Sands she felt was more detective work than history. She had succeeded in locating her primary source. But Compton's admission was not the holy grail of historical investigation which she'd sought. It was a suicide note, written by a bad man trying and failing terribly to redeem himself through a noble cause. The mystery of Slapton Sands had been more in the end than Professor Champion's dismissive anecdote. But it had been less, in the end, than what Alice had hoped to reveal. The Normandy invasion had succeeded, after all. The war had been won. What she had discovered hadn't mattered in the overall scheme of things.

Shame and remorse shaped the revenant Compton. Shame and remorse and his father's forgotten glory. Well. She'd let them lie intact. Compton had striven towards the end of his mostly misbegotten life for a nobility of purpose that had proved cruelly, catastrophically beyond him. But it was in the gift of Alice Bourne to do something noble and forgiving now for the poor man's wretched soul.

Later, they lit a fire together on the beach. His bike repaired, David had been to buy breakfast for them in Totnes. In his absence, Alice gathered wood from the beach for the fire and thought of the memories she would take with pleasure from her time in England. Canterbury Cathedral shimmering in the June heat. The first time she had heard John Martyn sing 'May You Never' on the jukebox of a Whitstable pub. Dancing shadows cast by glass on a vicarage floor. Knickerbocker glory, spooned from an ancient glass in the ice-cream parlour at Tankerton. Will Hay performing for an audience of one in a flickering, black and white world. And David Lucas, whoever David Lucas was, whoever he would discover himself to be. She'd take him away with her, too, ageless and intact, a part of the England that would live unchanging now in her mind for the rest of her life.

They had eaten their toasted bread and grilled bacon and kippers and were sipping tea and watching the waves when Alice Bourne took something from the pocket of her jeans and screwed it in her fist and threw it into the embers of their fire. It unfurled in the heat before burning with a bright, brief flame.

'What was that?' David asked.

'It was nothing,' Alice said. 'It was nothing of importance.'

Author's Note

I first visited Slapton Sands in the late summer of 2001 when a friend chose to celebrate his birthday by block booking a guest house there and inviting anyone who wanted to come over a long weekend. This old Victorian country house was a solitary building on a hill above Start Bay and the sands – more accurately shingle – stretched below it in a long curve extending as far as it was possible to see.

From the start it seemed an enigmatic, atmospheric location; not just because the owner of the guest house had the place littered with decades of mementoes. On the hungover morning after our arrival we went down to the beach. Waves broke violently and the wind shrieked and it was empty apart from a few distant figures struggling to stay grounded under the pull of sport kites. Partly to explore and partly to shake the morning after feeling, I set off on a run. And to the south of the sands, near the village of Towcross, was confronted by the surreal bulk of a Sherman Tank, dragged from the seabed in 1984 and left as a makeshift memorial to American dead.

The Sherman is a small tank, an awkward little vehicle with a stubby little cannon. This one had been painted with pitch, black over barnacles and rust. It looked incredibly sad and solitary, there.

Something awful happened at Slapton Sands. It happened in conditions of great secrecy in the spring of 1943. You don't need to be a psychic to sense it. You don't need a memorial, either, though the Americans certainly deserve one. The place is a wilderness of stones and water imbued with a deep and intimate feeling of loss. I've never believed in ghosts, and I've never been anywhere in my life that felt more home to them.

The Americans prepared at Slapton Sands for D Day because it so uncannily resembled the Normandy coast. They evacuated 13 square miles of South Devon in order to do it without being seen. Here, the citizen army of the United States practised what they would do for real on the Idaho and Omaha beach heads. Field Marshal Irwin Rommel had masterminded the Normandy defences and the German soldiers manning them were battle hardened. So practice for invasion was certainly required.

Opinions differ as to what went wrong at Slapton Sands. But Operation Tiger generally takes the blame. This exercise involved a small flotilla of American assault craft communicating, apparently, on an open radio frequency. It sailed without its planned Royal Naval escort and was raided by German E-boats dispatched from the French Coast. Three vessels were hit and almost 500 soldiers died. But that doesn't explain the accounts of officers from a British battle cruiser who claimed that during a planned practice bombardment, they were horrified to see American soldiers on the beach they were shelling. Nor does Operation Tiger address the persistent rumours of a mass grave at Slapton Sands. If the men died at sea, why did the Great Storm of 1953 expose so many infantry artifacts in one small location on the beach itself?

As a novelist, I was actually less interested in the secret than in the soldiers. Beyond the surf and pebbles, you could not imagine a location more English, with its gentle rise of verdant hills and stands of swaying trees. What must they have made of this empty place, these farm boys from Nebraska and street kids from Queens, pitched and tossed towards it aboard plywood boats?

There were three million American service personnel in England in 1943 and to a large extent, they kept themselves to themselves. They lived in their own camps. A Gi's daily beef allowance – shipped here from Australia – was as much as ration coupons would get a British adult in a month.

I set the novel in the seemingly endless summer of 1976. Sadly, I'm old enough to remember that one vividly. But nostalgia wasn't the reason – it was the year of America's bi-centennial; a year of analysis, breast-beating and navel-gazing done not by a red-neck populist

311

like Michael Moore, but by the likes of Normal Mailer and Gore Vidal. It was quite respectable then for American intellectuals to criticize their own country. It was even quite respectable to be an American intellectual.

I thought it would be interesting to have my protagonist – American, female – examine American heroism in a climate hostile to her country, her values and her beliefs. In 1976, America hadn't long lost its tatty war in Vietnam. It had almost seen a President impeached. In England, in 1976, we didn't seem to think very much of America. But then America didn't seem to think all that much of itself.

Slapton Sands is also about England. It is about the things about England that have changed and the things that never will.

Don't miss

Francis Cottam's enthralling new novel

A SHADOW ON THE SUN

To be published by Simon & Schuster
in April 2005

**POCKET
BOOKS**

This book and other **Simon & Schuster/Pocket** titles are available from your book shop or can be ordered direct from the publisher.

☐ 0 7434 6153 3 **Hamer's War**   £6.99

☐ 0 7434 4037 4 **Fires in the Dark**   £6.99

Please send cheque or postal order for the value of the book, free postage and packing within the UK; OVERSEAS including Republic of Ireland £2 per book.

OR: Please debit this amount from my:

VISA/ACCESS/MASTERCARD ....

CARD NO ....

EXPIRY DATE ....

AMOUNT £ ....

NAME ....

ADDRESS ....

....

SIGNATURE ....

www.simonsays.co.uk

Send orders to: SIMON & SCHUSTER CASH SALES
PO Box 29, Douglas, Isle of Man, IM99 1BQ
Tel: 01624 677239, Fax 01624 670923
bookshop@enterprise.net

Please allow 14 days for delivery.
Prices and availability subject to change without notice.